CW00537900

THE EARL I RUINED

SCARLETT PECKHAM

COPYRIGHT

This book is licensed to you for your personal enjoyment only.

This is a work of fiction. Names, characters, places, and incidents are either products of the writer's imagination or are used fictitiously and are not to be construed as real. Any resemblance to actual events, locales, organizations, or persons, living or dead, is entirely coincidental.

The Earl I Ruined
Copyright © 2018 by Scarlett Peckham
Print KDP ISBN: 9781731448064
IS Print ISBN: 9871641970709
BN Print ISBN: 9781641970747

ALL RIGHTS RESERVED.
No part of this work may be used, reproduced, or transmitted in any form or by any means, electronic or mechanical, without prior permission in writing from the publisher, except in the case of brief quotations embodied in critical articles or reviews.

NYLA Publishing
121 W 27th St., Suite 1201, New York, NY 10001
http://www.nyliterary.com

The EARL I RUINED

SECRETS OF CHARLOTTE STREET
BOOK TWO

SCARLETT PECKHAM

ABOUT THIS BOOK

She's beautiful, rich, and reckless ...

When Lady Constance Stonewell accidentally ruins the Earl of Apthorp's entire future with her gossip column, she does what any honorable young lady must: offer her hand in marriage. Or, at the very least, stage a whirlwind fake engagement to repair his reputation. Never mind that it means spending a month with the dullest man in England. Or the fact that he disapproves of everything she holds dear.

He's supposedly the most boring politician in the House of Lords ...

Julian Haywood, the Earl of Apthorp, is on the cusp of finally proving himself to be the man he's always wanted to be when his future is destroyed in a single afternoon. When the woman he's secretly in love with confesses she's at fault, it isn't just his life that is shattered: it's his heart.

They have a month to clear his name and convince society they are madly in love ...

But when Constance discovers her faux-intended is decidedly more than meets the eye—not to mention adept at shocking forms of wickedness—she finds herself falling for him.

There's only one problem: he can't forgive her for breaking his heart.

AUTHOR'S NOTE

Dear readers,
While this is a mostly light-hearted book, it contains flashbacks to a
moment of unwanted sexual aggression, and an outing of a character's
erotic tastes. If you are a sensitive reader, please do consult the reviews.

DEDICATION

For Chris, who makes the wildest dreams of wicked women come true in real life.

CHAPTER 1

Mayfair, London
April 1754

*L*ady Constance Stonewell awoke to a crisp spring breeze, birdsong streaming through her windows, and the sense that she was, for reasons she could not quite recall, inordinately vexed.

She flopped back against her vertiginous mound of feather pillows, annoyed to be wide-awake before her customary hour of high noon. A piece of paper came dislodged from the sleep-tangled mass of her hair and stabbed her in the cheekbone.

She squinted at the crumpled missive. *Potential Husbands for Gillian Bastian.*

All the reasons for her ill mood came rushing back.

She scanned over the names she'd written down the night before. Lord Avondale. *No, too libidinous.* Lord Rellfare. *Too bilious.* Sir Richard Voth. *Too poor.*

She balled up the scrap of paper and threw it on the floor, where it joined the pile of other names she'd rejected before she fell asleep. She caught sight of her haggard face in the looking glass and groaned.

This disaster with the Earl of Apthorp was giving her insomnia and making her look drawn. Which was unsurprising: she could always trust Lord Bore to find new, enterprising ways to drain her of her youth and beauty.

She sighed, and rose from bed, dabbing at a blotch of ink smeared onto her cheek. At least by now Gillian must have seen the poem and realized Lord Apthorp was not the saintly specimen of manhood that he so vigorously imitated. She could either decide she didn't mind a husband with a taste for the illicit and a penchant for hypocrisy or marry someone else. And Constance would come armed with a list of suitable alternatives.

It was the least she could do, having encouraged the match with Apthorp in the first place.

The door to her room flew open and a small child dashed in, clad in a frilly sleeping dress and a grown man's powdered wig.

She bit back a laugh. "Why, good morning, Georgie. What a fetching coiffure you have today. Will you be delivering an oratory at the Inns of Court?"

"I'm Lord Arsethorp!" he shouted, leaping onto her bed.

She snorted. Her cousin's three-year-old son had always lisped, but this was a new, rather amusing mispronunciation of Lord Apthorp's name.

She straightened the wig over his mop of blond curls. "It's *Ap*thorp, darling, but I must admit, I like your version better. You do rather resemble him today. Though he does not approve of gentlemen appearing in mixed company sans their smalls."

At least not that he cared to admit publicly.

"I'm Arsethorp!" Georgie insisted, jumping up and down on her mattress in a way that made her head ache.

"If you insist. Shall we go find the man himself and show him your ensemble?"

She draped her silk dressing gown over her shoulders and

smirked at her reflection. Apthorp frowned on her habit of meandering through the house in her *robe de chambre*. Provoking his prim sensibilities had been one of life's great pleasures even before she knew they were contrived and hypocritical.

She picked the child up and carried him down the corridor toward Apthorp's rooms. In truth, she'd been hoping for an excuse to speak to him ever since she learned his secret. But he kept scrupulously early hours, and she was almost never up before the stroke of twelve. They hadn't crossed paths in a week.

She paused at his door. "Here we are," she told Georgie. "Give it a tap."

The child smacked the wood with his palm. "Arsethorp!" he bellowed.

"*Ap*thorp, darling."

She waited, wondering if he would seem different now that she knew his sordid secret.

Or if, somehow, *she* would. To him.

She could not fathom why he'd played the Puritan all these years. Especially to *her*. She was friendly with plenty of dissipated rogues, circulating as she did among the theater set. She collected objects of scandal like other ladies collected hair ribbons and fine art.

To Apthorp's supposed never-ending horror.

Ever since his cousin married hers eight years ago, he'd been aghast at the company she kept, missing no opportunity to deem her continental and unladylike. He cast himself as the solemn future statesman, shouldering his heavy responsibilities with perfect bearing, in contrast to *her*, the frivolous, loud orphan who preferred hosting parties to doing charitable works, and collecting gossip rather than accomplishments. He made no secret that he viewed her as a naughty child who required constant supervision lest she be caught dangling from a chandelier in her nightdress. Or worse: inviting shame upon her family with her wanton, reckless ways.

And all the while he'd been—

"ARSETHORP!" Georgie shouted, kicking the door with his small foot.

There was no answer—to her disappointment as much as her relief.

Georgie giggled at his own antics, squirming in her arms.

"You're a very evil child, young Lord Lyle. Just like your wicked cousin Constance before you." She blew a noisy kiss onto his neck. "Apthorp must be down at breakfast. Let's present you to your nurse instead. I imagine she is looking for you. Just as the poor footman is no doubt looking for his wig."

They located Mrs. Williams in the children's nursery. The old woman was craning her neck toward some cacophony coming through the open window from the street below.

"Arsethorp!" Georgie yelled with renewed excitement, gesturing outside.

Mrs. Williams jumped and snapped the window shut, her face the color of *sorbet à la framboise*. "Lord Lyle! That's not language for a child to repeat." She shook her head apologetically at Constance and took Georgie from her arms. "Oh, heavens. Come, let's go apologize to whichever poor fellow is missing his hair."

Constance took the old woman's vacated position by the window and slid it open, curious at what she'd been observing on the street.

A news-rag hawker noticed her and waved. "New *Saints & Satyrs*, madam," he said, brandishing a paper with a saucy wink. "Lor' Arsethorp and the sinful—"

She slammed the window shut and backed away.

Arsethorp.

Oh God. Georgie'd heard that coming from the *street*? Could that mean—

No. She pressed her fingers to her temples. *Impossible.* She hadn't used his name. She'd sent it only to her usual, discreet audience of ladies, written in a code only they could understand.

It's a coincidence. You're overwrought from la⌐.

Nevertheless she walked briskly down the s⌐   ⌐y
needing to reassure herself that she was, indeed, im⌐   ⌐⌐
It was early enough that the man in question would n⌐
be at the breakfast table, tediously droning on about ⌐
points of irrigation or his favorite blend of tea. He would ⌐ ⌐ely
pause his diatribe to remind her in his patient, condescending
way that one mustn't appear at breakfast in half dress.

He would be as he always was: *insufferable.*

But Lord Apthorp's customary seat in the dining room
was empty.

Constance's cousin Hilary, and Hilary's husband, Lord Rosecroft, sat alone in silence.

They looked like someone had died. Someone they *liked.*

"What a glorious morning," Constance said, striving for
brightness despite the fact that her hands had gone damp.

"Is it?" Rosecroft glanced outside in irritation, as if good
weather were an affront to his foul mood.

Hilary just stared at her eggs. And being five months gone
with child, she never just observed her food.

"You're up uncommonly early," Hilary finally said. Her voice
was hoarse, like she'd been crying.

"How dare you malign my wakefulness? I always rise with the
horses," Constance retorted. She waited for one of them to either
laugh or reveal whatever was amiss. But they only exchanged a
pained glance, in that way that married people had of communi-
cating dire things without speaking.

She forced herself to acknowledge Apthorp's empty chair.
"Where is young Lord Bore this morning? Apthorp never misses
breakfast. He's so *inordinately* fond of his routine."

Hilary winced and placed a hand to her stomach, as if the
sound of Apthorp's name was so upsetting it roiled her unborn
child.

"Darling," she said. "I'm afraid something dreadful has

_ .ned. You see, there's been some untoward slander printed about Julian in a gazette."

"Lies," Rosecroft muttered. "Vile lies by those damned high-necked bloody—"

Hilary lifted a hand to calm his outburst. "Please, James."

Constance swallowed. "I see. Is it about ... his debts?"

Please let it be about his debts.

Apthorp's increasingly desperate insolvency was the sort of open secret that everyone in London knew but no one with proper manners mentioned. Such a scandal could be weathered. And had nothing to do with what she'd written in her circular.

Hilary sighed. "The details are not polite. Suffice it to say one of those vulgar gutter verses is going around and it dishonors him."

Rosecroft slammed his fist on the table. "No, it dishonors whatever bloody hack would write such chop without the decency to—"

"James," Hilary hissed. "You'll make yourself ill."

Perhaps not as ill as Constance felt. For she knew exactly what kind of hack would write such chop.

Oh God. What had she done?

How could it have gotten out?

She tried to fashion her face into a reassuring smile. "I'm sure it will pass quickly, whatever it is. After all, Apthorp's reputation is as spotless as they come. He's the most boring man in England."

His infamous dullness was precisely what had created her dilemma. Feigning a blandness one did not privately possess was misleading to the point of being treacherous when one was a gentleman presenting himself to a woman as a candidate for the lifelong office of her husband. Female happiness was routinely diminished by secrets male society insisted ladies were too delicate to countenance until after their weddings, when it was too late to object.

Constance considered it her duty to correct this imbalance using the arts at her disposal.

Namely, gossip.

"Perhaps Constance is right," Hilary said. "Perhaps we needn't fret, James."

"His bill is being read today in the Commons," Rosecroft thundered. "The evangelicals are handing out the papers to anyone with bloody hands. They spent the whole night singing outside Parliament. And with the election coming ..."

He trailed off, as if the dire nature of this was too obvious and tragic to merit explanation.

And, with a sinking heart, she saw that he was right.

After all, she only *pretended* to grow faint with boredom when Apthorp went on and on about his pending legislation. She knew the details of his precious bill well enough to recite the lines herself. He'd spent half a decade conceiving of these waterways and doubled his debts in the process. His entire future rode on the bill passing into law.

If it didn't, he'd be ruined. Totally, utterly ruined.

And a certain faithless hack who happened to share a roof with him would be responsible for his destruction.

Exactly as her brother had predicted when, with no small amount of rage, he'd banned her from using rumors to guide the hand of fate in the direction that she favored. That unpleasant disagreement had concerned her decision to expose his affair with his gardener in a national gazette, forcing him to marry her to save her honor.

Constance maintained she'd saved him from a dreary, loveless marriage to someone he disliked, in favor of the happy life he now enjoyed with the woman of his dreams. He maintained she'd treated his wife's future like a game of chance in a manner that was reckless to the point of cruelty.

They had agreed to disagree.

Or rather, he'd shouted at her vigorously and at length, in such a break from his famously cool demeanor that she'd worried for his heart. *You will destroy someone's life irrevocably with your gossip. Promise me you will not write another word. Or so help me, Constance—*

And, of course, because he was her closest living relative, and the man who had, however detachedly, raised her up from infancy, and the only person whose opinion she'd ever really cared about, she'd promised him.

She'd even meant it, at the time.

So he'd forgiven her for what she'd done, and they'd made peace. But not without a certain lingering wariness about her character on his part, nor a certain amount of tenderness on hers for being so villainously cast when she'd only been trying to help.

And not without his reminding her, whenever someone mentioned news more scintillating than the weather in her presence, that she was *not to write it down.*

If he found out that she had not only violated the only rule he'd ever given her, but done so at the cost of the reputation and financial future of a close connection of their family ...

He'd never, *ever* forgive her.

Which meant she had to *fix it.*

Urgently.

Before he found out, and she lost the only family she had left.

Again.

CHAPTER 2

The Strand, London
April 1754

There were several advantages to having one's life completely ruined.

For one, spirits tasted better. For two, there was no longer any reason not to consume them at four in the afternoon.

Julian Haywood, the Earl of Apthorp, winced down another searing slug of brandy. To be sure, inebriation was not the most salubrious solution to his predicament. But a wallow in one's cups might be forgiven when one had arisen from bed the most ascendant young politician in the House of Lords, and been reduced to an object of the nation's mockery by twilight.

The shrill shouts of the gazetteers drifted up from the busy street below his town house window. They were calling him … he almost couldn't bear to think of it …

Arsethorp.

Lord Arsethorp.

And that was the very least of it.

His most crucial piece of legislation had been delayed until the end of the month, when it would no doubt die of political toxicity, causing his debts to be called in and his mother and sister to be cast from their home. That is, if the humiliation of his ignominy didn't kill them first.

Certainly, it had killed his hopes of finally proposing to the woman he had loved these past eight years. His prospects for matrimony were as dead as his political ambitions, for no parents who had read the previous evening's *Saints & Satyrs* would allow their daughter within a hundred yards of him.

He couldn't blame them.

If he had a daughter, he wouldn't let her near him either.

Not because of the peccadilloes of which he'd been accused. The rumors were inaccurate—mostly—and in any case, he never took a lover who didn't share in his enthusiasms.

No. He would forbid any woman from marrying him on grounds of his sheer, asinine stupidity. For only a fool would allow himself to be ruined *twice*.

The first time could be forgiven. He hadn't known what he was doing when he'd staked the remnants of the family fortune on a pair of failing salt mines, and he'd spent a decade correcting that misstep. Proving he was not, in fact, incompetent. Building a coalition that would restore his own estate and the greater western Midlands to prosperity.

Now, for all his efforts, Westminster was covered in woodcuts of his flayed and reddened backside. He'd be lucky if he could afford to keep his holdings in another month of coal.

He poured more brandy in his cup. It splashed onto the table. *He couldn't even drown himself in drink properly.*

"God's elbow," he muttered. A weak invective, for in his penitent years he'd eschewed cursing. "Dam-*fucking*-nation," he tried again.

Yes. That was better.

More like how he felt: *alit with wrath* at whoever had exposed secrets that were supposed to be better protected than the royal jewels.

But mostly fury at himself. Because he was going to fail at a pursuit most men in his position seemed to scarcely need to try at. *Again.*

Faintly he heard a rapping at the kitchen door downstairs. That would be Tremont, his valet, with the effects he'd ordered sent here from his usual lodgings at his cousin Rosecroft's house in Mayfair.

Tap tap.

"Becalm thyself," he muttered. "No need to rush the gates of hell."

He walked down the stairs to the cellar kitchen and threw open the shutters.

The face that greeted him through the window was not that of his valet.

It was one Lady Constance Stonewell.

No. Oh, dear God. *No.*

She waved, gestured for him to let her in, and darted beneath the eave to protect her elaborate silver-blond coiffure from the drizzle.

What was she doing here? Someone was going to see her alone in his garden, and then they would *both* be ruined.

He threw open the kitchen door, put a finger to his lips to urge her silence, pulled her inside, and scanned above the mossy garden walls for roving eyes.

The garden was quiet. The shutters of the house next door were closed.

Of course.

No one lived on the Strand anymore. At least not the kind of people who would recognize the sister of the Duke of Westmead.

He stepped back inside and shut the door behind him.

"Heavens, Apthorp, what *is* this place?" she asked, wrinkling her nose at the damp. "Tremont said you'd moved to Apthorp Hall. He didn't mention it was abandoned."

That was because he'd not found the force of will to inform Tremont that his new lodgings had stood unoccupied since 1742, and had the mouse droppings to prove it.

A large false widow spider lowered itself from a rusted iron chandelier above his head and dropped directly onto Constance's gloved hand. She raised a pale, wry eyebrow and flicked it off. "Tell me, is it the ghosts that drew you here, or the spiders?"

He wanted to laugh, but if he did so, he would surely weep. And one did not weep in front of a woman like Lady Constance Stonewell.

God, she was a vision, with that ever-upturned mouth and those luminous blue eyes and hair as pale and silver as some fairy out of myth.

She leaned forward and touched his shoulder with a single, impossibly dainty finger. "Apthorp? Are you well?"

He found his voice. "You *mustn't* be here. I'm going to find a litter to take you home."

"No need, my coachman is waiting in the mews. I told him I'd be an hour. I need to speak to you. Have you somewhere more … tidy … where we might have a little chat?"

"Constance!" he said more forcefully than was polite. She was accustomed to his finest self—the one that was always a gentleman, no matter his true feelings. Perhaps his improper use of her Christian name would shock her into hearing him. "You *must* leave. Right now."

In answer she craned her neck, leaned toward him, and sniffed. Her eyes lit up with that glow of mischief that made her such a divisive presence in the nation's most aristocratic drawing rooms.

"Why, Lord Bore," she said, with a sly smile. "Have you been *drinking*?"

"Not nearly as much as I'd like to," he muttered. "Please, you have to leave."

She chuckled as if he had made a splendid joke and remained planted where she stood.

It physically hurt to look at her, standing in this filthy kitchen with her laughing eyes in her beautiful yellow dress, her pale hair frizzing in the damp.

He had to *save* her.

"Come with me upstairs. If you take a sedan chair and keep the drapes pulled, no one will know you were here. I'll send your carriage home."

"Very well, if you insist. But first, I must speak with you."

He drew a shaky breath. There was only one explanation for her resistance: she hadn't heard the rumors. Which, in keeping with his luck, would make today the *only time in history* Lady Constance Stonewell was not the first to know every scrap of gossip on two continents.

He had to do the honorable thing. The miserable, but honorable, thing.

He had to tell her what was being said about him.

He drew up his last shred of dignity. "Lady Constance, I hope you will forgive me for speaking of improper matters, but you see, there has been a scandal. If anyone were to learn you were here, you'd be—"

"As ruined as you are?" she cut in dryly.

He sank back against the door. "So you know. Of course you do. Everyone knows."

The amusement in her eyes faded. She looked up at the damp-stained ceiling and let out a shaky breath. "I know because I wrote the poem."

She nodded stiffly, blinking, as though she couldn't quite believe it herself.

His frantic desire to get her out of his house by any means necessary was suddenly replaced by a very still kind of quiet. A quiet that began in his bones and rose up through his blood. The kind of quiet the body undertook when the mind needed all the energy one possessed to make sense of what one had just heard.

A statement that could not—*must not*—be true.

He had never begged for anything in his life. He was far too proud.

But today, in this moment, he could only whisper a plea: "Tell me that I misheard you."

Constance glanced up into his eyes, then quickly looked away. "I suspect you will be very cross with me," she said in a low voice.

Cross was not the word. He gripped the dusty table to keep from retching.

She walked around it to come closer, the butter yellow of her dress collecting gray strands of dust as the hem dragged across his dirty floorboards.

She was saying things as she approached him, speaking in an uncharacteristic high-pitched clip that he barely understood.

"Please trust I didn't mean you any harm. It was only meant for the eyes of a few ladies. I was trying to avert disaster. But then, what is disastrous for Miss Bastian and what is disastrous for *you* are not quite the same, and in any case, I don't know how it came to be in *Saints & Satyrs*. But you see, all is not lost because—"

She was rambling, but her incoherence hardly mattered. His heart was so cracked that had she said his own name, he would have struggled to understand her.

"Why are you here?" he croaked out.

He could hear the misery in his voice and didn't care if she could hear it too, because for the first time in his life he did not care what she thought of him.

She turned, and looked at him, and her big blue eyes were soft and plaintive.

"To fix it," she said.

And then, as if by magic, the light in her eyes hardened into the bright cobalt glint he had admired in them so many times: a look of fierce, glittering resolve.

"Lord Apthorp, I am here to do what integrity demands when one's actions have, however inadvertently, ruined the reputation of another person. I have come to offer you my hand in marriage."

THE WORDS CAME OUT IN A GUILTY RUSH, DESPITE THE FACT THAT Constance had written the speech that morning and practiced it all day. She'd hoped to be eloquent and sincere in her remarks. To say the sort of thing a serious-minded person with integrity and forethought might say, were she as much that sort of person as she wished to be.

Oh, how she *wished* she were more that sort of person. She did aspire to be honorable and wise. But it was so difficult, when one was temperamentally haphazard and secure in one's convictions right up until the moment that one found oneself in one of these uncomfortable situations, when in retrospect a more cautious approach might have spared oneself a great deal of trouble.

And perhaps regret.

She chewed her lip and waited for Apthorp to react to her proposal.

She was not unaware that the concept of them marrying was absurd, but it was the only solution that might save them both, and they would not be the first aristocratic couple to embark upon a marriage of convenience for the sake of such salvation.

Besides, there was the chance, however slight, that his secret life revealed he was more intriguing than he let on. Perhaps she could inveigle him to join her among the ranks of people who lived wickedly and well without apology.

Or perhaps not.

After all, he was currently standing still and quiet with his eyes shut tight, like the very sight of her was hurting him.

Even in the darkness of his filthy cellar kitchen, his golden locks and symmetrical features made him seem more like a bronzed statue than a living, breathing man. He was so resplendently handsome it was ludicrous. And quite unfair.

Proximity to him had always made her feel windblown and rain-dampened and wretched, even on her most collected days. With his effortless beauty and courtly manners and perfect knowledge of the orders of precedence, he had always been everything she was not.

Though, looking at him in his ragged house, she was less sure.

He'd discarded the trim peruke he wore to Parliament, and his golden hair was short and mussed. The shadows beneath his eyes and at his jaw gave him an air of danger, despite the smoothness of his features. His linen shirt was open at the neck.

In all her years of knowing him—sharing a roof with him—she had never seen him quite like this. All … messy and undone.

Perhaps she should have ruined him ages ago, for in this state he was the single most compelling sight she'd ever seen.

His amber eyes shot open.

"Marry you?" he asked hoarsely. Like the words had been scraped from his throat.

That was not an auspicious start.

"Yes. I know it may *sound* slightly unlikely, but it's ingenious really. You see—"

"Constance," he interrupted her. He looked directly into her eyes, in a way he did not often do when pontificating over breakfast or correcting her use of a fork.

He stared at her so intently she felt hot.

"Yes?"

"*Stop.*"

He said it so quietly that for a moment she was at a loss. She searched his face, which looked even more haunted, somehow, than it had when she'd arrived.

He noticed her examining him and abruptly turned his back on her.

"Join me upstairs. If you please." He held out one of his long, elegant hands toward the staircase.

"Yes, of course." She moved toward the steps with the relief of doing something, anything, to break the tension.

He marched after her slowly, deliberately, as though his feet were composed entirely of anger.

"That door on the left, if you would," he said, in the tone an extremely well-bred pirate might use to direct a captive off a gangplank. A tone that implied "or else."

She stepped into an upstairs parlor, dim with dirty leaded windows. Between the rain outside, the disrepair within, and the aura of hostility emanating from the only other person in the room, it was very grim indeed.

"Shall I light a candle?" she asked. "*Have* you any candles?"

The dilapidation of his ancestral house was difficult to reconcile with his fine tailoring and even finer manners. She'd known he lacked for money, but he always took such pains with his appearance—his tailoring, his snuffbox, his fine imported tea—that this evidence of his true circumstances shocked her. His home looked like it had not been updated since the Tudors ruled the City. In fact, she rather liked it for its faint whiff of the Medieval.

She could play up its romantic character and fill it with very good wine and very amusing people. Yes. She was beginning to see how this would work. The narrative she'd craft for their surprising match.

They would be *interesting* together.

Apthorp bent and retrieved a crumpled broadsheet from a pile on the sofa and held it up so she could see it. It was a copy of *Saints & Satyrs.*

She swallowed. She would rather not directly confront the

evidence of the damage she had done. She would rather move right along to her brilliant plan for fixing it.

"Shall we discuss the terms of my offer?" she asked. "I think you will find it quite compelling."

Some muscle in his face spasmed and he inhaled deeply, as if the idea of marrying her was so suffocating he required extra breath. "No need."

Oh dear. She'd expected him to be annoyed at her, but the severity of his degree of pique was rather worse than she'd expected. She'd miscalculated. She should have led with an apology, then broached matrimony.

She widened her eyes and gave him her most doleful, sincere expression. "I'm *so* very sorry about this, Apthorp. Like I said, it was entirely an accident. I *do* hope you'll let me make it up to you. If you'll hear me out …"

She trailed off as he strode toward her, waving away her words. She had never noticed he was quite so tall. He held out a palm.

She stared at it, confused.

"Give me your hand. If you please."

Tentatively, she obeyed. He lightly gripped her fingers and led her to the center of the room, stopping her before the ancient desk that dominated the front half of the parlor.

"Stand here," he said, placing her like an actress on a stage.

He placed the crumpled gazette into her hands. "Read it," he said quietly.

The calm in his tone made her nervous.

"Read it? What, to *you*?"

"Yes." He turned and took a seat on a threadbare sofa opposite the desk and looked at her in a cold, stern way she had never seen before.

His usual deferential bearing was nowhere to be found. He seemed as certain of his powers as an emperor.

"Go on."

Her mouth went dry.

It had been one thing to write words of this nature. Reciting them aloud—in front of *him*, no less—was simply not a possibility. She did not handle embarrassment well. She would die of mortification, and her hopes of fixing this predicament were not high if her corpse was discovered in his parlor.

"I can't." She cleared her throat, which had begun to itch, and attempted to use his scruples against him. "It's not appropriate. For a lady."

He gave her a black, sardonic smile. Which she supposed she deserved, for he knew her well enough to know that she had never before much cared what was appropriate for ladies.

"If you can *write* it, Lady Constance, then I daresay you can *read* it." His tone was as poisonous and liquid as toxin in a tin of treacle.

And he was right.

But that didn't make it any easier. She drew a shaky breath.

"A Word of Warning about a Proper Lordling," she began.

"Louder, please."

She wanted to wring her hands. Instead, she squared her shoulders and cleared her throat and looked him directly in the eyes and bellowed *"A WORD OF WARNING ABOUT A PROPER LORDLING"* loud enough to be heard all the way in Southwark.

"By Princess Cosima Ballade," she added primly. Kind of Mr. Evesham to give credit to her *nom de guerre* when stealing her work without permission.

Apthorp waved his wrist in the air, signaling for her to proceed.

"This week," she began,
Princess Cosima must strike a chord
Of caution about a certain lord.
Marriage-minded ladies should be 'ware
That this man, who haunts the drawing rooms of St.
    James Square
—and indeed the halls of Parliament,
Where one notes with some lament
He is known to ramble on about the laws of decency
And the creek-heads of the Midland shires with equal
    frequency—

She winced. The verse was meaner than she remembered.
"Go on," he ordered.

Is in search of a wife possessed of fortune
Of which he might exchange his title for a portion.
You will know him by his manner fair, and courtly air
And by the beauty of his golden hair.

"Too kind," he muttered.

She looked up, and his face was akin to that of someone whose foot had been trampled by a milk cart. "If you're not *enjoying* this, may I stop?"

He leaned back and recrossed his ankles. "And miss the end? Many say that's the best part. Please, read on."

"Very well." She took a deep breath and recited the rest quickly, to get it over with:

Such a swain might seem a suitor most appealing
If one did not know the secrets he's concealing.
A reputation for virtue, calm, and gravity
Belies an inclination for depravity.
Princess Cosima must, out of duty, here announce:
His lordship belongs to a SECRET WHIPPING HOUSE
Where he's been espied by London's knowing sages—

"*Enjoying acts not fit for decent pages,*" Apthorp cut in, slowly, and with the excellent elocution he was known for in the Lords.

She stopped, but he gestured for her to read on. As she did so, haltingly, he closed his eyes and recited with her from memory.

"*A rogue in disguise as a paragon of virtue,*" they said
    together,
Is the kind of rogue most liable to hurt you.
Or, better still, to be the source of rue
On that day he comes to you
And beseeches—oh, wicked farce—
That his wife deliver pain unto his arse.

Eyes still firmly shut, he gave a long, slow clap at her performance. "Inspired work. Though you might have tidied up the meter."

She felt like her heart might burst from shame. She rushed forward and perched on the arm of the sofa on which he was rather imperiously reclined. "You must let me explain. You see—"

"I see," he said, "that there is nothing further to discuss. Follow your own advice, Lady Constance. Stay away from me."

He rose and stalked across the room to a decanter of brandy.

Her pulse beat wildly. She had not anticipated he might be so unmanageable. She had to fix this now before it spiraled out of her control.

As it was, there was time enough to correct the worst of the damage. But only if Apthorp agreed to her plan. And he had to, because if her brother found out she was the author of this poem before she'd fixed the situation, well. That would be it.

She'd lose him.

She knew better than anyone that one was not *entitled* to one's family's affection. One was not even entitled to one's home, or one's country. One had to win one's place through character and merit. And if one's character was susceptible to occasional lapses in judgment, one had to draw on the more reliable powers of beguilement, ingenuity, and wiles.

She clasped her hands before her. "Apthorp, please listen. This has all gotten out of hand. *Letters from Princess Cosima* is a private little note I send out to a tiny handful of ladies to share pertinent information about potential suitors—the kinds of things that men discuss at their clubs but ladies never learn until it's far too late. I had no idea the poem would find its way to *Saints & Satyrs*, or be turned into a song, or that the Spences would see it and drop your bill. I only meant to apprise Miss Bastian of your"—she winced, for this was delicate—"eccentricities … before she married you."

Oh, it was so dreadful she wanted to disappear.

"*Marry* Miss Bastian?" he repeated. He wrinkled his face, as though she was at once very tiring and very confusing. "But I don't even *like* Miss Bastian."

CHAPTER 3

*C*onstance narrowed her eyes at him like she thought he was playing a trick on her.

"Now is not the time to be coy, Apthorp," she drawled. "You all but told me you intended to propose to her. You asked me what kind of betrothal gift she would like."

Was she joking? Was she *daft?* He had not asked her about betrothal gifts because he wanted to marry Miss Bastian. He had asked her about betrothal gifts because he wanted to marry *Constance*.

Because he'd been in love with her so long that it felt as unremarkable as breathing. Because he'd dreamt of the day when he could finally tell her he adored her. Because he'd spent the past eight years trying to shape himself into the kind of man who had more to offer her than a pair of bankrupt salt mines, a crumbling earldom, and more debts than he was comfortable tallying in his own mind.

For years, he'd struggled not to make a fool of himself in front of her, not to let his longing seep out at every family supper and ballroom soiree and chance passing in the corridor of his cousin's town house.

Evidently he'd been better at it than he'd thought.

He counted to ten before speaking. "You mistook my meaning. I had no intention of offering for Miss Bastian."

She wrinkled her nose in a manner he'd always, until today, found very charming. "You gave every evidence of being *very* fond of her," she said flatly. "You've followed her around for months."

Only, he refrained from pointing out, because she was always, always *with Constance.*

He didn't answer. He turned around and busied himself retrieving his discarded clothing from the floor, because it made him ache to look at her.

She had always had an affinity for gossip. She'd always been cleverer with her words than she was careful. And she'd always been provocative—determined to bend the world to her very vivid vision of it.

Before, he had found these qualities poignant. They—along with her light, her charm, her mordant wit, her laughter—made her who she was. Irrepressibly, endearingly herself.

Now she just seemed reckless.

Cruel.

He did not want to hear more about her supposed reasons for exposing him. He did not want to imagine how little she must think of him to do so publicly.

In *rhyming goddamned verse.*

He just wanted her out of his house.

"I think it's time you took your leave."

She drew up beside him and put her fingers to his arm.

He froze. His body had yet to unlearn the wanting of her touch, and pricked in excitement at it even as his mind recoiled.

"Apthorp, I'm truly sorry. Please, listen. You haven't let me finish my proposal."

He wrenched his arm out of Constance's grip.

"No, I haven't considered it. And I don't intend to."

He was on the verge of shouting. He needed to becalm himself.

But for her to propose marriage—the thing he'd wanted so badly for so long—*now* when there was no hope of ever having it, when she'd proved there had *never* been hope, that he'd been *insane* for entertaining the idea—*Christ.* It was like some ghoulish fable: the greedy man granted the undeserved thing he'd always wanted, in exchange for his own destruction.

"Why not?" she asked quietly.

"Because the idea of marrying you after you've done such a thing is as preposterous as it is insulting, Constance," he shouted.

Her face did something he had not seen it do in years: collapsed.

Utterly fell, like he was seeing London's most self-contained and confident young woman transform back into the awkward girl she'd been when he first met her. Spirited and impulsive and sensitive and shockingly easy to injure.

She looked so hurt he felt unmoored.

But why should *she* be hurt?

And why should *he* care if she was?

Her mouth opened, but for once, nothing came out of it.

And then, as suddenly as it had appeared, the despair vanished from her eyes and she returned to her full height, like she'd reinflated with air.

"Ah. I think you have misunderstood me," she said with a dry smile. "I wasn't suggesting we *actually marry.*"

She shuddered theatrically. "Such would be the stuff of nightmares, would it not?"

"JUST THINK OF IT!" CONSTANCE FORCED HERSELF TO CONTINUE drolly, tossing her hair so that Apthorp would not see the fronds of humiliation that were trying to overtake her from within. "Outrageous Constance and Lord Bore, bound together for a miserable lifetime."

She made a show of shivering at the madness of the idea. And it *was* mad, so it was odd that his evident horror at such an arrangement should make her feel like she might burst into tears.

Why should she feel stung by his rejection? It wasn't like she *actually wanted* to marry him. She didn't even *like* him. He'd persecuted her for years.

"We needn't actually marry," she repeated, for if she paused, her voice might quaver and he might sense that she was acting. "We only need convince society we intend to long enough to restore your reputation and ensure your bill passes."

He crossed his arms. "My bill is dead."

"But that's not true. Rosecroft said it's only that the final reading's been delayed."

"A technicality. It will go back up in a month's time, but it won't pass without Lord Spence's votes, and there's no hope of getting them so long as his wife believes me to be a depraved sinner."

She smiled, relieved to be back on the solid footing of her strategy. For he was correct. Lady Spence was a leading sponsor of a pious low-church congregation, and spent her time trying to convert the aristocracy to her evangelical sect. Left to her own devices, she would certainly do everything in her power to stand in Apthorp's way, for there was nothing she loathed more than peers who failed to use their august standing to model Christian virtue.

But Constance did not intend to leave Lady Spence to her own devices. Constance intended to manipulate her one very obvious vulnerability:

"Lady Spence is my godmother," she said triumphantly. "The dearest friend of my late mother."

Apthorp appeared unmoved. "Yes. Your godmother, who has always disapproved of you nearly as much as she now disapproves of me."

She clicked her tongue. "Oh, Apthorp. Surely you, of all people, must know what disapproving people love."

"Urging their husbands to vote against notorious blackguard sinners?" he said darkly.

"*Reforming* notorious blackguard sinners. *Saving their souls!*"

He rolled his eyes. "You are even more ridiculous than I thought."

She glared at him. Imagine, her thinking all day that she might actually *marry* this man. She'd been so overcome with guilt it had made her temporarily insane.

"Just *listen*. We'll say we've been secretly engaged for years and were waiting for your bill to pass to marry. We'll dismiss the rumors about you as sordid slander by enemies seeking to block the waterways. My brother's blessing will be enough to vouch for your character with the City votes, and we'll spend the month winning over the Spences and any others until we have the numbers. When the bill passes, you can build your canal as you planned. And in the meantime, the promise of my dowry will appease your creditors."

She smiled at him. A fake engagement would save them decades of torturing each other. It was so tidy she wondered why she hadn't thought of it herself.

"It won't work, Constance."

"Of course it will."

He closed his eyes and took a long, slow breath. "You do realize no respectable gentleman would marry you if you did this. You'd be ruined."

She laughed. "Apthorp. No *respectable* gentleman would marry me as it is."

"Don't be ridiculous." He said it so gruffly she looked at him in surprise. Did he really think she was capable of attracting—

"Your brother's a duke," he added quickly. "You have eighty thousand pounds."

Oh. That.

"Yes, and a reputation for being as vulgar and indecent as I am rich. We both know I'm not a proper lady. You've made your thoughts on that subject clear enough for years."

His mouth fell open in offense. He looked genuinely aghast. "I've *never* said you weren't a lady."

She snorted. "No, you are far too polite to ever say anything as direct as that, Lord Bore. Instead you imply I cut my meat too indelicately, evade my chaperones too frequently, fraternize with gentlemen too indiscriminately, curtsy too abruptly, talk too loudly, and go on about plays and poetry too lengthily. One needn't explicitly call someone unsuitable to make the point."

He looked so horrified that for a moment she was embarrassed that she had revealed too much. And she had not even *mentioned* the incident with the rosebush, or the portrait gallery.

"Anyway," she said airily, waving it off. "It scarcely matters, as I don't wish to marry the kind of man who would covet some dull and dreary *yes m'lord*-ing flower of the realm."

That the concern in his face disappeared let her know she had arrived upon the right argument. She dug in for emphasis. "Imagine *me*, stuck in some rotting country pile amusing myself with charity baskets and sewing. I scarcely want to be a wife, let alone a dreary country countess. I want to write plays and travel and be free from the tedious strictures one must observe if one is a proper sort of lady. Being *improper* is my calling."

He maintained an even expression as he took in this speech, but she could tell by the way his eyes darkened that it stung him.

Good.

He crossed his arms. "Fine. But even if that's true, your brother will never go along with such a scheme."

Her smug serenity evaporated. He was right.

At the mention of her brother, Constance's face darkened.

For a moment, she seemed less certain. But then she tossed her head and rolled her eyes at him.

"He will, because he will not *know* about it. I will convince him we are in love."

"In love," Apthorp repeated.

She nodded. "*Madly.* For ages and ages. Ever since I caught you unawares and kissed you in a garden maze and you could not stop dreaming about me." She smiled at him bitterly.

The words were like a stickpin to his heart. Far closer to the truth than she could know. He chose not to acknowledge them.

"Westmead will murder me if he thinks I've dragged you into this. He'd be right to call me out."

"Unless he believes that my heart will snap in two without you. And he will. Because I will *make it so.*"

The stickpin became more like a dagger.

"And what of when we call it off? What will he think then?"

The light in her eyes went dark. Clearly, she had not thought this through. But if she wanted to pretend that such a plan had no consequences for her future, he would not.

She loved her brother and her family fiercely. Her loyalty to them was one of the things about her he admired.

"We won't ever tell him it was fake, of course. I don't wish for him to know that I exposed you, and it will not serve you to let anyone know we have conspired. If you will agree not to mention it, I'll simply run away."

"You'll *run away?*" he repeated. "What about your family? All your friends in London? Your plays?"

She smiled and shrugged, as though the things he had watched her pursue with a blind intensity for the past five years meant nothing to her, and he was foolish to think that they had.

"England is so provincial. I'm bored of it. I long for Paris."

"We're on the cusp of war with France," he ground out.

"Then I'll go to Genoa or Vienna," she snapped. "Where I go is not your concern, in any case. You needn't be so honorable. Your honor is *wasted* on me. Is that not clear?"

No, it isn't, he stopped himself from saying. He would not lower himself by conveying the appeal of intelligence and determination and a sparkling wit—not to mention cornflower-blue eyes and the kind of hair rarely found outside of poetry—to his betrayer.

She lowered her voice. "Apthorp, be sensible. If you won't save yourself, think of your mother and sister. They have no independent means and they will be destroyed by this. You have a duty to them. We both do. To *fix* it."

He closed his eyes. She was manipulating him. And it was working.

He *did* owe it to his family to salvage what he could of this disaster. It was bad enough they would be plunged into scandal on his account. But to tell them that the meager luxuries he'd managed to sustain for them—the good tea that was so important to his mother; the one new gown each year; the annual trip to Tunbridge Wells to take the waters and be seen living as though things were as they'd always been—he couldn't imagine telling them they would have to give them up.

How could he ask them to pay for his mistakes again, after all he'd put them through?

How could he ask that when there was a chance, however slim, that Constance's plan could work?

She wielded a not insignificant amount of influence in London society, after all, moving fluidly between aristocratic circles and the colorful world of the artists and writers she patronized. Her balls and salons were as legendary as her family's reputation for rebellion. Together, he and Constance would have the eyes of London on them. They would have an opportunity.

But could he stomach it?

Could he swallow down the hurt that rose in his throat like bile at what she'd done and the manner in which she'd done it?

Excuse her for believing that he, or anyone, deserved to be pilloried and shamed for doing what he liked in private? Lead a woman who felt such contempt for him around ballrooms and before their families as if she made him the happiest man on earth? And do it knowing they were lying to everyone they loved?

He inhaled and caught Constance's distinctive fragrance wafting near him, smoky and round, like frankincense and orange blossoms. A scent that suggested her formal gowns and fresh blond beauty belied secrets a certain kind of man would give anything to know.

He opened his eyes to find her perched on her knees before him in the posture of a supplicant.

Christ. The things he would have done, a day ago, to see her willingly in that position.

The chasm in his chest that had once filled with light whenever he thought of her boiled over with regret.

Of course he could pretend.

Of course.

He could, because adoring her came as naturally as drawing breath.

He had loved her for eight years. What was four more weeks?

"Fine," he said.

She looked up, and her eyes danced in that way that promised mischief, and for a moment, without thinking, he wanted to lean in and kiss her.

And in that moment he mourned. Mourned all the things he'd wanted that they would never have.

Places he'd imagined taking her.

Secrets he'd always wanted her to know.

Questions he'd always longed to ask her.

A thousand small moments they would never share.

She beamed at him. "Oh good. It will all work out, I promise. Perhaps we will even have a bit of fun staging our little drama. And when it's over—"

Her enthusiasm was more than he could bear.

"When it's over," he interrupted, "we will never speak again."

She looked up, startled. "Well, that could be difficult, given your cousin is married to mine, but certainly we can—"

"No," he interrupted. He needed her to really, truly hear him.

"It matters, Constance. It matters what you did. *It matters when you hurt people.*"

Her fluttering, her fidgeting—the nervous, playful energy that always seethed and popped around her—stopped.

He leaned down toward her so their heads were level. "For the next four weeks, I will be as fawning as any man has ever been in public. But here, between us, let me be honest: the things that you wrote about me are distorted. I have no idea where you heard them or what right you thought you had to print them. Such matters are *private*, and if you believe my tastes in bed make me so sordid as to be unmarriageable, you might have addressed the matter privately. To *shame* me with no warning, to make my family suffer—shows a lack of decency that I would never have imagined possible in you."

Her face went white as the rope of opals knotted around her neck.

"Julian," she said softly. "I didn't mean to—"

"Address me by my title. And spare me your excuses. What you have done will expose a place that deliberately operates in darkness because it is a sanctuary to people who the men and women *ranting* outside my door believe belong in hell for something that harms no one. People who are dear to me may be exposed in consequence, and people whose livelihoods depend on the discretion the place offers may suffer, and for what? So that the public may have the joy of righteous disapproval?"

He said this with extra pointedness, for Lady Constance Stonewell, the most rebellious young woman in all of London, was famously dismissive of conforming to society's expectations. That a woman who welcomed opera girls and dancing bears into her drawing room could display the precise combination of prurience and prudishness that drove people like himself into the shadows was an act of hypocrisy difficult to fathom.

She'd always mocked him for being careful with appearances. But people like her were the reason people like him needed to be careful.

"I suppose," she said quietly, looking even more miserable than she had when he'd made her read her poem, "that I didn't consider … that it did not occur to me …"

He held up a hand. "Just hear this, Constance. I'll go along with your plan for the sake of my family and my reputation. For the sake of my friends who will be endangered if these rumors continue unabated. But when this farce is over, regardless of where you go or what you do, you will do it without my friendship."

She chewed her cheek, looking absolutely shaken.

"I understand," she finally said. "And you have my word."

"Fine." He rose feeling stiff and empty, like his soul had given up and left his body in defeat.

"I'll print rumors of our engagement in my circular to get the ladies talking, and we'll convince my brother of our love tomorrow night at the Rosecrofts' supper."

He nodded. "I'll get you a litter."

He went outside and found two burly chairmen idling on the Strand, and led them up the stairs to the entry hall. Constance was waiting in the vestibule, her pretty gown soiled at the knees from kneeling on his floorboards.

She picked up her skirts and stepped into the sedan chair, drawing yards of cloth around her collapsed panniers so that it looked as though she were a princess nestled in a cloud of silk.

He looked away and nodded at the chairmen to remove her.

Constance stuck her head out the window of the conveyance. "Apthorp?"

Her blue eyes were misty and her cheeks were mottled pink.

"Yes?"

"You're right. I see that now. And I'm truly very sorry." Her voice broke, and before he could react, she closed the curtains.

His heart lunged painfully and he inhaled against the urge to pull the curtains open, smash his forehead to hers, and tell her that he would forgive her anything because the sight of her in tears did something to his organs that made it difficult to breathe.

But that was the gesture of the kind of man he could no longer afford to be.

And so instead he turned his back and walked inside so he wouldn't have to hear her muffled sobs.

He had four weeks.

Four weeks to save his life.

Four weeks to learn how to stop loving Constance Stonewell.

CHAPTER 4

Yesterday I wrote in error
About that lord with golden hair—
The claims about his sullied hide
Were invented by a foe who lied
In a scheme designed to kill
Lord Golden's most right-minded bill.

I must ask forgiveness of Lord G—
For subjecting him to mockery
And wish his lordship much felicity
In his future domesticity!
For one hears from sources very sound
He's betrothed to eighty thousand pounds.
Some call her the loveliest girl in town,
With her silver tresses and cunning gowns
(A claim that one cannot rebuke,
For she's the sister of a duke).

So here's to Golden and his bride—
With apologies to his wronged backside!

—LETTERS FROM PRINCESS COSIMA

*A*pthorp checked the knot of his cravat as he stood before the Rosecrofts' town house door.

Still exact.

He glanced at his gloves to ensure they had not collected dirt during the walk to Mayfair from the Strand.

Still pristine.

He made a final inspection of his cuffs—still impeccable—and cursed himself for stalling.

His valet had taken pains to return him to his usual standards of appearance. That he felt raffish and improper straight down to his liver was between him and his perfect tailoring.

He forced himself to raise his hand to the heavy iron knocker. Before his fingers touched it, the door swung open, revealing the very person he dreaded seeing more than anyone else: Constance's brother, the Duke of Westmead.

Looking even more irritable than usual.

"Apthorp," Westmead drawled. "I was curious how long it might take you to find the courage to actually knock at the door, but now I've grown bored of watching you merely stare at it. Do come in. You've arrived just in time. I'm absolutely itching to hit someone."

"Your Grace." Apthorp bowed, stepping inside the vestibule and trying to refrain from cowering at the threat.

Westmead slammed the door behind him so forcefully it echoed through the corridor and rattled the doors to the dining room thirty feet away.

No one stirred.

The house, usually a merriment of children, servants, and dogs on the evenings of the family's weekly Monday suppers, was conspicuously silent. Apthorp glanced down the corridor, hoping for some sign of Constance. But she, the coward, was as absent as the rest of the family.

Westmead folded his arms. "Have anything to say to me?"

Apthorp cleared his throat. "Where is Lady Constance?"

The duke smiled tightly. "I imagine she is hiding, lest she be called as a witness when I am tried for shooting you."

He sighed. "I gather you've heard the news."

"No, not 'heard,' Apthorp, for no one saw fit to speak to me. *Seen* would be the word. Seen in a *third-rate gazette* on my way inside a coffeehouse *in Shoreditch.*" He smacked a palm to Apthorp's chest and shoved him up against a wall. "Shoreditch, Apthorp. A group of fur traders were discussing news of my sister's impending marriage to a ruined cully this afternoon in *Shoreditch*. And so, may I ask: what in the name of *ever-living fuck* could you be thinking?"

Apthorp winced. "I apologize, Your Grace. I intended to speak to you, but the gazettes got ahead of me. I submit, the situation is not ideal."

"'Not ideal.' Mmm. Do you mean the bit where you *cocked up* the bill I've spent two years touting for you, or the bit where you somehow—in contravention of all *sense*—betrothed yourself to my sister?"

Westmead could be caustic at the happiest of times, but he was usually tightly controlled. The sheer force of his anger felt like a blow to the ribs and lingered, aching.

Mostly because Apthorp agreed with him.

Westmead had been his closest ally in politics, the unlikely champion of his bill when he'd had little beyond determination to recommend him. And Apthorp had not only failed politically but gone and yoked his failure to the man's only sister without so much as a word of warning.

His behavior was exactly as noxious as the duke's disgusted stare implied.

"Your Grace, I'm sorry. None of this was my intention."

Westmead worked his fingers in the air, like he was looking for a neck to throttle. "Don't speak to me of intentions, Apthorp.

What I'd like to speak about is *decency*. A quality which before today I would not have said you lacked."

"First let me assure you that the rumors of my supposed dissipation are exaggerated. You need not worry that—"

Westmead held up a hand to stop him. "Spare me. That isn't what I mean. Whatever you've gotten yourself into at Mistress Brearley's is your private affair."

"Mistress Brearley's?" he repeated. The question was disingenuous, for he knew exactly to whom Westmead referred. He simply could not imagine how *Westmead* knew of her.

"Don't play innocent with me," Westmead growled. "I'm an investor in her club. While I'm baffled by your carelessness in allowing your membership there to become gossip, you don't need to explain your tastes to me. Your *tastes*, whatever they may be, are not my concern."

Apthorp stared at him, not sure whether to be relieved or more alarmed. "Thank you, Your Grace, for your broad-minded—"

"Which of course does not change the fact that you will *not be marrying my sister*." Westmead's eyes drilled into his.

Apthorp swallowed and tried to ignore that Westmead looked at him like he'd grown mold. "With respect, Your Grace, I'm afraid I *will* be marrying her. She has agreed to be my wife. To my tremendous honor."

The duke's lips curled. "Tremendous honor. I see. Or rather, I don't. I *don't* see, Apthorp, because I keep getting stuck on the small fact that Constance cannot *stand* you."

"Can't stand him?" an offended feminine voice trilled. Constance came sailing up from the lower stairs, dressed in a shimmering pink gown with hoops so wide she resembled a schooner made of ballerinas. She was flushed and slightly disheveled, with strands of dust clinging to her hair, exactly as they might had she been eavesdropping in the service cupboard below the stairs. Which, given her history of doing exactly that whenever anyone in the house was peeved with her, would explain her absence.

"What rubbish, Archer," she said, reaching the landing as she caught her breath. "I adore Apthorp."

Westmead whirled around. "*You.* What do you have to say for yourself?"

"Surprise!" She threw out her arms in his direction, as if in expectation of a joyous embrace. "Isn't it wonderful!"

"Wonderful?" Westmead repeated. "What in bequaking Sodom are you *thinking?*"

"I'm in love!" she cried. "Rapturously in love!" She spun around, letting her skirts swish about in festive circles. "Oh, Archer, I've been dying to tell you, but I was worried you might try to stop me."

He came and put two hands on her shoulders, forcing her to stop spinning. "I am, without question, going to stop you."

"Oh, don't be tiresome," she chirped, shrugging him off. She wobbled backward, precarious in her hoops and heeled slippers. "I'm so delighted I might swoon."

Apthorp darted forward and pressed a hand to her shoulder to prevent her from careening into a credenza. She smiled fondly and took his other hand in hers. "My hero," she whispered in his ear, just loud enough for her brother to hear.

Westmead looked at both of them with the half-focused squint of a man suffering from vertigo or nausea. "What scheme is this you two have concocted?"

Constance wrinkled her nose. "Scheme? I finally find the courage to profess my love for the man I've pined for since girlhood, and you accuse me of a scheme? That is cynical even for you, Archer."

"Constance. You can't possibly expect me to believe you want to marry *Apthorp.*"

Apthorp tried not to be offended by the degree of derision in this statement, however much he might privately agree with Westmead's position.

"Whyever not?" Constance asked. She reached up and cradled Apthorp's face, cupping his jaw like he was a priceless piece of pottery in a museum. "Is he not the most handsome man you've ever seen?"

Apthorp tried not to be moved at the idea she found him handsome.

Was that just for her brother's benefit? Or does she really—

Westmead closed his eyes and averted his face, as if the sight of his sister touching Apthorp might render him blind, reminding him the question was moot.

"Constance, it has not escaped my notice that you have displayed nothing but contempt for Apthorp for half a decade. You have addressed his Christmas gifts to 'Lord Bore' since 1749."

Constance gave her brother a long-suffering sigh. "I was *flirting*, Archer. Haven't you ever been flirted with?" She paused, and looked up conspiratorially at Apthorp. "Upon further reflection, no. I daresay he has not."

Apthorp choked back a snort of laughter. Constance fluttered her eyelashes at him, evidently pleased to be found amusing. Dear God. Despite his impulse to despise her, it was enjoyable, this feeling of being in league with Constance. It was exactly the thing he'd always wanted.

"Very well," Westmead interjected, forcing the rupture of their small moment. "Apthorp is your great love, then? The man you feel you deserve? *Him?* A person who does nothing but lecture you on how bothersome and vulgar you are?"

Apthorp froze. He felt Constance freeze beside him.

Was that true?

Given that she had made exactly the same observation the day before, he could only surmise that he was … *guilty.*

He ticked through half a decade's interactions. Since she'd arrived from France at fourteen, she'd been such a bold, fanciful creature that he'd worried she would say the wrong thing to the wrong person. He'd sometimes offered her discreet advice about manners and comportment, but only out of a desire to protect her. He'd meant to help her see that her bold ways left her open to criticism.

He had *never* meant to imply she was unfit.

Before he could think of what to say, she recovered her composure with an airy wave of her wrist.

"Well, I *can be* bothersome and vulgar, when it serves my purpose. It's part of my charm." She looked at him with an arch smile. "Clearly, it worked on Apthorp, didn't it, darling?"

He nodded with everything he had.

Westmead plucked her hand from Apthorp's arm and spoke to her with a voice like gravel. "Constance, I regret I have not always been the most attentive or affectionate of brothers. If I could go back and be a better guardian to you in the years when you were small, I would. But in light of what happened to our mother, I have made certain you would never need to marry any man you did not choose. So I beg you, before you make a mistake that is irrevocable, consider whether there might not be some person out there whom you cherish, and who would cherish you in return."

Constance glanced up at Apthorp, and for first time he saw uncertainty in her eyes. He couldn't blame her. That speech made *him* want to weep with sentiment, and he was the villain of it.

There was only one thing he could possibly offer in response: the truth.

He stepped forward and met Westmead's eyes. "Your Grace, I have loved your sister since I was eighteen years old. I regret I hid my feelings behind a stiff exterior, but it was only because I did not want to prevail on her to consider my suit until I felt confident I could be the kind of husband who deserves her. It is the tragedy of my life that I will never be that man. And the miracle of it is that your sister would have me anyway." To his astonishment, his voice cracked.

Both Constance and Westmead stared at him, as shocked as he was by his display of emotion. He turned to the wall and collected himself.

Constance came and put a comforting hand on his shoulder. "Oh, my darling. There, there."

She turned to Westmead. "Don't you see, Archer? He acts aloof, but only to protect his tender heart. Is it not human to hide our vulnerabilities?"

Apthorp took a minute with the wall. In truth, saying these words to manipulate the duke only made him feel worse. For once, mere days ago, he would have meant them virtuously. Using them in the service of this gambit was a travesty for which he would not soon forgive himself.

Nor soon would he forgive himself for making Constance feel he had rebuked her for the very qualities that made her exceptional. He could see that beneath her laughing dismissal of his criticisms was real hurt. How had he never noticed it before?

Westmead had begun to pace. "If all of this is true—and I am not saying I *believe* you—then why am I reading about it in a bloody gazette?"

"Apthorp wanted to ask for your blessing, but I forbade him," Constance said. "It's my decision whom I marry. I shouldn't need your permission."

"Nor should I need yours to call him out."

"Call him out?" she said coldly, the girlish effusion suddenly so absent from her voice it was chilling. "What purpose would that serve?"

"Justice."

"No. Think clearly. It would merely amplify the scandal. And you are far too shrewd to do that. What I suspect you will do is welcome my intended husband into our family and make a great show of seeing that anyone who attempts to cut him understands they do so at their peril. And then you will help him save his bill."

"You overestimate my powers to protect him or you," West-

mead thundered back. "If you betroth yourself to him, your reputation will be damned and there's nothing I can do about it. You're
going to be the talk of the whole nation. And for what?"

"I enjoy being the talk of the nation. Have you not noticed my
concerted efforts to engender just that effect for years? And
besides, no one is more adept at shaping reputations than myself.
I have a plan. And if you hold me in as high regard as you say you
do, you will grant me the capacity of knowing my own will and
letting me see it through."

Westmead rubbed his temples, looking from his sister to
Apthorp and back again. "I see that you're both determined. What
I don't yet see is why."

"Because I love him," Constance said, in a tone so simple and
believable that he once again wanted to weep. "I *love* him, Archer.
I know it might be hard for you to accept that, given I have always
made a point of hiding it before. I know you only want to protect
me. But *you* don't need to. *Apthorp* will."

Damn him if his traitor's heart did not swell at these words.
Damn him if he did not resolve to somehow make them true.

"Westmead, give us the evening to convince you," he said
quietly. "If you still doubt my sincerity, we'll call the whole thing
off. You have my word."

Westmead shut his eyes. "Fine," he said. "Convince me. Otherwise it's dawn with dueling pistols."

Constance leapt up and threw her arms around her brother,
her steely demeanor suddenly so featherlight Apthorp wondered
if he'd dreamt it. "Thank you, Archer. I knew you were a romantic
at heart. Now come, both of you. It's time for supper and
everyone is waiting."

As soon as her brother turned and stalked down the hall to
the dining room, Constance latched on to Apthorp's arm to shore

him up. He had the look about him of a man who had eaten day-old cockles and was about to pay the price.

"That was brilliant, your little speech," she said. "So moving even *I* nearly believed you."

He shifted away, but she clutched his arm more tightly. She was aware she was holding on to him in the manner of a child squeezing an uncooperative cat, but she did not feel any steadier than he looked, and it soothed her nerves to touch him. Now that she'd started, she couldn't seem to stop.

He paused and turned to look at her. "You realize Westmead doesn't believe us."

"Not yet. But he will."

She said it more to reassure herself than to convince Apthorp. And what she meant was that *he must.* Because she'd heard every word her brother had said from her hidden spot beneath the stairs, and when he'd revealed he was an investor in the whipping club, she'd felt like she might plummet through the earth. She would *prefer* to plummet through the earth than to see his face if he found out what she'd done.

For what Apthorp had said about the club serving as a haven for people who risked judgment had lingered with her bitterly for hours the night before, like the flavor of raw garlic on the breath. Neither she nor her brother had ever fit their birth-appointed places in society. For her part, she had made this a point of pride, adopting fellow outcasts and eccentrics and burnishing their odd qualities, as she did her own, with vast supplies of insouciance and money. Her brother had gone a different route, disguising his sensibilities beneath a cold exterior and keeping mostly to himself. She did not wish to think too deeply about how a secret whipping house might feature into his private comforts. But if such a place had given him respite from the desolation of their family's past ... well.

It was enough to know that Archer invested only in concerns that he believed in. If he championed the place, it must be something he cared about ferociously. And she couldn't stand to see her brother hurt.

She could *never* let him know she'd been the architect of it.

Apthorp stopped walking and forced her to look at him. "Constance, you don't have to do this for me. If we reverse course *right* now, it will not be too late to change your mind."

She gave him her most serene smile. "I am not doing this for *you*. I am doing this because I made a mistake I am determined to repair. Just agree with everything I say at supper."

He glared at her, looking boyish in his petulance and not the least bit in love with her. She tapped a finger to his scowling lips. "And pretend you *like me*."

He removed her fingers from his mouth and placed them over his heart, smiling into her eyes like she was a precious object.

"Better, my love?"

She smirked at him, pleased that he could mount a show of false adoration at will, even if the sight of her seemed to repel him. They would need that skill.

"Quite. Now, then. During the meal I'm going to excuse myself to freshen up. When I do, I want you to wait five minutes, make an excuse, and follow me down the corridor toward the billiards room."

Hilary poked her head through the double doors to the dining room. "Oh, there you are. Do come to the table before Westmead overturns it." Her eyes fell to where their joined fingers lay pressed to Apthorp's chest, and the corners of her mouth drew up.

"Oh my, you two. I *knew* it, you know. I've been telling Rosecroft you had an attachment for years."

Constance gave her cousin a conspiratorial smile, though she was not sure how poor Hilary had come to that conclusion, given that prior to this week she and Apthorp had communicated mostly in veiled insults.

They followed her into the dining room, where the family was assembled in their usual positions. At the head of the table sat

Rosecroft. To his left, Constance's sister-in-law, Poppy—the Duchess of Westmead—and beside her the duke, who was looking surlier by the minute.

In the year since he had married, her brother had become far more fluent in expressing his emotions. This was charming when it manifested as tenderness for his wife and baby, but far less agreeable when he was angry. He no longer stared at you in cool dispassion when he wanted to murder you; he took great pains, and exercised considerable verbal precision, to let you know.

"Thank you all for welcoming us," Apthorp said to the assembled family. "I apologize if our news has caused you shock. We did so wish to tell you privately. We are baffled by how rumors reached the papers before we had the chance."

"Yes, they're an affront to decency, those dreadful hacks," Constance said. She was pleased Apthorp had taken the initiative to distance her from the gossip.

"Well," Hilary said, lifting up her glass. "I suppose a toast is in order? Rosecroft, will you do the honors?"

Rosecroft stood and raised a glass. "To the unexpected news," he began.

"*Salut,*" Archer said, and gulped down his entire glass of claret in one swig.

Rosecroft, who had clearly intended to say more, cleared his throat uncomfortably and sat back down.

Hilary looked at Archer and shook her head. "I don't know why you are behaving as if this is a shock. It's been clear to me they care for each other for years."

"Yes!" Constance nodded vigorously, shooting her cousin a grateful smile. "You were all rather dense not to see it."

She heard her brother grinding his molars from halfway across the table.

Poppy, no doubt hearing it too, cleared her throat. "Well, my dear, you could perhaps forgive the rest of us for being taken aback. The two of you *were* rather convincing in your dislike for one another. Perhaps you could tell us how this … attachment … began?"

"Oh yes," Archer drawled. "Do. I can't wait to hear this confabulation."

"It's not a confabulation," Constance said, pleased at Poppy for the opening. "More like … a *conspiracy*."

Archer slammed his glass on the table. "Damn it, Apthorp. I warned you—"

Constance reached across the table and put her hand on her brother's fist. It was touching, in a way, how angry he was. She was rather shocked he cared so much.

"No, I mean I conspired with a rosebush to make Apthorp fall in love with me. Years ago. In the maze at Rosemount, a few days after James and Hilary's wedding. It was entirely my fault, you see."

Because things that went awry in their family usually *were* her fault, this seemed to mollify her brother. He, and everyone else, stared at her, waiting for the story.

Of course, that meant she needed to invent the rest of it. Quickly, and with feeling.

She had always found the best way of making a convincing narrative was to base it upon truth and embellish it until it fit one's purpose. She closed her eyes and tried to recall the exact emotions of that dreadful day.

"It was that first summer you summoned me back to England," she told Archer. "I'd been in France for so long I'd developed an atrocious accent—do you remember?"

They all nodded.

"It was before we realized Tante Louise was ill, and so every time she was meant to chaperone me, she fell asleep, poor thing. And I, being the terror you all adore, took advantage of it by sneaking off onto the grounds when I was meant to be resting in my room. That was when I realized that Apthorp had a habit of strolling through the garden maze every afternoon at three."

Apthorp looked at her oddly.

"At the convent school in France, I was never around young men, and certainly none that looked like Apthorp." She gestured at him, to seem helplessly lovestruck. "Forgive me for being forward, but you all *have* noticed what he looks like? Has there ever been a more beautiful man?"

It was rather a relief to be able to acknowledge Apthorp's prodigious beauty out loud for once, instead of merely sneaking jealous glances at him from the corner of her eye.

"Get on with it," her brother said, looking like he had eaten a rat.

"I was an excitable girl of fourteen, as you remember, and Julian was the newly minted earl, all serious with newfound purpose and therefore scarcely aware of my existence. And you *know* I can't stand to go unnoticed."

They all exchanged pained nods.

"I tried all sorts of tricks to catch his eye. Asked about his sister, hid his books, tried to persuade him to play in my theatricals. He ignored me. Naturally, I began to plot."

"Naturally," her brother muttered. A good sign, as it meant he did not entirely disbelieve her tale. Which was fair, as so far every word of it was true.

"I had been reading Tante Louise's books when she was sleeping—she was fond of those wicked memoirs by French courtesans that summer—and they filled my head with ideas of seduction. I thought if I could only catch Apthorp alone and declare myself to him, I would instantly bestir his passions."

She could see her brother's face becoming man-killing again, so she reached out across the table and patted his hand. "Spare us another threat of dueling pistols, Your Grace. I will put you out of your suspense: it didn't work."

Hilary and Poppy chuckled. Even Archer and Rosecroft seemed to relax a bit. Constance didn't dare look at Apthorp, lest she lose her nerve. Instead she plastered her face into a rueful smile and leaned in, to draw their sympathies.

"I waited for Tante Louise to fall asleep, put on my prettiest dress, and arranged my hair like a sophisticated older girl. And then I slipped into the maze and waited behind an urn near the bench where I knew he liked to read."

"*Waited* would be a mischaracterization," Apthorp cut in. "I would call it crouched in hiding."

She nodded in complete agreement, surprised he still remembered. "Yes, exactly, and as soon as he arrived, I jumped out and threw my arms around his neck and tried to kiss him." She bit her lip. "I was, er, not very good at it."

"She nearly relieved me of my ear," Apthorp summarized. "Drew blood."

She felt herself coloring. "Well, only because you leapt out of my way. I was aiming for your cheek."

"Christ," Archer muttered.

"Needless to say," she went on, "instead of winning a courtly suitor, I received a severe scolding, a warning that I risked bringing dishonor upon my family, and Apthorp's promise to tell Archer what I'd done if I did not behave. Naturally I burst into tears and ran away."

"Poor dear. It must have been embarrassing," Poppy said softly.

"Oh, *humiliating*," Constance agreed. For some reason, she could still not look at Apthorp, though the memory was so old you would think it would be stale by now. "I thought I might actually melt of shame. I went back to my room and wept for hours, and that evening I pretended to be ill so I wouldn't have to face him at supper."

Here, she did peek at Apthorp. He once again looked rather green, and didn't meet her eye.

"The next morning I awoke in a very morose mood, determined to do something desperate and poetic like drown myself in the lake or cut off all my hair. But then I noticed there were flowers on my windowsill. A mess of crimson roses—all different lengths hacked off with a pocketknife and tied with twine. It was the ugliest bouquet I'd ever seen. But attached was a note and to this day, I can still recall every word. It said: *Dear Lady Constance, please accept these flowers as an apology for my harsh words to you. And with them, my assurance that while you are far too young for suitors now, you will no doubt receive many more bouquets in due time from gentlemen who will admire your spirit, intelligence, and beauty. Until then, I hope you will take to heart the sentiment that strikes me when I look at you: that the best things are worth waiting for. With warm regard, Apthorp.*"

To her shock, she found she could barely say the final line, because she had to wipe away a tear. Rather pathetic, given that the truth of her story had ended with Apthorp summarily dressing her down and forgetting the matter entirely.

"So you see," she said, "from that day on, I loved him. Because he is sensitive and kind, even if he does sometimes deserve the name Lord Bore."

She used a serviette to dab her eyes.

"Excuse me," she said, rising from the table. "I really must freshen up."

APTHORP GLANCED AT THE CLOCK AS CONSTANCE LEFT THE ROOM. It was half past seven. He had five minutes.

The family was quiet. He was not the only one, it seemed, who was oddly shaken by the emotion of Constance's story.

She was wrong to think he'd been unaware of her that summer. He'd been intrigued by the precocious young lady with the captivating air. But she was four years his junior, and not yet out, and not accustomed to English manners. It would have been appalling to think of her as anything other than a child, and one in need of his protection.

Besides, he was preoccupied. His father had died the year before and while he'd no doubt meant to get the estate in order long before it became his heir's problem to sort out, the elder earl had not counted on his heart suddenly stopping at the age of eight and forty. With the title came a new reality: the estate was bleeding money and carrying heavy debts. His mother was frantic that no one should know their circumstances. To stanch the flow, something had to change.

Apthorp's strolls in the garden had not been the idyllic pastime of a carefree young man. He'd gone outside so his family would not see him rifling through investment strategies, trying to parse silt from ash, and coal from granite, and the costs of borrowing against the estate's future gains—concepts he had not been trained in and strained to understand. He'd been desperate to hide how desperate he was becoming. How inadequate he was to the task.

Such had been his state when a small presence had come barreling at him and nearly knocked him off his feet into a rose-bush, gnashing at his ear. He'd been so alarmed he'd pushed her away before he'd realized what, much less who, she was.

Perhaps, in his surprise, he'd been less gentle than he ought.

He remembered that she'd cried and he'd felt bad. But soon enough, his thoughts had traveled back to his accounts, his diminishing coffers, the absurdity of a man so young propping up an estate nearly as old as the kingdom itself.

He'd not noticed how he'd hurt her.

So the end of her story—the kind note, the flowers, the respectful words of admiration—was a fiction.

He'd never apologized for wounding her.

And now that he recalled, she'd never looked at him the same way again.

If he'd reacted better in that startled moment, would it have changed the course of both their lives?

"Well," the duchess said, turning to him and breaking the

silence, "don't leave us in suspense. Did you send her a bouquet expressing your admiration when she came of age?"

He cleared his throat, which had grown thick with regret. "After that day, I never stopped thinking about her. When she returned, three years later, she'd grown up. I couldn't believe the transformation."

"I remember," Hilary said. "It was at that dreadful, rainy house party we had at my lodge in Devon. You spent the entire week gazing at her. You pulled me aside and asked me how many seasons young ladies waited before they married."

He winced at the memory of that trip. "Well, by then things had gone so badly with the mines I couldn't have proposed."

That, and he had gathered her affections were trained elsewhere.

"Didn't stop you this time," Westmead muttered.

Apthorp glanced at the clock. It had been seven minutes. He was late.

"Excuse me," he said, rising. "I want to see that Constance is all right. The past two days have been a trial for us both."

Before anyone could object, he went down the corridor where she'd fled. There was no sign of her. He poked his head into the billiards room, but it was empty.

He tried the sitting room, but succeeded only in startling a maid who had been cleaning up the tea remains in silence.

"Constance?" he called out in a low voice. At the end of the hall there was only the closet used for powdering wigs. Surely she was not—

A small, ink-stained hand shot out of the door, grabbed him by the wrist, and pulled him inside.

CHAPTER 5

$\mathcal{S}$he knew him by his footsteps alone. That precise clipped pace, the moderate thump of a well-kept heel articulated under a (she imagined) slender but finely muscled calf. He never shuffled or stomped. He walked the way he did everything: elegantly.

She reached out from behind the closet door and grabbed him.

Perhaps with too much force, for he came careening toward her in a half stumble and nearly crushed her against the shelves.

"What are you doing?" he gasped, bracing against the shelf above her head to find his balance. The closet was small, just big enough for two adults to stand in. It was lined with wig stands and jars of powder and smelled heavy, like starch and milled soaps. And now, like the woody, balsam scent of whatever Apthorp used to oil his hair.

"Waiting impatiently to be discovered weeping in the wig closet by my future husband," she said irritably. "Who is four minutes late."

"May I ask why you are in the wig closet?"

"Because wig closets are just the improbable, tucked-away kinds of places that young lovers go when they wish to steal a moment of privacy to offer each other comfort outside of the prying eyes of their extended families."

He glanced at her face in the shadows.

"You appear decidedly dry-eyed."

"Can you please get on with it?"

"Pardon?"

"Hurry. When we're discovered, you can't be freshening up your peruke. Kiss me."

He inched backward into a stack of smocks. "Absolutely not."

"Must I do everything?"

She latched on to his shoulders so that he could not escape and, before she could lose her nerve, planted her lips on his.

She had not taken the initiative to kiss anyone since that first fumbling attempt on Apthorp all those years ago—and it was harder than it looked to do it properly, without accidentally eating someone's nose or clacking into his jaw with one's forehead. She felt like a mole nosing in the dark for a berry on a bush just slightly out of reach. Under her fumbling lips Apthorp went completely rigid. She stood up on her toes, trying to get better purchase.

He yanked his head out of her reach. "My God, what are you doing?"

"Kissing you. My brother will come looking for us at any moment. We must be locked in a passionate embrace."

He wiped his mouth with the back of his hand, his eyes flashing with some emotion she couldn't place.

"You know, Constance, you really must learn to ask permission."

He must really learn to stop lecturing her, but now was not the time to press the issue.

"Please just kiss me." It was imperative that when Archer found them, they be engaged in something more convincing than a discussion of the etiquette of courtship.

Apthorp stared at her, as if debating something in his mind.

"Constance, may I kiss you?" he asked in an official, courtly tone, like he was modeling correct behavior on which she might be tested later.

"Obviously."

Gently, he took a hand and tipped her mouth up to his. Gently, he put his lips to hers.

Given what she knew about the secret ways he spent his time, this pretension to gentlemanly delicacy was rather laughable. And they did not have time for it.

She snatched his head in her hands and mashed her face to his, trying to mount a more persuasive display of ardor before anyone witnessed this chaste, practically nonexistent peck.

She felt a rumble beneath her hands.

His shoulders were shaking.

With *laughter*.

She gasped and pushed him back. His shoulders hit the shelves, causing a wooden wig stand to fall onto a sack of lavender-scented powder, which erupted in a cloud that itched her nose. She immediately fell into a coughing fit so violent that, half-weeping with laughter, he pounded at her back.

"You cow," she said through gasps. "Because of you, we will both suffocate."

He stilled, clearly trying to restrain his mirth. "I'm sorry."

"What is so unbearably humorous?"

"The fact that you are mauling me in the powdering room."

"I was not *mauling* you. I was evincing passion."

His lip quirked up. "In my experience," he said softly, "that's not how passion works."

"No? It works by tiny mincing nibbles at my lower lip?"

"It *builds*. Lovers have to get to get a feel for one another."

"Sounds dreadfully dull."

He stared at her lips for a beat too long, then glanced up into her eyes.

"I assure you, Constance, it isn't."

She wanted to be angry at him, but she could not fail to notice that his eyes no longer held the ire they'd borne when he'd looked upon her yesterday. His gaze was earnest. Like he wanted her to understand something that was important to him.

She found herself at a loss for a response. Because for the first time, she was connecting the rumors about this man and his salacious nocturnal predilections to the person whose eyes lingered on her face rather more kindly than she'd have expected of a hellraking letch, yet with a knowledge in them that made her shiver.

"Haven't you ever been properly kissed?" he asked softly.

She stuck out her chin, embarrassed to admit that she was far less bold in her private behaviors than the devil-take-it portrait she liked to affect in public. "Of course I have."

He bit his lip. "Not by anyone who knew how to do it properly, apparently."

She knew exactly whom he meant, and he was right, but it was surly and impudent of him to point it out, for after his reaction to her in the garden maze at Rosemount, and that dreadful scene in Devon, she'd avoided any man who'd betrayed the slightest interest in providing demonstration for five years. She had not wished to be mortified again.

And she still did not. Particularly before a man who had just the day before reacted with visceral *revulsion* at the idea of marrying her.

"Fine," she shot back. "I confess. I am ignorant of your debauched ways. Maybe had I spent as much time as you cavorting in a *den of fornication*—"

He let out a sound of absolute shock that she had said that.

"You want to be kissed properly, you wicked girl?" he growled.

"As I *said*—" she began, but before she could finish, he put his finger to her chin to tip up her mouth, twined his hands behind her head, and kissed her the way she had imagined lovers kissed.

None of that boring, mousy *nibbling*.

His mouth was on hers, his tongue was against hers, and he

was using it to claim her. It was knowing and erotic and demanding and she felt like she would drown.

And not with passion. She couldn't breathe.

The portrait gallery and the smell of tobacco and the feeling of being trapped came rushing back.

"Stop," she cried, wrenching her mouth away.

His hands fell to his sides and he broke away immediately, moving back against the shelf behind him.

"Constance? I'm sorry. I didn't mean to scare you. I'm so sorry." He looked stricken.

"No, it's my fault, I told you to do it," she said quickly, stunned by her own reaction. "It's only ..." She trailed off. She felt overwhelmed and shy. She realized what the problem was, but she didn't want to say it: she was not *good* at kissing. It alarmed her and she didn't understand it. And she loathed —*loathed*—being observed undertaking tasks at which she did not naturally excel.

Especially by Apthorp.

"I don't know how to do it," she admitted darkly.

Slowly, he relaxed. "That's all right. There's no right or wrong way to kiss a person. Only the way that you like."

She glared at him. "I don't *know* what I like."

He bit his lip, like he was holding back a smile. "Ah."

"Don't gloat."

"I'm not gloating. I'm thinking. Perhaps let's try it the way I like, shall we?"

She nodded, hating this, wishing she could run away, but knowing that they really did need to be caught by her brother, and not at debating her inability to be seduced.

"Close your eyes," he said softly. His voice was gentle, and there was no longer any laughter in it.

She did.

"Lean back against the wall and relax."

She tried, but she was nervous. She waited for his lips again, holding her eyes shut tight. Instead his fingers lightly traced her cheek.

"Ideally," he murmured, "lovers enjoy each other's touch." His fingers brushed the back of her neck and landed at her nape, where the small hairs that always evaded her pins fell against her skin. His warmth made her shiver.

She heard him inhale.

Slowly, deliberately, he put his lips to the pulse of her throat.

It felt warm and feathery. Soothing.

"Do you like that?" he said softly, into her neck.

"Yes," she admitted.

"Me too," he said, almost to himself.

He ventured higher, dragging an airy line up to a place below her ear. Something crackled inside her, like he had dragged a flint across a fire steel and elicited a bloom of sparks.

His hand came to rest behind her, on the small of her back. "That's all right? Me touching you?"

"Yes."

His other hand caressed along her rib cage, just above her waist. "And that?"

"Yes," she made herself say. She felt at war with herself: very much inclined to like his touch but very reluctant to admit it to him.

His hand rested on her side and did not draw her forward toward his chest nor move up to her breasts. She wished it would do one or the other. Or both.

His mouth, too, remained just so, nuzzling her neck as his fingers stroked that dreadful, lovely spot along her nape. It felt safe, soft, like she was dissolving into light. Then he brought his lips to hers and took her lower lip. It was similar to his first attempt to kiss her and now she understood it.

It wasn't nibbling.

It was dancing.

Flirting.

Promising something else.

He let out a soft sigh, one that made her think perhaps the same feelings that were rising up in her were rising up in him.

"I would like it," he whispered against the corner of her mouth as his fingers rubbed small, molten circles over the fabric of her dress, "if you would kiss me back."

She hesitated, certain she would somehow do it wrong again and ruin this delicate, exquisite demonstration. But when his tongue resumed its passage near her lips, she brought her own mouth to his, lightly. And just like that, it clicked. She didn't *need* to think.

Her body told her what to do.

Her body told her that if she tasted him, he would like it, return it, let out another sigh of pleasure.

That he would hold her closer.

That she would kiss him back as earnestly as he was kissing her.

And just like that, she was kissing him exactly like a lover.

And she was not *pretending* that she liked it.

He'd never expected her to be so innocent.

Given her boldness in kissing him in the garden maze, and what he'd so excruciatingly happened upon in Devon, he'd assumed she had enjoyed flirtations since. When, in weak moments, he'd imagined making love to her, he had assumed she would not come to him a virgin.

Which was fine. He was not a virgin either.

Far from it.

But the woman in his arms was no experienced temptress.

She had been so apprehensive she was shaking.

But now, holding her just so, he felt the shift. The moment when she realized she liked his hands on her. When she discovered that place where one noticed little beyond skin and heat. When she realized one could separate from one's mind and became a creature of one's body.

He would never forget what it was like to hold Constance Stonewell as she realized what it felt like to want someone.

It changed everything.

What had started as a game to call her bluff was now too altogether real. He was kissing her in a powdering closet and he wanted very badly to do so much more than kiss her.

He tried to hold himself in a gentlemanly way, so that the telltale hardness rising at his groin would not frighten or embarrass her.

But when she leaned against him and stroked his cheek and let out a little moan, it was so honest that he abandoned his precepts of virtue and grazed against her, just for a fraction of a second. Long enough for her to feel him. Long enough for him to feel her.

He wanted her to feel him and know that he was not pretending either.

Because, damn it, they might never be this close again, and after all the years of wanting her, he wanted her to know.

He *needed* her to know.

Her eyes shot open and looked up into his.

He stared back, letting her see it in his eyes. Telling her that if she could read his mind, she was welcome to the confession pouring out of him.

The years and years of longing.

She held his gaze. Then she cocked her hip and rubbed against him and he was lost to understanding.

She paused uncertainly, and observing that he had not moved away—for how could he bring himself to move away?—she brought her lips back down and kissed him sweetly.

Fuck.

He fell on her like a wave, pulled her up against him so she was molded directly to all the places where he was hard, and put his mouth on hers while his body made a woman of her. He gave her the kind of filthy, erotic kiss that began in the hips and ended somewhere in the brain, a kiss that was not so much a kiss as a way of making love with all one's clothes on. The kind of kiss he had told her new lovers did not exchange before they knew each other's bodies.

Well, he'd been lying. He had wanted her for too many years to pretend that he did not want to fuck her filthily and well and in such a way that she would never want another—

The closet filled with light.

Hands came down on his collar and yanked him into the corridor.

A fist slammed into his jaw.

"I see we don't have to wait for dawn," the Duke of Westmead growled. "I'm going to murder you right now."

Oh, don't take him just quite yet, Constance wanted to protest as her brother peeled Apthorp off her body by his neck. *I was enjoying him immensely.*

She sighed as Archer shoved poor Apthorp against a wall and yanked his fussy wig right off his gorgeous head.

He looked *so* much better without it.

"Have you no respect?" Archer was shouting. "Do you *want* me to call you out?"

She bit back a smile. There was nothing like the sound of one's brother threatening to dismember one's *faux fiancé* to make a girl feel smug. The force of the duke's rage could only mean one thing: her plan was working.

She stepped forward and pried her brother's hands away from Apthorp's neck. "Stop it, Archer. You're going to hurt him."

"Yes, Constance, that is exactly my intention."

She shoved her way between them, separating them with her shoulders.

"Don't injure him. He was only comforting me."

"He was doing quite a bit more than that."

Indeed, he had been. She still felt as if she were made of jelly that hadn't quite set up. Who knew *Apthorp* was capable of turning a woman into a quivering dessert?

Not that pointing out this shocking fact would mollify her brother's anger.

"You needn't act like an innocent kiss between two people about to be married is cause for execution," she said. "Need I remind you the way you conducted yourself with Poppy when you were engaged? If *she'd* had a brother, you'd have been dead long before the wedding."

Archer turned on his heel. "Come with me. Both of you. Now."

He strode down the hall.

She took Apthorp's hand. "Are you all right?" she whispered.

"Never better," he said, licking away a bit of blood where his lip had caught a tooth.

A wave of tenderness for him rose up in her chest, surprising her.

"Poor man." She pulled a handkerchief from the pocket in her gown and dabbed the blood away.

He reached down for his wig and attempted to mold it into some semblance of its original shape.

"Don't bother. I like you better without it. You look agreeably dissolute."

"I do?" He looked startled but not displeased. But then his face returned to a grim line. "Constance—" he whispered, adopting the rather self-serious tone he always took when he was about to bore her with a pontification upon correct behavior.

Instead of listening, she spun on her heel and followed her brother down the hall. She was not prepared to discuss the oddness of what had just happened, and in any case her brother would certainly not wait for them to parse the strangeness of her intense desire to drag Apthorp to her bedchamber.

When he didn't follow her, she reached back for his wrist and pulled him after her down the hall, hoping a show of brisk congeniality would reassure him that they did not need to litigate the fact that he had just kissed her in a way that left her vibrating from her belly to her heels.

He let her. He seemed as dazed as she felt.

Westmead threw open the door to the billiards room and gestured at a sofa.

"Sit down," he ordered them.

They sat, side by side, like two naughty children.

"Be honest," he growled. "Is there a need for a special license?"

"No, Archer!" she sputtered, trying not to laugh at the idea she might be carrying Apthorp's child. She suspected Lord Bore would no sooner take her virtue prematurely than he would parade through Windsor Castle in his small suit, his performance in the powder closet and a certain illicit members' club notwithstanding.

Apthorp cleared his throat and took her hand in his. "Your Grace, I sincerely apologize that I let my emotion and affection for your sister overcome my gentlemanly propriety just now. I assure you that Constance's honor is safe in my hands. There is no undue haste; if you are amenable, we will post banns and be married at St. James's Church after the parliamentary session concludes."

Archer paced, his black frock coat trailing him like the feathers of a crow. She distracted herself from her nerves by discreetly tracing her middle finger along the inside of Apthorp's palm. When he subtly squeezed her hand, as though to shore her up, it made a prickly feeling dance upon her spine, rather like the sparking of joy at unexpectedly good news.

"Fine," Archer said suddenly. "If you want to do this foolish thing, I will not stand in your way."

Ah, but victory was warm. She could feel it flooding through her like the waters of a soothing bath.

She gave her brother her meekest, most grateful smile. "You are so kind, Archer. Of course, it goes without saying that we will need to do something about Julian's waterway bill. If it's allowed to languish, our future will be limited to my dowry, which I doubt will be sufficient to keep me in the immoderate comfort to which you have made me accustomed."

She winked at him. Her great facility for spending his money was an old joke between them. The kind that took its humor from profound veracity.

Archer was not amused. "If you expect this marriage to redeem his reputation, you will need a very clever plan to carry it off. The evangelicals are still parading in the streets as we speak."

"My dear brother, have you ever known me to lack for a clever plan?"

Constance had truly missed her calling on the stage. Apthorp could have sworn she'd felt it just as deeply, what had happened in the closet. And yet now she was her usual effervescent self, sharp and fizzy as a brut champagne.

He, on the other hand, could just barely get through his lines. Kissing her had made pudding of his brain. His head was still thick with the incense and jasmine her skin exuded when he'd brushed his lips along the hollows of her collarbone.

God, she was disarming. Lush and vulnerable as a dewy maiden when touched, yet canny and self-possessed as a woman twice her age when speaking. And yet despite her airy tone, she gripped his hand like he was her sole attachment to this earth. He simply didn't know what to make of her.

Westmead glared at him, and he realized he'd been caught

staring at her in wonder. He lifted his eyes to the duke's angrily tapping fingers.

Westmead turned his eyes back to his sister. "I never doubt your ability to craft a plot, Constance, but even with the most careful management, I am not certain any amount of coin or influence can repair the damage that's been done to Apthorp's bill."

Constance waved this off. "It can. I have it all worked out."

"Does *he*?" he drawled, raising a brow pointedly at Apthorp as though to ask if he was sitting on the sofa in silence because he had a head injury, or if he had merely ceded his will to Constance.

It was possible he *did* have a head injury. Westmead's fist had alighted on his jaw with all the delicacy of a cannon blasting into a puddle. But more likely, the trouble was that he simply could not outthink the outrageous pleasure of feeling Constance Stonewell's finger rubbing circles on the inside of his palm.

"We have a strategy," he affirmed, pulling his hand away. "Though it will not surprise you that the social aspect of it rests with your sister."

Constance smiled at him like a cat who'd been served foie gras.

"Indeed," she said. "First, we need the family to make a show of support. It needs to be understood that to cut Apthorp is to cut the Rosecrofts and the house of Westmead. We'll start with a public appearance in the Rosecrofts' box at the opera tomorrow. You will grace society with one of your rare outings and make a great show of being protective and intimidating and Apthorp's greatest friend."

"That won't be enough," Westmead said. "This goes beyond operas and ballrooms. If we can't win back political support—"

"We can. I intend to enlist my godmother's support. She will help us with the evangelicals. She might even pick off a few Tories."

Westmead laughed. "Lady Spence? Not likely. Her impulse will be to cut us both entirely. She's flirted with the idea ever since your stunt with those foxes on Boxing Day."

"Nonsense. She has been itching to save my soul ever since you sent me to the nuns. You will seed her sympathies by requesting guidance in preparing me for marriage in the absence of our mother. Say I've gone wayward like my father. I'll handle the rest."

Westmead nodded, as though this was a normal conversation. It was terrifying to watch them when their full powers were aligned. The duke and Constance had gone from being outsiders of ill repute—dispossessed children of the most infamously dissipated man to grace the peerage in a century—to influential members of society in the span of the last half decade. Westmead had furnished the financial power and amassed a bloc of seats in the Commons, while Constance had beguiled the beau monde with her charm and lavish entertainments and ability to make intriguing introductions.

He needed to think clearly or his own will would be lost to the house of Westmead's machinations. He did not intend to be treated like a hapless damsel in distress; when it came to politics, he was capable of captaining his own redemption. And if he wasn't, he deserved the failure that awaited him.

He cleared his throat. "Your Grace, I am confident of the political equation. I'll bolster up the borough votes first—they've been with me all along and will fall in line as soon as they see your support is assured. The Midland shires will benefit from the waterway and will therefore succumb to political pressure—it's an election year and constituents will not take kindly to a vote against their interests. If Lord and Lady Spence can bring us back the evangelicals, we can make up the numbers. But it will take incentive."

"What incentive?" Westmead asked. "It's too late to rewrite the bill."

"Not political incentive," Constance said, meeting Apthorp's eye with an approving nod, like she could read his mind. "Social incentive."

He was impressed that she caught his meaning so easily. Once again he felt a pang of pleasure at being her ally. And an equal measure of loathing for enjoying it so much, given how poorly it reflected on his dignity. He needed to do a better job of remembering this was all *pretend*.

"Dare I ask what you have in mind?" Westmead drawled.

"An engagement ball, of course," Constance said. "An evening so unforgettable that the entire city will live in fear of missing it. An invitation people will do *whatever* they must to secure."

"Exactly," Apthorp said. "We'll host the ball the day after the vote and make it understood that anyone who does not count themselves among our allies will be unwelcome."

Westmead looked at the two of them with an expression that bespoke either dyspepsia or grudging admiration. "You," he said to his sister, "are a terror. And you," he said to Apthorp, "should not encourage her."

"I assume that means we have your support, Your Grace?" Apthorp asked.

"I will do what I can. But that still leaves the matter of this unpleasant chatter. We will need to uncover whoever is behind the rumors. Constance, excuse us. I need to speak to Apthorp privately."

THERE WAS NOTHING CONSTANCE LOATHED MORE THAN BEING dismissed from a room so that a pair of men who lacked a fraction of the gifts she had for shaping public opinion could attempt to discuss the flow of news *in private*.

"I think I'll stay," she said. "Whatever you wish to discuss with Apthorp you can say in front of me. We're to be married after all."

Her brother gave her the driest stare imaginable, a look with all the humidity of a particularly arid day in the Sahara. "Go."

"No," she parried with equal precision.

"I'd prefer she stay," Apthorp said, surprising her. "I have no secrets from my future wife, and even if I did, I would think it safe to venture she has as firm a grasp on London hearsay as the most committed journalist on Grub Street."

She rewarded her dear, clever pretend beloved with a fond smile. "Thank you. It is so kind of you to notice my accomplishments."

She returned her attention to her brother. "It is clear to Julian and I that the rumors were planted by a political enemy," she said, before Archer could mount an argument. "I shall very discreetly make inquiries to see who might have ties to *Saints & Satyrs* and reason to oppose the waterways."

Her poem could not have found its way to Henry Evesham's circular by accident, after all. Nor, she suspected, had the rumors found their way *to her* by accident. Someone had told her about Apthorp's nocturnal predilections deliberately, to use her. And she *hated* being used without gaining something in return.

"Is everything all right?" Hilary asked, startling all three of them by appearing in the door with Poppy at her side. "We heard quite a lot of shouting."

"And what sounded rather like someone being thrown into a wall," Poppy added, narrowing her eyes at her husband.

Constance remembered she was meant to be in the throes of infatuation and rose to her feet. "Everything is wonderful! Archer has given us his blessing. Julian and I will be married as soon as the season is over."

"My darlings, what exciting news!" Hilary cried, rushing forward to draw Constance into a hug.

Constance made a show of twirling around in raptures, nearly knocking an ancient suit of Rosecroft armor over with her skirts. "I'm going to plan a ball to celebrate the engagement. It must be the most spectacular one yet. Poppy, will you help me with the flowers? I think lilies. *Thousands* of them."

Poppy winced. "Lilies are quite heady. Thousands might cause your guests to suffocate."

"Nonsense. And of course I will need entertainment. Perhaps I'll hire the opera dancers again."

"Please, not the opera dancers," Hilary said weakly. "Anything but those opera dancers."

Apthorp turned to her with a fond, shy smile, perfectly in pitch. "My bride shall have opera dancers if she wishes. Anything her heart desires." He was proving a better actor than she'd thought.

Hilary smiled at him. "The spirit of a happy marriage if ever I heard it, cousin. Will you join Rosecroft for a brandy? He's taking it on the terrace, given the warm night."

"No, I must take my leave," Apthorp said. "I need to write to my mother to inform her of the happy news. Thank you all for your kindness. I am humbled by your forgiveness."

"I hope you will be very happy," Hilary said.

"I have every confidence we shall," Apthorp said, looking at Constance with a gaze that was warm enough to make beads of sweat bloom along the back of her neck.

Hilary shot Poppy a look, as if to say *I told you so.*

"I'll see you out," Constance said, offering Apthorp her arm.

"That went well," she whispered as he led her toward the entry hall. She used the pretext of lowering her voice to draw even closer to him, because she was enjoying the newfound pleasure of brushing up against his side.

"Did it?" he sighed absently. She glanced up and his face was utterly devoid of the serene joy he'd displayed moments before. He looked depleted.

"Are you quite all right?" she asked.

He paused, massaging the stretch of skin around his temple. "I must say, I do not love the feeling of lying to my family, or to yours."

The darkness of his tone should not have knocked the air out of her, but it did anyway.

Because she was being thick. He was not happy about what had just occurred. He had, of course, been *pretending*. And she had let herself get swept up in his fond smiles and sentimental speeches and his ardor in the closet, forgetting she'd written the script herself.

"It is unpleasant," she said quickly. "But it's necessary."

"Yes," he said in that weary voice, looking rather hollow about the eyes. "It is."

"Well." She straightened her spine, hoping to seem unreduced, even if she suddenly felt wilted. "Good evening."

He nodded and walked out the door into the night.

And she, fool that she was, could not help but admire how elegantly the line of his coat fell as he descended the stairs to the street.

CHAPTER 6

"**G**ood evening, my lord," Winston, the Rosecrofts' butler said when Apthorp returned the following day to join the party headed to the opera. "Lady Constance awaits you in the orangery."

"The orangery?" he asked, with a wince for his formal attire. A glass room designed to catch the sunlight was not the ideal environment for a well-starched cravat.

"I'm afraid so," Winston said with a sympathetic smile. "Shall I take your coat?"

"You'd better."

He found Constance pacing back and forth in the warmest section of the room, clad in a pink gown so voluminous that it swished against the foliage as she walked.

Her brow was dewy with exertion.

She was lovely.

Not lovely, he corrected himself. *Sweaty.*

He'd spent the day rebuking himself for feeling far too much affection for her after their tender moment in the powder closet. Arriving at Parliament to a sea of disgusted faces and vulgar innuendos had been all the reminder he needed that she was dangerous, however lovely it might feel to make her tremble at his touch. He needed to harden himself to her, or the next month would be an unremitting torture.

Unfortunately the part of him that principally wished to harden at the memory of her shuddering against him was not his heart but, alas, his cock.

And the way she was currently smiling at him, very much like she was remembering too, was not helping.

It was unbecoming of a gentleman to slaver over women who hadn't asked to be the objects of his fantasies. As a general rule he kept his amatory attentions limited to his compatriots on Charlotte Street, where his lovers did a fair bit of slavering themselves.

But the shock of hunger that had lit up in Constance's eyes when he'd given her a proper kiss had awoken some primal part of him that could not let the image go. He wanted to see that look again. He wanted to make her shaky with a single word whispered in her ear, or a bold command on a scrap of paper pressed into her hand. He wanted to sit beside her at the opera and make her come without removing a single stitch of clothing.

He wanted her to see him as he truly was. Which was a gentleman, yes.

But one with a *preternatural* talent for fucking.

Which meant he could look forward to a month of pure frustration. Because outside the orderly arrangements he made on Charlotte Street, gently bred virgins were not fair game for men with any scruples. And he had many, many scruples. Abandoning them would make him exactly as bad as the man he most despised.

"Ah, you've arrived," Constance said, walking toward him. "And you haven't worn your wig."

She winked at him. *Winked* at him.

He blushed, for he had dispensed with his peruke for exactly the reason she intuited: because *she* preferred him without it.

You have to stop this.

"Come, stroll with me," she said, offering him a satin-clad arm. "I have excellent news."

He remained posted by the door, where he might inhale the cool, calming air of the dim marble corridor and not the intoxicating blend of amber and lilac or cedar and tuberose or smoke and bloody *lust* that seemed to curl around her in a cloud of pure temptation that made him so irritable he wanted to rip out his own hair.

"I'd rather stand where I can breathe," he demurred. "Why are you marching about in here? You'll give yourself a fever."

"I always pace the orangery before the opera. It improves my dull complexion." She sashayed prettily on her heel and began another lap.

He stopped himself from pointing out that her complexion was luminous, and one could not look at her skin without wanting to stroke it to see if it was indeed as soft as it looked. Which, he now knew, it *was*.

Stop. It.

"Where are the Rosecrofts?" he asked, trying to keep the edge out of his voice.

"They'll be down soon. I hoped we might have a brief word alone. You see, I've discovered something I suspect might be helpful." She gave him a mysterious, pregnant smile, like a Madonna in a sacred painting.

"And what is that?"

"A clue to the mystery." She waggled her eyebrows playfully.

Was she *flirting* with him?

He wanted to shove his fist into a wall. *Why* could she not have flirted with him a week ago? *Why* must she discover a taste for it now, when they were alone, and he was trying his best to remember to loathe her for what she'd done, or at least refrain from picturing her bodice tugged down below her dewy breasts, and failing on both counts?

He steeled his face into a grim line, determined to get hold of himself. "Explain."

"Well, you see"—she lowered her voice conspiratorially—"I had a fitting at my mantua-maker's today and made some subtle inquiries, for Valeria Parc dresses all the most scandalous ladies in town. Tell me, have you had any ... *confidential* dealings with an actress at the Theatre Royal?"

Something pinched in his neck.

He had a strong presentiment that wherever she was going with this question would lead to even greater personal risk to his privacy than she'd already created. And what's more, he did not know how to answer her, for given the nature of his nocturnal activities, he'd known many, many women. And not in such a context where one asked their occupations.

"Not that I recall," he said brusquely. "Why do you ask?"

She lowered her voice. "Oh, don't be nervous. It's quite all right if she's your mistress. I'm no longer easily shocked where you're concerned, Lord Bore."

"What?" he hissed, glancing behind him through the open doors to make sure she had not been overheard. The hall was empty. He strode over to where she stood beneath an orange tree. "I have no mistress. And you should not allude to such things. It's not appropriate."

Hypocrite. Stop inhaling her.

She rolled her eyes. "Apthorp, my dear, fretting about what is appropriate between us now is like worrying one does not have one's parasol whilst drowning in the ocean."

"I'm not in the mood for jokes, Constance. What is the relevance of the Theatre Royal?"

The teasing lightness left her face, and she straightened her spine.

"I believe the woman who spread the rumors about you might be an actress there. I have yet to find her, but when I do—"

"Don't," he cut in sharply.

There were indeed things she might uncover if she went pawing through his past. Things far more ripe for scandal than a peer with a proclivity for whipping. But her learning them would not *improve* the situation.

She crossed her arms. "*Don't?* We agreed I would investigate who exposed you yesterday. With my brother. Don't you recall?"

"I recall that *you* exposed me," he said evenly. "No investigation is required. I implied otherwise to keep Westmead from guessing your involvement. I assumed that was obvious."

"It most certainly was not," she said loftily. "After all, I did not *invent* the rumors about you. I heard them at Lady Palmerston's. If someone is trying to harm you by spreading tales, we must look into it, lest they imperil our plan. This woman is connected, I'm *certain* of it. Just leave it to me."

At her condescending tone, he lost his grasp on civility. "*Certain of it*, are you? Like you were certain I meant to marry Miss Bastian? Certain I'm a flagellant? Forgive me if my faith in your powers of deduction is not high."

Injury lit up her face. "I see."

He cringed for letting his temper get the better of him, but he was *right*. She was not nearly as omniscient as she believed herself to be, and it offended him to his core that she insisted on meddling in affairs he was perfectly bloody capable of handling himself.

And above all, he could not trust her with any more details about his past. There was no telling what she would think of him or whom she would share it with.

"The carriage is waiting!" Rosecroft called from the stairs.

"One moment," Apthorp said over his shoulder. He leaned in and whispered to Constance in a low voice. "We will continue this discussion when we have more privacy. You must tell me everything you know, and then you must promise me that will be the end of this. *Promise* me."

"Why should I?" she whispered back. "Because you have proven you are so *competent* at handling things yourself?"

He breathed in sharply, and her eyes flashed with something smug.

She must have been paying more attention to him all these years than she'd let on, for one could not aim a barb with such precision if one had not made careful study of the target.

She wanted to hurt him.

Well, fine. It had worked.

"I don't need to be reminded that I've made mistakes," he said quietly. "My entire life is one long vivid reminder of it. I'd like to prevent *you* from following suit."

Her face softened, slightly. "That came out harshly. All I mean to say is that I can fix this, Apthorp. You only need to trust me."

"My God," he said, sinking back against the wall. "What I trust is that you have *never* met a problem you weren't tempted to make a thousand times worse."

She let forth a bright, acidic laugh. "Ah, yes. I suppose this situation is all *my* fault. I suppose *I* am responsible for your affliction."

"What affliction?"

She smiled and batted her eyelashes. "Your desire for *unnatural* acts, my lord. Is that not what really ruined you?"

He felt like she had slapped him.

To say such a thing when he'd already explained what Charlotte Street meant to him, and what she'd risked by exposing it, proved she had no business anywhere near the truth.

He turned on his heel and began walking for the door, so he wouldn't have to look at the victorious expression on her face. Then he thought better of it, and turned back to her.

"I don't have an affliction," he said in a low voice. "I am perfectly capable of regulating my desires. But, Constance?"

"Yes?" she said, glaring. He leaned in and inhaled the burnt vanilla of her perfume from the bare curve of her pale throat.

"Don't call them *unnatural* until you try them."

On the way to the opera, Apthorp made polite conversation with the Rosecrofts, as though absolutely nothing were wrong.

That was because he was evil.

Only a very wicked man could appear so serenely unaffected when she was so angry she could breathe fire and singe his perfect eyebrows right off his perfect head.

She knew she had done badly by him. She had accepted her culpability. She was going out of her way to make amends. She was doing so at the ultimate cost of her own *family*.

And for all that, he chastised her for doing the very thing upon which they'd agreed.

She should not have provoked him, but his maligning of her character was too rich to swallow blandly when she *knew* he was not innocent. She had not *invented* his Wednesday evening pastimes, even if she had been wrong to expose them.

Imagine, holding her wholly responsible for his *secret member-ship in an illicit brothel*. At the best of times, men felt entitled to freedoms that women would be stoned for, but he'd surely known his actions were not sanctioned by society when he'd made a habit of them. There was a price for freedom, as she well knew. If one wanted to be free, one had to bear the risk of being damned.

Besides, she was no villain. Everybody *loved* her. She'd spent her entire adult life *ensuring* it. And tonight she intended to remind him of that fact.

"We're here," Hilary remarked, looking out the window. "And the crowd is enormous. Are you sure you're up to this, Constance? You look fevered."

Fevered indeed. More like *aflush with the fire of vengeance.*

"Oh, indeed. I have never been more thrilled to attend the opera in my life."

She waited for the others to exit the carriage as she took a moment to pinch her lips and smooth her gown. Then she accepted Apthorp's hand and stepped down onto the pavement.

She held herself poised and swanlike before the swarming mass of jeweled ladies, bewigged gentlemen, alewives, and begging children, letting them take in the sight of her and Apthorp together in public for the first time.

She shifted her shoulders, so that the silver threads in her pink dress would catch in the golden sunset light and make her glow.

The throng stilled. "It's Lady Constance!" someone squealed.

She smiled. With a dramatic flick of her wrist, she released the silver lace that held her train and stepped forward, allowing her skirts to fan out behind her in a shimmering wave to the approving murmurs of the crowd.

"Repent!" some woman squawked from somewhere in the crush of bodies. "Repent, ye filthy cull!"

She paused.

"Look at Cunny and Arsethorp, fine as can be!" a man shouted from somewhere closer.

The crowd erupted in a sound she had not heard directed at herself in years: *laughter*.

She smiled and tossed her head and charged onward, clutching Apthorp's arm. As a child, she had learned the first lesson of mockery: reacting to it is the surest way to invite more abuse. She would ignore her persecutors and let them read about her triumph in tomorrow's papers. She sailed through the theater doors, all but dragging Apthorp after her, and braced for the usual onslaught of waves and bows from her friends.

Not a soul looked up.

The artistic gentlemen of Covent Garden seemed unusually preoccupied in purchasing refreshments and locating their seats. Fine ladies' backs turned just as she and Apthorp neared them.

They were *deliberately* avoiding her.

It sent her back in time. To arriving in France and discovering that she was everything a little girl ought not to be. To returning a decade later to discover her hard-won adopted mannerisms now made her queer, forward, uncommonly direct.

She'd fought her way through that. She'd beguiled, charmed, and bought anyone who didn't mind her oddness, and made herself bored by or indispensable to those who did, until she had amassed the kind of influence that, when accompanied with unconscionable wealth, made one impervious to judgment.

She'd thought that she was *immune*.

"Why, if it isn't Lady Cunny's cully," a man's cultured voice drawled from somewhere a few paces away.

She turned sharply, violating her own rules by trying to locate the source of the titters. The whole crowd seemed to undulate with quiet laughter.

Apthorp tightened his grip on her arm and continued strolling casually to the Rosecrofts' box, an expression of mild amusement fixed on his features.

Either he was a marvel of equanimity or else he was stone-deaf.

In any case he was elegant and stoic, while *she*—the master of appearances—was becoming unsuitably upset.

She had been so certain that her popularity would serve as a layer of protection for them both. For the first time a horrible thought crossed her mind: *what if she wasn't enough to save him?*

Her slipper caught on a half step, and she tripped over the hem of her dress, stumbling forward. Apthorp gently righted her before anyone could notice.

She clung to him, wishing he could make her disappear.

"It's all right," he said in a low, soft voice. "Don't let on that you notice. It will pass."

His voice betrayed no sign of being bothered.

He's accustomed to it, she realized. She'd never considered it before, but he must have endured years of pretending not to notice what people said about him after he'd made his bad investments.

In fact, it now occurred to her he'd never reacted to the many rather mocking things *she'd* said to him. She'd called him Lord Bore a hundred times without him ever flinching.

"Don't forget to breathe," he said into her ear.

She inhaled and relaxed her posture. Usually she hated being told what to do, but it was soothing, under the circumstances, to not be the one in charge.

"Good," he murmured. "Now lean up and say something amusing to me."

Her mind went blank. "I can't think of anything amusing," she whispered in his ear. "I can scarcely remember my own name."

He laughed softly, like she'd made a private, intimate kind of joke. "It doesn't matter what you say," he whispered back. "Just say it like you mean it."

She turned and grinned up into his pretty amber eyes. "What a dreadful situation."

"Isn't it?" He smiled back.

"No one has been so rude to me in years, no matter how awfully I've behaved." She met his eye. "And I've had my regrettable moments."

She hoped he understood that she meant she was sorry for all the times she'd said things that, perhaps, were not quite nice. Things that might have made him feel a bit like she felt now.

His eyes went dark. "We've both had our regrettable moments," he said quietly.

Was that ... an apology for what he'd said in the orangery?

She paused, trying to read his odd expression, but her brother's voice called out her name. They turned to the sight of Archer and Poppy.

Archer clapped Apthorp on the back in a hearty, affectionate manner that was no doubt designed to discreetly inflict pain. She felt the eyes of the crowd observe this signal of his blessing.

She hoped desperately they absorbed the message.

"Constance, have you heard the news?" Poppy asked. "It seems you and Apthorp are not the only betrothed couple making your debut. Your friend Miss Bastian is promised to Lord Harlan Stoke. It is said they plan to marry in *one month's* time."

"*Pardon?*" She felt like she might faint.

"Are you quite all right?" Poppy asked.

She was not all right.

Gillian Bastian was a fellow refugee who'd been raised in Philadelphia and deemed hopeless when she arrived in London in search of a titled husband to strengthen her family's ties to the Crown. Always sympathetic to a fellow *déclassée*, Constance had ushered Gillian into her closest circle of friends and set about making her a figure in society. When that had been accomplished with some success, she'd moved on to securing the girl a husband.

Namely, Apthorp.

In all the months they'd been in league together, arranging pretexts for him to call, analyzing his every move for some hint into the progression of his feelings, Gillian had never mentioned an attachment to Lord Harlan.

A brisk engagement implied a long-standing history between the couple, and perhaps the anticipation of their vows. If Gillian had been anticipating vows with the likes of Harlan Stoke, she'd surely been in no imminent danger of marrying Apthorp.

It made no *sense*.

But more immediately distressing than this lapse in friendship was how *stupid* it would make Constance look to the man currently holding her by the arm.

No, not stupid. Careless.

She glanced up at him to see whether he had made the same connection.

His face had gone the color of alabaster, and was just as rigid.

∿

"How wonderful," Constance said in an absolutely miserable tone. "I suppose we should offer them our congratulations."

Apthorp nodded, because he could not count on himself to speak. He followed Constance out of the box, trying to steel his face into an impassive line.

Vindication was, in normal circumstances, very elevating. But any joy he might otherwise take in proving that Constance had been wrong was overpowered by his revulsion at the name of Harlan Stoke. And at him marrying some harmless girl like Gillian.

"I'm sorry," Constance said in a low voice, glancing at him. "I truly don't know how I got it so wrong."

He said nothing. He had not yet collected himself to the point that he trusted he could speak without shouting.

"Please don't be angry," she said.

"I'm not angry," he ground out. "Not, in any case, at *you*."

"I feel so foolish," she said in the smallest voice he'd ever heard from her.

Her regretful tone brought him back to himself, and their need to assert their purpose here. He tried to smile at her. "Never mind. They're not our concern. Let's circulate about the room before the curtains. It's important to pretend to be enjoying ourselves."

She clutched his arm more tightly than was decent. Because he was upset, he allowed himself to take in one strong, fortifying whiff of myrrh and gardenia and squeeze her back. It made him feel better.

"What if no one acknowledges us?" Constance whispered, letting her gaze dart about the room. He'd never seen her so unsure of herself. At least not in half a decade. It made him want to draw her closer, protect her from the stares he—they—were attracting.

"They will," he said firmly, scanning the room for friendly faces. "Look, there's Avondale. He's thoroughly dissolute. He'll happily be seen with us. We might even *improve* his reputation."

He lifted his hand to the marquess, whose eyes lit up in greeting.

"Well, well," Avondale said, clapping his hand on Apthorp's back. "Lady Constance, I hear you've snagged yourself the least eligible man in all of London."

The quip seemed to restore Constance's spirits. "Lord Apthorp's reputation for vice is second only to yours, my lord," she said sweetly. "But I have made my peace with second best."

Avondale threw back his head and laughed. Others noticed. Avondale was popular and wealthy. His approval would ease the way for them.

"Are you looking forward to the opera?" the marquess asked.

Constance smirked. "I've heard the aria is lovely, but it seems Lord Apthorp and I are the real focus of the evening's entertainment."

"My dear, with you in that gown, who would bother looking at the stage?" Avondale gave her a grin so wolfish it was physically painful to watch, but Constance only laughed and did something attractive with her fan.

God, she was good. Apthorp knew she was distressed, but to look at her bantering with Avondale, you'd never know that moments before her hands had been shaking as she'd clutched his arm.

Out of the corner of his eye he spotted Cornish Lane Day, his ally on the waterway bill in the House of Commons, and someone who had never looked wolfishly on anything other than a piece of legislation. Apthorp beckoned him over gratefully.

"Lord Apthorp," Lane Day said with a bow. "My sincere congratulations."

"Thank you," Apthorp said. "Lady Constance, allow me to introduce you to Mr. L—"

"Oh, Mr. Lane Day needs no introduction," Constance said, switching fluently from the knowing, flirtatious manner she had used on Avondale to a tone of demure respect pitched perfectly to the serious young politician. "I hear such glowing things about his speeches in the Commons."

"Surely you flatter me," Lane Day said, looking floored.

Constance leaned in and shook her head. "Not at all, sir. I've been eagerly following your success in the election, and I can't say how long I've wished to meet you. I know how grateful Lord Apthorp has been for your skill in guiding his bill through the Commons."

Lane Day's smile bloomed, for if there was one thing he had a weakness for, it was politics. "The legislation will be a great thing for the Midland shires. The price of coal is far too dear without a reliable means of transport."

"Indeed, it is a scandal," Constance said solemnly. "I intend to work tirelessly on behalf of the people of Cheshire and I hope we can be allies. In the meantime, if there is anything I can do to be of service in securing an advantage in the vote, I hope you will let me know. The hospitality of Westmead House is entirely at your disposal."

Lane Day beamed at her. "I shall keep that in mind."

Avondale smirked at her blatant political pandering. Apthorp was so proud of Constance he could have kissed her. He'd always suspected she'd make an admirable partner in politics, with her instincts for flattery and favors. He'd not suspected she had an ear for policy as well.

Out of the corner of his eye, he saw Gillian Bastian and Lord Harlan Stoke rounding the corner toward them. The hair on his neck stood up.

Constance followed his gaze. "Excuse us, gentlemen. We must congratulate my dear friend Miss Bastian on her happy news."

She turned and inclined her head at the approaching couple with a warm expression, raising her fan.

Lord Harlan whispered in Miss Bastian's ear. Apthorp saw in Stoke's eyes what was about to happen.

"Constance," he hissed, touching her elbow. But she had

already fluttered her fan in friendly greeting, drawing interest from the crowd.

For the briefest of moments, Gillian paused, training her eyes on Constance. And then she picked up her skirts, turned with a dramatic pivot, and walked in the opposite direction without a word.

Constance stopped abruptly, fan still held aloft.

"Did you see that?" she breathed.

He had. Everyone had.

She stared up at him. "She just cut me. *Gillian Bastian* just cut me."

Her big, beautiful blue eyes went misty.

Christ. Was it possible that the indomitable hellion Constance Stonewell—moments before at her most confident and insouciant —was on the verge of *weeping*?

He stared at her, struck dumb.

It's an act. It's always *been an act.*

She was not entirely the haughty, saucy woman she presented herself to be. She just worked very, very hard at pretending that she was.

For some reason, this broke his heart.

He pressed his fingers lightly around her wrist until she looked up at him.

"Smile," he said softly.

She obeyed in a dazed kind of way.

"Lean up like you're saying something light and clever and above all *cruel*, then laugh."

With empty eyes, she did as he instructed, though she whispered only nonsense words—swishes of air with no meaning that tickled his ear.

He shouted with laughter and gazed down on her like she'd said something so cutting he was shocked.

"Perfect," he murmured under his breath. "Now take my arm

and go directly to the box. If anyone approaches, smile and wave, but don't stop until you regain your composure."

For once, she did exactly as he said.

"Sit there," he told her, pointing to the seat nearest the wall, which was partly hidden behind a curtain. He sat down beside her and shifted the bottom of the drape with his shoe, moving it so that she was shielded from the view of the crowd, but he was fully visible, lest there be any question of decency.

He felt her shaking.

"It's all right," he said softly. "No one can see you."

She put her knuckle to her lips and leaned against the wall.

"Constance," he whispered urgently. "Don't let them hurt you. It's me they wished to slight. Stoke despises me. He has for years."

Lord Harlan summered in a property several miles from Apthorp Manor and had proved himself to be the very worst kind of neighbor. They hadn't spoken in two years, but when they had, it had nearly erupted into violence.

Constance looked up at him with haunted eyes. "I doubt he could despise you more than he despises me."

He wanted to ask her what he meant by that, for he had always wondered what had ended their brief friendship, but she shook her head in agitation. "I always expect the worst of Lord Harlan. But Gillian is my *friend*."

He reached out and squeezed her hand. "I'm sorry."

He wanted to say *he* would be her friend.

That they would make other friends together. *Better* friends.

But of course, that would be a lie.

Because she was planning to leave in one month's time. Because of *him*.

Had he known she was so vulnerable, he would never have agreed to this. But now that he had, it was too late. They'd already written out their futures. There was no comfort he could offer her.

"I just don't understand," she whispered to the wall.

He took her hand. "It's very simple. Lord Harlan's a rakehell. With a brief engagement, Gillian no doubt feels her own reputation is not strong enough to survive proximity to a scandal."

"I suppose I thought I was above such treatment." She laughed, a bitter sound that chilled him, for he knew what it felt like to be brought down to size.

"Foolish of me, I'm sure you'd say. Or well deserved."

"No," he said instantly. "I would *never* wish to see you hurt."

He cleared his throat, looking away from her. "And it will pass. We have a plan."

"Right," she said shakily, taking his hand in both of hers. She jutted out her chin, yet squeezed him like she needed him for strength.

It made him want to gather her up and take her out of this place and withdraw somewhere safe and private where he could explain that she'd become entangled in something more complex than she fully understood.

But he couldn't explain, and so he must be careful.

He couldn't change what he'd already agreed to. But he would not let her suffer more on his behalf.

It was a marvel. Apthorp was quietly keeping her from falling apart.

Who knew he had such talents?

She squeezed his hand, and he squeezed hers back.

She needed to pull herself together. For his sake.

"Constance, Lord Apthorp," her brother said, striding back into the box. "Look who I found."

She looked over her shoulder and directly into the penetrating gaze of Lady Spence.

Collect yourself. This will be your only chance.

Apthorp leapt to his feet and made a deep bow. "My lady."

Lady Spence's narrow eyes did not move from Constance's tear-lined ones.

Constance made a rapid calculation. Lady Spence had never been fond of her, and it was a risk to show vulnerability before a foe. But if there was one thing she knew about her godmother, it was that the woman enjoyed being right.

And so Constance craned her neck and blinked, allowing a single tear to roll out of her eye and trail tragically down her cheek.

She tilted her head away poetically, mopping up the tear like she'd been caught.

"Lady Spence!" she said, rising to curtsy. "What a relief to see a friendly face."

Friendly was the last word she would use to describe her godmother's penetrating gaze. But at the evidence of Constance's discomposure, the old woman looked at her with greater interest.

"I saw what happened," she said without preamble. "As did half the room. The cheek of that colonial. I told you not to consort with her type."

"You were all too right. I regret I didn't listen."

"I can't say I'm surprised, given your circumstances." The old woman looked meaningfully at Apthorp, eyeing him like she might meat rotting on her parlor floor.

Constance ignored the insult and wrung her hands. "Oh, Lady Spence, I'm at a loss for what to do! You can't imagine my distress. All around us I hear the vilest whispers, all because of slander printed in some dreadful paper. None of it is *true*, of course, but the timing is so unfortunate." She paused, as though to stifle a sob. "I'm desperately afraid for our future."

Lady Spence sniffed. "As you are right to be. I made clear to Westmead I don't approve of this match at all. I can't fathom why he hasn't blocked it."

Apthorp did a remarkable job of not reacting to this discussion of his own unsuitability.

Her brother only chuckled. "Lady Spence and I agree I am far too lax a guardian and you need taking in hand," he said cheerfully. "I suggested she might find it in her heart to reform you."

Constance sighed. "*Normally* I would contend I am not in need of reformation, but this week has been so difficult that I am chastened. I would be grateful for your advice, Lady Spence. It is a fretful thing to prepare oneself for marriage without a loving mother here to guide me. I so wish I weren't an orphan."

Lady Spence gave her a long, appraising look. "I shall do what I can for you. However, I might lament your choice of suitors."

Constance pressed both hands over her heart. "Oh, I am so grateful."

"*If* you'll agree to surround yourself with respectable people," Lady Spence added. "I'm hosting a small luncheon with several members of my congregation tomorrow. Join me and I will see what can be done for you. Perhaps it's not too late to make a proper lady of you yet."

"How kind. I would be delighted to attend."

Lady Spence glared pointedly at Apthorp. "And bring him with you. I expect he would benefit greatly from the example of my minister."

Apthorp produced that bland, gracious smile she'd watched him use on everyone from the vicar to the king for years. The one she'd dismissed as hopelessly boring. "I'd be honored, Lady Spence," he said with touching humility. "Thank you."

Lady Spence nodded at Westmead, who escorted her out of the box.

When they were alone, Apthorp turned to Constance.

He was silent. And then his face crinkled up into an absolutely charming smile. "Lady Constance. My word. Is it possible your wicked plan is working?"

She put her hands over her face and put her head on his shoulder and laughed in pure relief. He put an arm around her, laughing too, his chest rumbling beneath her shoulder.

The curtain opened, and the crowd went quiet, and they stopped laughing.

The soprano sang, and for the next three hours there was no one to perform for.

But she could not help but notice that for the duration of the opera, neither of them even tried to move away.

CHAPTER 7

*T*he servant who greeted Apthorp at the door to Lady Spence's town house the following afternoon was so hoary and gray that he looked like a ghost from the fire of 1666.

"The Earl of Apthorp," the servant said, announcing him to an overwarm room furnished with tapestries that appeared to predate the Stuart line. Apthorp bowed to his hostess, who sat sternly in a chair next to the fire, and to Constance, who sat beside her with her hands folded demurely in her lap.

She smiled at him sweetly, in the exact way she had the night before when he'd awoken her at the end of the opera, after she'd fallen asleep nestled into the crook of his shoulder.

When no one had been watching.

"Allow me to present you to my friends," Lady Spence said. "This is Mrs. Henry Mountebank, whom I'm sure you recall from her many noted essays on theology."

"Of course," he said, hoping he would not be struck down instantly for lying.

"And Reverend Keeper, the minister of our congregation. And of course Mr. Henry Evesham, whose name you will know from his most affecting reports on vice."

Apthorp froze.

That name he *did* know. For Henry Evesham was the editor of *Saints & Satyrs.*

A curate-turned-journalist with evangelical leanings, Evesham was enjoying increasing renown for his crusading gazette calling out the city's vices. His stories exposing procurers and serial bigamists had endeared him to the more pious members of the House of Lords, who'd recently invited him to testify on what could be done to protect the city's innocents.

Lady Spence's message in inviting Evesham was clear: it was a none-too-subtle threat to fall in line.

"A pleasure, Lord Apthorp," Mr. Evesham said. He looked nothing like the spectral figure one imagined of a crusading man of letters. He was tall and wide-framed, with hands and feet like shovels and intelligent green eyes that held the kind of restful clarity that must come with the certainty one is ordained for heaven.

How nice for Mr. Evesham.

"It's an honor to make your acquaintance," Apthorp said, making it his personal mission to seem utterly unperturbed by having been invited to break bread with the man who'd slandered him.

"Lady Spence, thank you for inviting us here today," Constance said. "Lord Apthorp and I have been so eager to become better acquainted with your congregation."

"I'm glad to hear it. As Mr. Evesham's writings can attest, there is a creeping wantonness in our society that those of us with the privilege of nobility possess a duty to expunge."

She looked at Apthorp meaningfully, the way a long, black eel might regard you as it coiled itself around your ankle in a swamp. Christ, but he despised people of her ilk, with their penetrating judgments. He rewarded her with a smile that he knew from years on Charlotte Street set off his jawline to its best advantage and turned his eyes on Constance.

"I agree," Constance said with a beatific smile that belied any awareness of the undercurrent of hostility in the room. "Mrs. Mountebank, Lady Spence recently sent me your essay on the sacrament of matrimony. There is much I'd like to learn from you. It is my dearest wish to be a loving wife in the spirit of Christian rectitude."

"I am surprised to hear that," Mrs. Mountebank said coolly. "One so often hears your name attached to frivolity and idle pleasure."

Apthorp cleared his throat. "It is no surprise to *me*, Mrs. Mountebank. Lady Constance's accomplishments may be unconventional, but everything she does is designed to bring joy to others. Surely there is virtue in a heart as large as hers. I have no doubt that she would be an asset to any cause your congregation put her to."

Constance glanced up at him in surprise.

He met her gaze head-on, for he meant what he'd said. Few people displayed more determination to spread happiness and good fortune to those around them than Constance, and it annoyed him to hear her rudely maligned by a room of supposed Christians.

He considered himself a man of faith, but he believed above all in the morality of conscience. Enough time on Charlotte Street, where bishops sinned as freely as the laity, had convinced him that the performance of public virtue did not always bear on private scruples.

"I have no doubt Lady Constance's talents would benefit our cause," Evesham said pleasantly. "Her persuasive skills are as legendary as her evening balls. I've long been an admirer."

"Have you?" Apthorp asked, taken aback that they were acquainted.

"Mr. Evesham and I have had the pleasure of debating several times at Mrs. Tremaine's quarterly salon," Constance said. "Though never, regrettably, on the same side of any argument."

"Nevertheless, each time, I find myself musing on Lady Constance's thoughts long after the debate has concluded," Evesham said.

The two of them exchanged a smile from across the room.

Apthorp didn't like it.

Why had Constance neglected to mention, in their discussion of her poem mysteriously finding its way to *Saints & Satyrs*, that she was acquainted with its editor?

"We weren't discussing intellect," Mrs. Mountebank said tersely, interrupting his thoughts. "We were discussing character. There is a difference, Mr. Evesham, wouldn't you agree?"

Constance nodded before Evesham had a chance to answer. "You are quite right, Mrs. Mountebank," she said. "I have much to learn about fulfilling my Christian duty. And I intend to make a careful study of it."

"I should hope so," Lady Spence sniffed. "I have feared for your soul every since your brother sent you to those Papist nuns like a Jacobin. And I should hope Lord Apthorp will not stand in your way."

Before he could react, Constance looked the woman directly in the eye and smiled so sweetly that the ice in her voice when she spoke came as a shock.

"Anything virtuous in my character I have learned from the example of my future husband. Lord Apthorp is the most solemn, earnest, and conscientious man I've ever had the honor to know. Devoted to his family and his tenants. Exceptionally committed to his duties in the Lords. And *kind*. Which is a quality many otherwise good souls lack, wouldn't you agree?"

Lady Spence clamped her lips so tight they turned white at the corners.

"And," Constance added, her tone resuming a mellifluous lightness, "you cannot deny he is handsome."

Evesham leaned back in his chair and chuckled. "Lady

Constance, you've made your poor intended blush. I see the rumor that yours is a love match must be true."

Apthorp's cheeks burned brighter at having been observed reacting to her compliment. He wished he could steel himself to the acute pleasure that gathered in his gut when she expressed appreciation for him. But the flare of pure emotion that rose when she came to his defense nearly obliterated his composure. He was, God help him, *aflutter*.

Reverend Keeper, seeming perturbed at the earthly turn to the conversation, attempted to reestablish a godly tone. "Lady Constance, I'm flattered to hear of your interest in our congregation. I imagine you will be able to do many good works as the Countess of Apthorp."

Constance gave the man a blinding smile. "Oh, indeed. The people of Cheshire have suffered this last decade. We are fortunate that my dowry will assist in providing them some ease. Perhaps, if you are able, you might come to lead a service on the estate. For, beyond material comforts, it is my fervent wish to build a new church, where we can offer sustenance to our tenants' souls."

"I had no idea you were so pious, dear." Lady Spence said with an air of pronounced skepticism. "Nor so charitable."

Constance let out a self-deprecating laugh. "My lady, to my deep regret, you are correct. I have scarcely taken an interest in my own soul, let alone that of any other. But hearing Lord Apthorp speak with such emotion of his people's plight has awakened in me a desire to help." She paused and locked eyes with Lady Spence. "In that respect it's a misfortune that the legislation Lord Apthorp was hoping for seems destined not to pass, as it would have improved their lot immensely, and freed my funds for more heavenly causes. But we shall try to do what we can for our tenants even without the waterway, as is our duty. A new church will have to wait, alas."

Lady Spence and her goddaughter exchanged a look.

"Is that right?" the old woman drawled. "Well then, Lord Apthorp, how convenient you are here with us. Let's sit down to luncheon, and you can tell me more."

IF APTHORP'S DETERMINED POLITENESS HAD STRUCK HER AS BLAND in the past, Constance began to see the wisdom of his methods over lunch.

While she preferred to procure favors using the blunt tools of flattery and innuendo, his were subtler means. He crisply laid out the virtues of his bill, responding to all of Lady Spence's questions with sound reasoning and good humor. He did not fawn or pander, but he was self-assured, polite, respectful, and thorough. By the second course he had, without directly asking for it, received her pledge to discuss his bill with her husband.

He then engaged Reverend Keeper in a long, enervating discussion of the minister's recent trip to a revival in Cornwall, nodding along as though it were as scintillating as one of Mr. Evesham's accounts of the procuresses at Seven Dials.

And he did all of this under Evesham's penetrating gaze, never once betraying any discomfort at his presence, nor awareness of Lady Spence's aggression in inviting him.

It was a talent, his bland exterior. In all the years she had dismissed his dullness, she had failed to notice that his affability required as much calculated performance as her theatrics did.

By the end of the meal, if he had not quite gained the trust of Lady Spence, it was obvious that at the very least the rumors about him were fading in the presence of his respectful manner.

"You know, Constance," Lady Spence said as they rose to leave, "when you smile, you are the very image of your mother. She was a beauty, the late duchess."

Constance bit her lip. "So I'm told. It pains me not to have known her."

"Well, I am sure it is a solace that you will now have the maternal guidance of Lady Apthorp," Lady Spence said. "Such a lovely woman, the countess. Exquisite manners."

Constance had not set eyes on Apthorp's mother in years, and scarcely knew her, but she was not about to admit this.

"Oh yes. A tremendous comfort. I hope she will treat me as her own daughter."

Apthorp, she noticed, looked away at the mention of his mother and appeared more eager to leave.

"Perhaps, Lord Apthorp, your mother will accompany you when you bring Lady Constance to visit our congregation," Lady Spence said. Her tone implied this was less a suggestion than an order.

Apthorp smiled. "You are too kind. My mother would no doubt love to join us, but unfortunately her ill health does not allow her to travel to London. The bad air is a strain."

Constance looked at him in surprise. She had heard nothing about Lady Apthorp being in poor health.

Lady Spence frowned. "She has not mentioned such invalidism in her letters. Surely the countess would be an asset in bringing out your future bride to her advantage. Lady Constance would benefit from her skillful chaperonage. Do invite her." She looked meaningfully at Constance.

Constance smiled reassuringly. "We shall do everything we can to convince Lady Apthorp to brave the pestilential air. And if we are lucky enough to be honored with a visit, we will indeed bring her to your chapel."

Apthorp shot her a grimace, warning flashing in his eyes.

But she failed to see any harm in making such a promise.

In fact, now that Lady Spence had suggested it, she thought it was an excellent idea.

❧

APTHORP HELPED CONSTANCE INTO A CARRIAGE AND MADE OFF eastward toward the Strand, fighting back a smile.

They had been set up to be humiliated and they had triumphed.

Constance's scheme was working better than he had ever imagined. It was working so well he was finding it increasingly difficult to believe their natural partnership and growing ease with each other was not real.

Of course it isn't real. It's a performance.

But which parts?

"Lord Apthorp," a voice called from behind him. He turned to see Henry Evesham striding after him down the street.

"I'd hoped for a word with you in private," Evesham said, catching up. "I wonder if you might spare a moment."

"Of course," Apthorp said. "I'm walking east. Care to join me?"

Evesham smiled. "Thank you. I'll be frank and warn you the matter is delicate."

Apthorp labored not to show his unease. "Oh?"

"I'd like to ask for your assistance in an investigation I'm pursuing."

"I would be happy to oblige if I can be of service," he lied affably, grateful for years of covering his true feelings behind stiff courtesies. "How might I be helpful?"

Evesham gave him a tight smile. "I'm sure you are aware that my calling is to rid the city of vice."

"A noble calling."

"I assume, as a peer of the realm, you share this desire?"

"Of course," Apthorp said. "One sees the most appalling things in London. Maidens abducted and forced into prostitution. Predations upon children. Procurers who trade in despondence and disease. I hope you are directing your efforts toward the most vulnerable among us." It would be a nobler use of his efforts than shaming whores and mollies in his pages.

Evesham nodded. "Of late I have been investigating a growing moral pestilence: houses of iniquity."

"Oh?" London was littered with such places, from lavish pleasure houses peopled by cultured courtesans to squalid Seven Dials brothels filthy with rats and syphilis. He was not opposed to efforts to protect harlots and culls alike. Fornication would always be bought and sold. But if Elena Brearley's club had taught him anything, it was that it could be done so with an eye to fairness, pleasure, and good health. "You are wise to advocate for reform and regulation."

"One establishment in particular is the subject of my special interest," Evesham went on. "I've heard of a place in Mary-le-Bone where all manner of vile eccentricities take place. Violence. Depravity. Sodomy." He lowered his voice. "All practiced in secrecy by aristocrats who possess wealth enough to keep their vices hidden."

Apthorp kept his expression blank, even as his blood went cold. Was this man truly going to exhibit the cheek to address Elena's club with him directly? On the bloody streets of Mayfair?

He wanted to push him against the wall and say depravity was in the eye of the beholder.

"Fascinating," he drawled instead. "Yet I fail to see how such a place could overawe the plight of kidnapped children and helpless girls. Perhaps you should redirect your efforts there."

Evesham sighed, as though he was as pained as Apthorp. "I don't disagree with you that such crimes are graver sins in the eyes of God, my lord, but I will be candid. A humble scribe must answer to his readers' interests. Noblemen with sinful predilections are good for circulation, and I am beholden to my publishers."

"Your publishers must have prurient tastes," Apthorp remarked.

"If that is true, my lord, they are not so unlike their betters." Evesham shot him a meaningful sideward glance. "From the tales

I've heard, it seems many of your fellow peers believe themselves above the laws of decency."

"As do many members of the clergy, alas," he said evenly.

"Most upsetting, such hypocrisy," Evesham agreed. "Perhaps, armed with your knowledge, I might do my part to unravel such abuses."

"What is it you're suggesting I can help you with, Mr. Evesham?" If the man was going to accuse him of something, he'd had enough of dancing around the charge.

"I'm sure you're aware I printed a poem suggesting a person not unlike yourself in description might have some familiarity with the notorious establishment I am investigating."

Trust a man of letters to be as tortured as possible in making a very simple point.

"Any such resemblance is coincidental, I assure you. But your poem was amusing. Lady Constance and I had a long and merry laugh about it."

"I'm sure. But I understand that you have encountered no small measure of difficulty as a result of the ensuing talk, spurious though I'm sure you'd say it is."

Evesham smiled in a manner that, though not unkind, communicated clearly his belief that it was not spurious at all. A manner that suggested they both understood the ways of the world and were above the pretense that they didn't. Apthorp would almost like him for this attempt at candor, were Evesham not suggesting that he help betray the secrets of consenting people who had asked the world for nothing more than the tolerance to do what they liked harmlessly in private.

Apthorp slowed his pace, narrowing his eyes to signal they were not allies in this matter.

"The political climate is mercurial. One finds oneself the subject of whispers when it is convenient for one's rivals to have them believed. They rarely coincide with the truth."

Evesham nodded in a way that made clear he understood he'd

been dismissed. He paused, as if reconsidering. "I see. A nasty business, politics. Nevertheless, I wonder if we share a mutual interest in locating the source of such whispers. I'm a great admirer of Lady Constance and wish her every happiness. I have no wish to see her embarrassed. If you were to assist in my investigation, I would, in return for such a favor, keep your involvement in strict confidence. Whatever it may prove to be."

Apthorp stared at him. The man seemed to be offering this in *good faith*, as though the implication of what he was saying was not enough for a less restrained man to bash him in the face with his walking stick.

"I will overlook what you're suggesting, Mr. Evesham, and thank you not to mention such topics in the same sentence as my future wife."

"I mean no offense, Lord Apthorp." He said this so flatly that Apthorp almost wanted to believe he meant it. Who *was* this man, and what was he about?

"Whatever you mean, Mr. Evesham, I have no interest in perpetuating the slander against me by appearing to take an interest in it."

Evesham leaned forward and clasped his hands in front of him.

"Of course, my lord. I should only note that any person helpful in my efforts to rid the city of vice can be guaranteed a degree of discretion that he will not enjoy if he is found to be complicit in perpetuating it later. I hope to do good in the world. I invite you to do the same. Should you recall any further information, I hope you will write to me."

Evesham took a card from his coat and held it out.

Apthorp made no move to take it. "I would urge you not to sit at home waiting for my correspondence, Mr. Evesham. This is my turn," he said, nodding at the corner. "Good day."

Evesham stared at him for a moment, as though deciding whether to say more.

Wordlessly he returned the card to his pocket, bowed, and walked on.

Apthorp ducked into a public house and waited a few minutes until he was sure the hack was gone. And then he doubled back down the street toward Mayfair.

He needed to speak to Constance.

Before Evesham did.

CHAPTER 8

*L*ady Constance Stonewell had always intended to fall wildly, extravagantly in love.

Eventually.

The timing of this condition was, regrettably, outside her control, for it depended on the arrival of a man.

Assuredly this gentleman she awaited would be handsome, though the exact cast of his features was not of paramount importance. And he would be clever, though he need not be his generation's greatest wit, as she was cunning enough for them both. He would be kind, though not so kind that his manners lacked a suitable degree of edge, and loyal, though most principally to her.

The precise dimensions of his make and character were fungible, for the important thing about him was that he would be the first person in living history to want her *exactly* as she was.

She would not have to disguise her love of devilry nor her too-tender heart to be found winning. She would not have to exercise beguilement to captivate his interest nor dampen the contours of her character to maintain it. He would adore her wholeheartedly and without reservation and above all without the least imposition of her will. He would be wholly, unconditionally insane for her, and that's how she would know he had, finally, arrived.

Since she had not encountered a fellow even remotely resembling this description in all her days, she had never spent much time imagining what being in love with *him* might feel like.

But now, as she sat at her desk, making arrangements for her new life in Genoa after an afternoon of feigning lovestruck bliss, she wondered.

Would it feel like pride at his ability to charm her godmother while an assembly of disapproving Methodists tried not to swoon over the absurdly pretty way he held his fork?

Would it feel like pretending to fall asleep beside him at the opera so that she might rest her head against his neck, where she could smell his skin?

Would it feel like lying up awake remembering the contours of his body as he'd pressed against her in a closet, unable to resolve the tension that welled up at the memory because, regrettably, he wasn't in bed with her?

It mustn't. For if it *were* like that, would she not be joyfully embroidering marital linens, rather than making discreet arrangements to flee to the Continent alone?

"My lady?" Winston said, tapping gently at her door. "Lord Apthorp is here to see you."

She jumped. How odd. It had been only an hour since they'd parted.

She tucked her letters in a drawer and followed Winston to the parlor, where Apthorp was waiting, staring prettily out the window. Without his wig, positioned in the sunshine, he was so luminous he seemed to emit light.

Was that what it would feel like to see the man you were in love with? Would he be so beautiful he looked as if he glowed?

"Oh, young lovers," she said archly, lest he sense that the sight of him made disorder of her heartbeat. "They simply cannot bear to be parted for more than an hour's time."

He glanced up. "Ah. Thank you for seeing me. I hope I'm not intruding."

"I shall forgive you. You must have been pining for me dreadfully to rush back to me so soon."

"Dreadfully," he agreed. "I confess, I never stop."

She bit her lip. His ability to *quip* still came as a surprise, given he'd been so humorless for years. She wished he'd displayed more of *that* talent rather than his less charming abilities to chide, harass, and tutor her.

His eyes traveled down to her face. "You've got something on your cheek," he observed.

She put her fingers to her skin. "Do I?"

He laughed softly. "Ah. Ink's the culprit as ever, Lady Constance. It's all over your hands."

She smiled, though in truth she was annoyed she was appearing before him splattered in drops of brown sludge, given his current state of summery radiance.

"Regrettably, Lord Apthorp, I am famously indelicate with my quill."

He met her eye, but if he caught the double meaning in her words, he didn't show it. Instead, he walked toward her, taking off his gloves.

"Here, let me." He reached out and gently dabbed at the skin beneath her left eye with his thumb.

He frowned. "I've only smudged it."

She held her breath, very much hoping he would not notice that she had, for some reason, started shaking at the onslaught of his touch.

He licked his thumb, steadied her chin in his other hand, and rubbed more firmly at her skin. She was not sure if it was pleasure or mortification that made her close her eyes and simply let him.

"There. Good as new," he said, stepping back.

She was glad he'd withdrawn his hand before she'd rubbed her cheek against his palm like a cat. "Thank you. I shall inform my lady's maid that there is a rival for her position. Now, then, what brings you here?"

"I'm concerned we may have a problem with Henry Evesham," he said.

She had suspected he was unsettled by her acquaintance with the scribe. His face, when he'd gathered that they knew each other, had gone so blank she had worried Lady Spence would notice and declare victory early. But he'd played it off quite skillfully.

"Don't worry. It was impudent of Lady Spence to invite him to lunch, but you handled it just the right way. In fact, you were perfect with her. She would probably have offered to sponsor your bill herself if you'd agreed to bring your mother to town. You *will* invite her, won't you?"

"I'm afraid that isn't possible."

"Why not? Is she truly ill? You've never mentioned it before."

"She's not ill, no," he said in a manner that implied she would be rude to ask further questions. He turned his back, once again gazing out the window in the haughty, superior fashion of Lord Bore. It was kind of him to return to form just in time to remind her of the reasons why she'd never liked him.

She went to stand beside him, where he could not evade her. "You know, Apthorp, bringing one's mother to town seems a far easier way to secure Lady Spence's favor than attending weeks of revivals and gospel studies. And don't you think she'd enjoy a few weeks of the season? Your sister could accompany her. They must be bored senseless rusticating in Cheshire."

"Well, Constance, had you ever spent any time rusticating in Cheshire, you might discover it's not entirely charmless," he said, an edge to his voice.

"Of course. I didn't mean to cause you offense," she said evenly, for he was not addressing the substance of her points, and she did not like to be dismissed when she was right.

"You haven't," he said, *obviously* lying. "But that's not what I came here to discuss. Please let the matter drop."

He looked pointedly into her eyes, as if waiting for her solemn oath. But she did not make unreasonable promises to people who failed to explain themselves, even if they became less handsome when they were cross with her.

"I simply don't see why you won't invite them if it will be helpful to our cause. Why don't you ever wish to explain yourself?"

A tendon in his jaw twitched. "I don't want them involved in our engagement, Constance, because of the way that it will *end*. The scandal will horrify my mother and reflect poorly on my sister. Remember, not every woman can afford to be as blithe as you about her reputation."

Ah. As usual, it was about her money, and his lack of it. Nothing made men less willing to speak sense to you than knowing you had something that they lacked.

The old, familiar note of judgment in his tone was all the reminder that she needed that she was *not* in love with him. Not even slightly.

"Very well. I assume you did not come here strictly to forbid me to bring shame upon your family with my wealth and dissipated character, so what would you like to discuss?"

"The matter you mentioned last night," he said briskly, now every inch old, humorless Lord Bore, "concerning the actress. Might we sit?" He gestured at the chairs in the center of the room.

"Certainly." She walked past the chairs and sprawled in a rather insolent pose on the sofa.

He perched stiffly across from her, as if by achieving the perfect degree of straightness in his spine he could straighten out the aspects he found wanting in her character. "I must insist you tell me everything that you're aware of, and then give me your assurance you will not probe any further."

If there was a single word she hated having leveled at her, it was *must*. She liked it even less when paired with lofty masculine dismissal of her proven abilities. If he did not trust her to help, she saw no reason to be candid. She knew the potent effects of *her* investigative powers; of *his*, she had grave doubts.

She yawned. "All I know is that the woman who was spreading rumors about you appears to be connected to the Theatre Royal. You were probably right to dismiss it as idle speculation. I'm sure I was being dramatic in thinking it was anything beyond coincidence."

Apthorp looked at her gravely, in a manner that conveyed he was not fooled. "You must tell me *exactly* what you know," he said. "In detail. From the beginning."

How bothersome. She vastly preferred her fake betrothed when he was giving touching defenses of her character or cuddling her in the shadows at the opera. Where had *that* man gone?

She decided to start *very* early in the story. Perhaps he would grow so bored by the circuitous nature of the tale that he would leave her to get on with the business of saving his life in peace.

"Well," she drew out, "I suppose our odyssey begins when I decided to match you to Miss Bastian."

He drew up his brows in a rather forbidding fashion. "You were *trying* to make a match of us?"

She had been quite assiduously trying to do just that. Why he looked so *outraged* by this notion, she could not hope to understand.

"I was indeed. Did I not make that clear before?"

"You said you thought I wished to marry her. You did not mention you were attempting to *induce* such an outcome."

He said this as though he had just discovered she had attempted to have him deported to New South Wales rather than to secure him a wealthy bride he had everything in common with.

"You needn't look so unhappy. I was trying to do you both a favor."

He smiled tightly, with no warmth. "Would you consider it a

favor if I tried to inveigle *you* into marrying someone entirely unsuitable?"

"Miss Bastian is not unsuitable. She is rich, attractive, poised, and fashionable. I thought you suited one another. I thought you were *alike*."

He looked like she'd put a fish bone in his tea. "Alike. I see. And I assume it has not escaped you that Miss Bastian is vapid, tiresome, and dull?"

No one was less pleased with Gillian Bastian at this moment than herself, but even so, his contempt of her friend was irritating. Miss Bastian was *not* vapid, precisely—more like singularly focused on her own interests, which were mostly limited to shopping. A pursuit that Constance did not find dull in the slightest.

"Is she vapid, tiresome, and dull, Lord Bore? Well, you can see how I thought she was perfect for *you*."

He glared at her, profoundly unamused. Then he stood, walked from the chair to the window, pressed two fingers against the glass, and was silent. His stillness made her vaguely nervous, so she was relieved when he finally turned back around.

Until she saw his face.

His eyes were lit with such a strange, dark energy that she could not tell if he was moved by anger, calculation, or some foreboding combination of them both.

"If you think *dullness* is what I'm after, Constance," he said, inspecting her face carefully, like she was a portrait of herself rather than a person, "then you should be much, much more careful. For one wonders if you understand anything about me at all."

His eyes met hers, and he smiled in a way that held no warmth, and yet, somehow, made her feel like she was burning.

No. She *didn't* understand him when he looked at her like that. And she was no longer certain she ever had.

∽

WHAT LADY CONSTANCE STONEWELL COULD NOT IMAGINE, because she was far more innocent than she knew herself to be, was that dullness had never been among the traits he coveted in ladies.

His tastes ran to naughty women.

And if she called him Lord Bore one more time, he might set about teaching her in vivid detail the many, many other things she had misjudged about him.

He was tempted to begin this very moment, because the expression on her face—like she was seeing him for the first time —made him itch to cast off years of hiding his attraction to her behind good manners.

He wanted to find the nearest powdering closet and demonstrate just how very bad his manners could be.

Were it only that he did not need to get the *blasted* story of his ruin out of her.

"I digress," he said, removing his eyes from her face in such a way that he was sure she would feel the loss of his gaze and *miss* it. "You intended to marry me off to Miss Bastian. And then what happened?"

"Well," she said, her voice rather more shaky than it had been, "the night of Lady Palmerston's masque, I was watching you dance with Gillian." She coughed, and seemed to recover her composure. "A woman in a stunning navy gown came and struck up a conversation. Her dress was a fabric unlike anything I'd ever seen. Gorgeous. I'd love to get something like it—"

She was nakedly stalling. "Get to the point, Constance."

She pursed her lips into a precious little rosebud. "I *am*. If you knew anything about poetics, you would infer the gown shall feature later as a relevant detail."

"Please, then, continue," he gritted out.

"She observed it was your second dance with Miss Bastian and asked if I thought you had hopes for her. I said I thought good news might be imminent. She became very quiet. And then she whispered that she hoped Miss Bastian would not suffer regrets, given what she'd heard about your Wednesday nights."

Wednesday nights. That was, indeed, a rather specific detail.

"She mentioned Wednesdays?"

"Yes. And she said it in such a mysterious, ominous way that I, of course, immediately asked her what she meant."

"And what did she say?"

She glanced up at him from below her long, pale lashes and smirked. "But don't you know?"

He fervently hoped he did not.

"Constance. What *exactly* did she say?"

"She said she hoped Miss Bastian had a taste for leather. And observed that it's often the prettiest men who are the most perverse."

Ah. Not nearly the whole of it, though the word *perverse* sent a flash of irritation through him. His practices were *not* perverse. "I see. And from this, you determined I enjoy a whipping and exposed me in your papers?"

At the word *whipping*, Constance blushed, which pleased him in a way he was not proud of. The petty wounded man in him liked knowing she was not as nonchalant about these matters as she acted. The petty wounded man in him wanted to leave her with the distinct impression that there were many, many things about which a person like himself might educate her.

"As you might understand," she said primly, "I was taken aback. I wanted to ask her what she meant, but the dance ended and she moved off into the crowd before I could gather my wits."

He tapped his fingers on the window, no longer pleased at all. He should really inure himself to how little he had meant to her, but each time he learned a new detail, the extent of her indifference stung him fresh.

"Am I to understand," he said, "that you destroyed my reputation over a rumor from a *total stranger*?"

She winced. "No. In fact, I intended to ignore the rumor

entirely, because it was so laughable. I mean, *imagine*, Apthorp, *you* frisking about a bawdy house."

He turned around, stepped forward, and looked directly in her eyes.

"Yes, Constance. *Imagine.*"

She blushed so deeply that, despite his barely checked fury, he had to bite his cheek to keep from smiling in a most unseemly way.

"In any case, I had no intention of pursuing the matter, until later that same evening when you asked me about betrothal gifts."

What he would give to take that moment back. It had been pitiful. He'd found her alone in the Palmerstons' library, for once not attended by Hilary or her motley of friends, and she'd asked him whether he thought his bill would pass, and he'd been so flattered by her interest, so thrilled to be alone with her, that the words had just slipped out.

What do you think a lady might like if a man who loved her were to declare himself?

He was determined not to color at the dreadful memory. "So you gathered from my question that I intended to propose to Miss Bastian."

"Yes. And from thence decided I should make sure you were not, in fact, perverse, as Gillian is quite particular about men, and I had encouraged the match."

"Particular about men? My God, she's about to marry *Harlan* bloody *Stoke*. Do you have any idea what he's—"

"Yes," she shot back. "I *do.*"

Her face was now crimson. He thought back to that week in Devon—one he'd tried fervently to forget—and had the uneasy feeling that something even less savory had transpired there than he'd originally suspected.

"You must understand," she said, before he could formulate that uneasy feeling into a question that possessed the degree of delicacy it merited, "that I had no idea Gillian was attached to him. She'd given me reason to think she was very fond of you. So for my own peace of mind, I decided to look into it."

"Look into it how?" He was instantly awash in dread at the notion she'd done more probing. There was a reason he'd always been on his finest form in Constance's presence; her chilling aptitude for discovering people's most inconvenient secrets.

"Since the woman mentioned Wednesdays, it seemed easy enough to simply consult your diary."

"You read my diary?"

"Well, you *do* tend to leave it on your desk, where anyone could find it." She said this defiantly, like the fact that it had been *possible* to invade his privacy excused that it was *childish* and *wrong*. "And since you were living here at the time, I simply asked my maid to distract your valet while you were out, went inside your rooms, and consulted your notations."

He thought back, with sickening panic, to what he might have written about his activities on Wednesdays. He exhaled. Nothing detailed enough to be incriminating. He rarely recorded his day in more than snippets.

Session at Charlotte Street with L. Naughty girl. Left bruises.

M. tonight. Purchased ropes for the occasion.

Saw F. Christ, the sounds she makes.

Snippets that were, nevertheless, just colorful enough for an inexperienced girl to form conclusions without understanding anything at all.

That she could somehow have such a detailed and yet incorrect picture of this most absolutely private aspect of his life was so offensive and intrusive that it made him want to gag.

Instead, he said only: "How dare you?"

She stuck out her chin. "I'm tired of being vilified for doing what I thought was right. I invite you to live as a woman and enjoy the choices we are blessed with, and then judge me for sharing information about what men do in private. I have kept such secrets before, out of discretion, and lived to very much wish that I had not. I didn't mean to harm you; I only meant to protect Gillian. And however much I regret that my words were used against you, you cannot deny that they were *true*. Were they not?"

He was not going to answer that. If she was going to be so smugly righteous about her own moral superiority, she could account for why she had not told him the truth from the beginning.

And now he wondered how much she might be leaving out.

"Here's a question, Constance. Why didn't you tell me you know Henry Evesham?"

She sighed, like he was being tiresome. "I make it my business to know *everyone*. You know that. Don't change the subject."

"I'm *not* changing the subject. How did he come to receive your poem?"

She gasped. "You aren't suggesting that *I* gave it to him?"

After today, there was little about her he would not believe.

"Did you?"

"Of course not!" she snapped. "If I had *wanted* to ruin you, I would not be subjecting myself to this public *indignity* of having to pretend to *like you*."

They glared at each other, and he believed her, but not in such a way that made him less inclined to seethe.

"Finish your story. How do you know the woman is an actress if you don't even know her name?"

"Yesterday I saw a sample of her gown at my dressmaker's." She paused. "You will recall I *did* say the gown would be important. We call that foreshadowing."

"Get on with it."

"That particular gown has only been sold to one person: the costumer at the Theatre Royal. Which means the woman was likely an actress. My mantua-maker is going to inquire who the dress was worn by. And then we'll have another clue."

"No," he snapped. "I already asked you not to pursue this. Do *not* consult further with your dressmaker. And whatever you do,

THE EARL I RUINED

do not say a single word to Henry Evesham. He's circling the story and I don't want him to think that either of us is taking the slightest bit of interest in it."

"Fine," she said. "Do you have any further unreasonable and self-defeating demands or will that suffice?"

"That will suffice. Good day."

He turned around and walked briskly for the door.

"Wait," she said coldly, half-rising from the sofa.

He could only assume she was going to apologize, so he paused.

"Forgive me for being frank, as I know you *despise* it when ladies display candor. But since today is Wednesday, I would be remiss if I did not ask you to break your usual appointment."

He stared at her. Her expression was defiantly blank.

"You must be *joking*."

She rose fully to her feet. "I assure you, Apthorp, I am not."

To think what had been going through his head at lunch. *This is how it would feel if she really were in love with me.* And the traitorous thought that came after it: *What if she wasn't pretending?*

Bile splashed up in his throat for indulging in such foolishness. The only thing that was real was her low opinion of him.

He shook his head. "My God, the things you think of me."

"Not think," she corrected quietly. *"Know."*

He was so angry he was shaking. He looked at her long and hard.

"You know *nothing*, Constance. And though you believe courtesy to be beneath you, I would ask that while we must bear each other's company, you grant me the small decency of considering what you are implying about my character when you say such things."

"All I'm implying is that your usual Wednesday habits are not conducive to our current goals," she said with infuriating calm.

"I wouldn't observe my usual Wednesday habits, Constance, because in addition to being very foolish with Evesham circling, it would show a distinct lack of *care* or *respect* for my supposed future wife. Would it not?"

"Yes," she said peevishly. "It would."

He threw up his hands. "And yet you think I would do it anyway? You think I would risk humiliating you for a *fuck*?"

She was silent, her face pinched into a bitter frown.

He moved closer to her, until he was close enough that she was forced to look at him. "You are very quick to assume that I am a careless person. Someone who harms other people without a thought to the consequences. Have you ever stopped to consider *why* that is?"

She stared at him angrily. "I don't know what you mean."

"Oh, I think you do. You're observant enough to have gathered that we often loathe the qualities in others we most dislike in *ourselves*."

CHAPTER 9

*A*pthorp's meaning hit her like a sack of bricks between the shoulder blades, making it difficult to breathe. The old familiar claim. Wicked, harmful Constance. Never to be trusted.

"I see," she said slowly, so he would not hear that she was trying not to cry. "You believe I think these things of you because they are true of *me*. You think *I* harm people."

"Well, don't you?" he asked quietly.

She shook her head, wiping moisture from her eyes. "I don't know why I'm surprised to hear you say that. You've always thought poorly of my character, so why would you not believe me to be cruel?"

"Not cruel," he said. *"Reckless."*

That bloody word. How she *hated* that word.

"Yes, you've thought me reckless ever since that day in Devon, haven't you? Well, perhaps you're right about me. Perhaps I *am* reckless. Because I wasn't trying to get *his* attention that bloody day—I'd been trying to get *yours*. And for my *reckless* efforts, I have been rewarded with no end to your low opinion of me ever since."

She turned and left the room and slammed the door recklessly behind her. She stomped recklessly through the marble hallways and managed to avoid being caught recklessly weeping until she was halfway up the stairs, where she recklessly collided with Rosecroft on the landing.

"Constance! Whatever is the matter!"

At his concerned tone she threw herself onto his shoulder and recklessly wept.

"I hate him," she seethed. "He is *so* unkind."

"Who?"

"Your bloody cousin bloody Apthorp."

Beneath her soggy cheek, Rosecroft's shoulder rumbled gently. He patted her back, moved aside, and dug in his pocket to offer her his handkerchief.

"Bloody Apthorp, indeed," he said, sounding as much amused as he was sympathetic. "Had your first lovers' quarrel? Don't worry, my dear. You'll be able to extract all sorts of tender moments from the lad once you've forgiven him for whatever he's done to aggrieve you. It's all part of the fun." He gave her a wink.

His good-natured amusement made Constance cry harder, because this was not a lovers' quarrel. This was an *enemies'* quarrel, and it had been quietly brewing ever since she returned from France at seventeen.

In keeping with her character, she had acted impulsively. And in keeping with his, he had held it against her ever since.

"I'm going to my room. Tell Winston not to let anyone disturb me."

She heard Rosecroft chuckling to himself as she marched up to her bedchamber, where she drew the curtains, climbed onto her bed, and stared miserably at the ceiling.

She regretted every moment of that odious party in Devon. She'd been so excited to return to England. After her humiliating sojourn in her native country at fourteen, she'd gone back to France determined to remake herself into a woman who'd never again be subject to rejection. She would gain the upper hand not by fitting in, but by being so clever she would not have to.

And so as soon as her final year in convent school was finished, she'd descended upon her aunt's apartment in the Marais and made it her sole purpose to observe the elegant, arch French ladies who peopled her aunt's salons. She apprenticed herself in the absorption of their secrets. How to emphasize one's supposed flaws to exaggerate the singularity of one's beauty. How to dress to devastate. How to draw a man's eye without so much as looking at him. And most crucially: how to read the room.

By carefully observing, one could sense when there was advantage to seeming mysterious and striking, or humble and attentive, or beflattering and generous—and adjust oneself accordingly. This, it turned out, was Constance's inborn gift.

The art of influence, she'd discerned, was not in being perfect but in being the right thing for the right person. Being admired and indispensable to everyone—floating on a sea of fizzy *bons mots* and favors—was far more restful than cultivating intimate relationships that pinned one down. For when one was truly known, one could be judged insufficient, and dismissed.

Having polished herself into a gem with enough facets to sparkle in any kind of lighting, she completed her studies by learning how to flirt. She quickly discovered she'd been doing it all wrong. If a man caught your fancy, you didn't *announce* it. You certainly did not lie in wait for him in a shrub, as she had attempted with Lord Apthorp. *Mais non.* If you wanted a man's attention, the most critical thing was to never, ever directly let him know. Instead, you made him notice you. And once he did, you made him think you *hadn't* noticed him.

And so when her brother summoned her back to England to assume her place in the family, and Hilary announced she'd arranged a small house party in Devon to welcome Constance before her first London season, she had made it her mission to put these lessons into practice. She would leave the English stunned.

Particularly those who had looked askance at her on her previous visit.

Particularly her cousin's altogether too-handsome relation, that stiff, rather mean fellow, the Earl of Apthorp.

And she was in luck: he was among her cousin's guests.

She could still remember how his eyes had widened the day she'd walked into the room in a dress that was every inch the Parisian style, cut daringly low, with mismatched jewels twisted around her neck in a column that covered her throat, and her pale hair piled up so high it grazed the doorframes. She did not look English. She did not look girlish.

She looked *sensational*.

And once she was certain that he'd noticed, once she'd felt his eyes trailing her about the room, she'd made a point to speak to everyone in residence but him. To write theatricals in which she did not cast him. To yawn when he went on in conversation. To make it known she found his habits dull.

It worked.

She could *feel* him watching her. She never openly acknowledged him, but she made jokes in his range of hearing that she thought he'd find amusing, and pretended not to notice when he smiled. She hinted her desire to be escorted here and there in London, so he might overhear and invite her for a drive on their return to town. And then, she'd gone in for the kill: she'd lavished her attentions on the person at the party he seemed to like the least. Lord Harlan Stoke.

Her flirtations began harmlessly. Whispered words at dinner. Permitting him a second dance. Allowing him to draw her portrait as they sat on a blanket in the sun. All of this timed, of course, to be observed by the real object of her fascination.

She thought she had Lord Apthorp exactly where she wanted him when he'd asked her for a private word at a luncheon picnic.

She'd been giddy thinking he would finally declare himself. Instead he'd pulled her aside to deliver a lesson in deportment: "I can see you have a tendre for Lord Harlan, which is natural. But not all men are kind. You must be careful not to put yourself in a situation where you might be harmed."

She'd been so embarrassed at his condescension she'd wanted to kick him. Instead, she'd said an icy thank-you for his solicitude, gone back to the picnic, and thrown herself even more thoroughly at Harlan Stoke.

For if she could not make Lord Apthorp jealous, she could at the very least *provoke* him.

In fact, the idea of finally provoking him out of his calm, polite, patronizing manners gave her a delicious little thrill. She imagined strategies she might employ to finally make him lose his temper. She imagined doing something so beyond the pale— breaking into his room and leaving her handkerchief among his starchy shirts, or her card between the pages of his diary—that he'd be so incensed he'd break his own tedious code of propriety and come storming up to her room to dress her down in private. She imagined being undressed when he arrived. She imagined him locking the door and telling her that if ladies wished to act like wicked girls, they would be treated with due wickedness. He might even take her over his knee and ...

It was just a fantasy, of course. If he were to actually try such a thing, she would no doubt scream and assail him with the nearest piece of firewood, or push him out her open window.

But the *idea* of it. Him, all passionate with anger, eyes dark and trained on her, perhaps with his cravat untied or his shirt untucked, perhaps without his wig. His hands reaching for her, strong and masculine ...

It was quite the tableau to imagine as she fell asleep.

Especially when her gambit with Lord Harlan seemed to work.

Lord Harlan was what the French would call *une proie facile*— easy prey. Each time she made a bold remark, he returned it with something more outrageous. When she touched him with her fan, he nudged her shoe beneath the table. When she wore a low-cut dress, he made no effort to hide his appreciation for her breasts.

And Apthorp noticed. Every time she laughed at Lord Harlan's filthy jokes or read a pert passage of poetry aloud to him or joined him in flagrantly cheating at whist, she could see it drove Apthorp mad to watch her be so brazen.

It was *delightful* fun to make him stew.

But still, he kept his composure. And soon he had to leave. As his remaining days grew numbered, and *still* she had not gotten what she wanted, she became more and more annoyed.

Reckless.

And so on his final day in Devon, a boring, endless rainy after-noon during which Lord Apthorp attended to his correspondence while the others wrote silly poems and drew comic portraits of the dogs, she decided to take her last chance to win the game once and for all. She'd stood just within his range of hearing and made a show of whispering to Lord Harlan to join her in the picture gallery across the sunken garden from the house, so she could show him the sculpture of Leda and the Swan, the gem of the collection.

She knew Apthorp would disapprove of her being alone with Lord Harlan, and would therefore contrive to follow them. Perhaps he would mar the polish of his impeccably shined boots darting over the rain-soaked path across the garden. Perhaps he would yell at Lord Harlan for besmirching her maidenly honor.

It was a petty gambit, but it amused her.

Until she found herself alone with Harlan Stoke.

For it seemed Lord Harlan also knew how to read a room. And it turned out *he* was not the easy mark.

She was.

In the empty gallery, he dropped all pretense of decorum.

"I like your type, Lady C.," he'd purred into her ear, drawing up far too close for comfort. "We Englishmen should send all our prettiest girls to France."

She'd tapped him with her silver fan and flounced away to inspect a second-rate statue of Athena. "You're too kind," she said over her shoulder. "But I'm afraid not every female specimen returns as finely molded as myself."

"Oh, you're finely molded," he said in a low voice, once again moving much too near her. "I'd rather look at *you* draped in gauze than a piece of marble."

She began to feel uneasy. But she did not wish to seem provincial, and anyway, he was only playing the game that she'd invented. So she merely batted her lashes and said, "Oh, Lord Harlan, you shocking man," as she moved out of his reach and waited for him to perceive she was not interested.

But her degree of interest had not proved relevant to his.

"Let's have a go at staging one of your theatricals," he'd murmured, closing the distance she kept reasserting. "You play Leda. I'll play the swan."

She backed less subtly away, and he stepped closer, until they were standing flush with a wall of drapes that protected the paintings from the light, and there was nowhere else for her to go.

"Why don't you show me your artistic form," he said lecherously, running a cigar-stained finger along the neckline of her bodice. "I suspect it's far more beautiful than the art."

"Dear Lord Harlan," she said airily, though her pulse was beating like a rabbit in her throat. "Have you never been to a gallery? The art is on the *walls*. But this collection is insipid. Come, let's return to the others. I want to arrange a game of *vingt-et-un* and relieve you of your money."

He edged so close that her shoulders pressed into the curtains and she could smell his breakfast on his breath. "Not just yet. There's more beauty in this room I'd like a look at."

And then his hands had been everywhere at once.

His mouth was wet and suffocating, leaving moist trails

slugged upon her neck and throat. His fingers smelled like damp tobacco. She tried to edge away, to politely signal he'd misread her cues. But the more she wriggled, the more forcefully he writhed against her and the more frightened she became.

"Stop it," she'd whispered, but she was scared, and her voice was so faint she could scarcely hear herself, and he'd dragged his rotten lips up to her face, and tried to kiss her on the mouth, and it was so awful that she'd jabbed the filigreed edge of her silver fan to his neck and scraped it from his neckcloth to his ear, not stopping until she felt the tip meet bone.

"Damn you!" he'd hissed, rearing back with outrage in his eyes. She'd tugged her bodice and her skirts back into order, furious, unable to look him in the eye, praying the faint stubble at his jawline had not left telling marks along her neck.

Just then the door had opened.

And there he was.

Lord Apthorp.

Looking from her, flushed and disheveled with her gown askew, to Stoke, panting.

"We're busy, Apthorp," Stoke had sneered, whipping around.

Apthorp had stood completely rigid, looking from Stoke to her.

"Lady Constance," he said in a voice that was not angry, but something worse: gravely concerned. "Do you need assistance?"

Still so aghast and humiliated she did not trust her own voice, she could only shake her head.

He jerked his chin in silent acknowledgment and shut the door without a word.

Wait, she'd wanted to cry. *It isn't what you think. It was a game, and he broke the rules.*

Stoke had only adjusted his cravat and smirked at her, like it had all been a joke. "For a girl who acts like a tart, you kiss like a bloody goat."

Tears had welled up in her eyes as he'd sauntered from the room.

Later, she'd found a curl of his skin dangling from the serrated blades of her fan.

She'd burned it in her fire like a witch.

Neither Lord Apthorp nor Lord Harlan Stoke had spoken a word to her for the remainder of their time in Devon. Apthorp left that very night, indicating he'd been called earlier to Cheshire.

But Stoke had remained for a week, and had made no secret of his contempt for her.

First he made a show of courting all the other girls, just to see if she was watching. He found his most willing audience in Lady Jessica Ashe, who was just fifteen. The poor girl looked like she might faint from pleasure when he spoke to her, and soon became his favorite, following him around like a loyal, lovesick puppy.

I should warn her about him, Constance had thought. *He'll probably paw her too.*

But she'd felt so numb and guilty and sickened by her part in what had happened that she'd just ignored the unfolding flirtation and said nothing.

And when, not a year later, there came to be whispers about Lady Jessica … a girl who'd gotten into trouble, and would never have a season …

She *hated* that she had not sounded a warning.

She promised herself that the next time she had an inkling a man did not play by the assigned rules, she would act.

She would use her innate gift for observation to fashion herself a position in the world that gave her information others lacked. And she would use it as a scythe.

Not because she was *cruel*. Not because she was *reckless* in matters such as this.

Just the opposite: because she had learned her lesson.

Women must *protect* one another.

And if, in the same spirit, a *man* was being foolish and short-sighted, well, by God, she could protect him too.

Yes. She would do exactly as she always had: use the information she possessed in the service of what her gut told her was right.

And so she pulled herself out of bed and sat down at her desk and took out her most effective weapon: her quill. She wrote until she was ink-speckled and exhausted and the action she must take was starkly written on two letters.

One addressed to Gillian Bastian. And the other to Apthorp Manor, Cheshire.

She sealed them and delivered them to Rosecroft's secretary to be put into the post.

And then she summoned her maid to remove her gown and dressed in her coziest old nightdress from the nuns and curled up on her bed, too tired to even climb beneath her swans-down quilt though it was only half past eight, and slept.

Until a knock at her door roused her at half ten.

"Lady Constance," Winston said. "I'm sorry to disturb you so late, but Lord Apthorp is here, and he requests a word with you."

THE ROSECROFTS' PARLOR WAS DIM, THE LAST EMBERS OF THE FIRE dying low. Apthorp anxiously adjusted the ribbon tied around his gift.

"You're nervous," Rosecroft observed, swirling brandy in his glass.

Apthorp glared at his cousin. "Not nervous. Just impatient."

Rosecroft grinned and stretched his legs lazily before the fire. "Constance has been in a state ever since you went tearing out of here. I don't like to see the girl upset."

Neither did he, apparently. He'd left here determined not to speak to her again until he *must*, and by the time he was halfway to Westminster, the guilt of what he'd said and how he'd left things was so urgent he'd gone tramping out to procure the kind of silly, sentimental gift that had its roots in made-up stories.

Why had he pressed an argument with her, when speaking candidly only ever seemed to make things worse? Why could he not just ignore the thing she'd done a week ago and grit his teeth around bland pleasantries until he could get on with the bloody business of forgetting her?

But the truth was obvious enough that he could not avoid it no matter how angrily he stomped along the dirty streets.

Because it goes back longer than one week. Far longer.

Years.

He'd always hoped that if he ignored it—the kernel of unhappiness between them that they'd never spoken of—it would simply fade away, like a bad dream. He'd hoped that by the time he could be honest with Constance about his feelings, a few unpleasant moments in their youth would be irrelevant.

But it *was* relevant, clearly. It had become a kind of constant, seething tension that roiled beneath their every conversation. If he didn't address it now, it might very well combust before his bill passed.

And then this torture would be for nothing.

"I did something I regret," he said to Rosecroft, not quite knowing if he meant this afternoon, or years before, or all the other times that, looking back, were colored by that moment in the portrait gallery.

"It happens," his cousin sighed. "You're smart to have a word with her before she goes to sleep. If you want my advice, never let bad feelings linger overnight—they only turn to rot."

Clever of him, then, to let them linger for five years.

"Apthorp?" Constance asked in a tired voice, walking into the room. "Have you come back for another round of persecuting me?"

He rose. She was in a voluminous white night rail of thick

cotton that swallowed her from the top of her neck to her toes. He'd seen her many times in her fashionable silk dressing gowns when she'd swanned into breakfast late as he was leaving, and been indignant at her habit of traipsing through the house in such unsuitable attire. But this prim ensemble, though it covered more of her, somehow made her seem more exposed.

He wanted to tell Rosecroft not to look at her.

"Forgive me for disturbing you so late," he said.

She said nothing, but her eyes conveyed she was not pleased to see him.

Apthorp glanced at Rosecroft. "I don't suppose you would give us a moment of privacy?"

Rosecroft sighed. "I'll be on the terrace having a cigar." He gestured at the French doors off the parlor. "With the door open. Don't be pert. And don't make her *cry*."

Constance waited, arms crossed over her breasts, as his cousin went off, whistling.

"Why are you here?"

At her contemptuous tone he felt shy and ridiculous, but nevertheless reached down and held out his offering. "I brought you something. By way of amends."

She gingerly took the fat armful of red roses that he'd coarsely tied into a bouquet with garden twine.

"How perfectly hideous," she said coldly.

He was capable of giving a woman an elegant bouquet, but he'd thought perhaps it might be more meaningful to give her the inelegant one that she'd imagined in her story about the maze.

Now he felt foolish. She didn't remember.

"Uh, yes. I'm sorry they're a mess. It was a kind of a joke—a poor one, rather—er, a reference to your—"

She looked up and met his eyes. "To my tragic little story about my broken heart?"

He swallowed. "Yes."

"You realize it was *fake*."

He closed his eyes. "I know. Would you read the note?"

She unfolded the card he'd attached to the bouquet. "*Lady Constance,*" she read aloud warily. "*Please accept these flowers as an apology for my harsh words to you. Not just this afternoon, but in years past.*"

She paused and looked at him uncertainly. He bit his lip and waited for her to read the rest.

"*Please know,*" she continued, her voice softer, "*that despite the strained moments in our history, there has never been a time when I did not admire your spirit, intelligence, and beauty. I regret that I ever made you doubt you had my high opinion. I know these next three weeks will be a trial, but I hope that we can endure them as friends.*"

She looked up at him, and her eyes were fierce with some emotion. "Friends? Is that what we are to each other? I'm not sure we ever have been."

He didn't know the answer. A week ago he would have said they were. But it seemed he'd not fully understood how she'd perceived him.

"I'd like to be," he said finally. "I think this would be easier if we were."

She sank down onto the sofa that she'd reclined on so imperiously earlier in the day. "If you wish to be my friend, perhaps I should be frank. You have never seemed terribly fond of me. As far as I can tell, you formed a low opinion of me in Devon, and have disapproved of me ever since."

He sat down beside her, trying to muddle through his own feelings about the torture that had been that week in Devon. How she'd arrived, looking like a vision. How he hadn't been able to take his eyes off her. How, at every turn, she'd signaled he was not the kind of man she deemed worthy of her interest.

Lord Apthorp is uncommonly pedantic about soil drainage, is he not?

Who will be the hero in my scene? I won't ask Lord Apthorp—he is far too busy with his letters to engage in such trifles.

What a grim young man is your Lord Apthorp. Why does he come here, if all he does is read his books and make notations in his ledger? Were no charming gentlemen available?

She'd made no secret of finding him a bore. Or worse: slightly absurd.

And having just lost the remainder of his family fortune in a humiliating, public way, neither he, nor the rest of England, disagreed with her. He was proving himself to be exactly the kind of errant peer his father had always warned him not to be: irresponsible and incompetent. Unworthy of his place.

He'd *despised* himself that summer.

He'd wanted out of his own *skin* that summer.

If it had not been that the Rosecrofts had insisted, he'd never have gone to that house party, for any time he set foot in public, all he heard was the whispers.

Imagine being asked to do so little with so much, and still managing to piss it all away.

Constance's obvious contempt for him had only confirmed his low opinion of himself. Because he'd craved her admiration, and he'd known that as he was, he'd never warrant so much as a second glance.

That week had changed him. He'd resolved to dig his way out of his shameful state, to reshape himself into the kind of man who merited respect.

The kind of man who could eventually be worthy of a girl like Constance Stonewell.

But maybe he'd also resented her, for being what he could not have. And maybe that had been unfair of him. Maybe it had made him childish, at a time when she'd needed him to be the older, wiser soul.

"I didn't disapprove of you, Constance," he said, navigating around the dryness that had overtaken his throat. "In fact, I thought *you* disapproved of *me*. You seemed a bit—"

"Dismissive?" she offered. "Taunting?" She sighed and leaned back into the cushions, looking at the fire. "For such a legendary letch, Lord Apthorp, one wonders if you understand the simplest things about young women. I did not behave that way because I didn't like you. I behaved that way because I wanted you to *notice* me."

"I see," he said, blowing out a breath because he instantly *did see*, now that she had pointed out the obvious. He dearly wished he could go back in time and kick his oversensitive, underobservant younger self in the shins.

"Forgive me. I simply thought ... well, and then it seemed you had taken a fancy to Lord Harlan Stoke, and I did not wish to—"

He did not know how to go on, because he was not sure what exactly had happened in the picture gallery, only that she had very clearly wished for him to leave her there when he'd walked in on it.

"Now that I know the way you conduct yourself on *Wednesdays*," she said meaningfully, "I think it is unfair of you to hold me in low esteem for what happened in the gallery."

"Constance, I *don't*."

Her mouth was grim. "No? Your manner has always suggested that you thought I had allowed him improper liberties. And I didn't."

He turned toward her, so his face would be out of the shadows from the fireplace. He wanted her to see that he was being fully honest. "I wouldn't *care* if you had taken liberties with him, or with any other gentleman. I merely took your seeming attachment to him as confirmation that you would not welcome my interest. And so I didn't extend it. Even if I wanted to."

She was quiet. "You wanted to?"

He laughed roughly. "Yes."

They were both silent. She fiddled with the petal of a rose.

"Constance—I don't wish to pry, but if you were not there because you welcomed his attentions—" He bit off the words, unsure of exactly how to continue but needing, *needing*, to ask, because it was possible he had failed her in more ways than one, and he could not live with himself if he had.

"Lord Harlan has a reputation for ..." He swallowed. "He didn't *hurt* you, did he?"

Her face went dark. "No. Not as such." She met his eye. "He was ... briefly overexuberant in his attentions. I made my lack of enthusiasm clear and he did not continue."

Overexuberant. He wanted to go find the man and pull him out of whatever club he was half-soused in and thrash him until he bled.

"You were right to warn me about him," Constance added. "I wish I had listened."

He leaned forward and took her by the shoulders.

"Just know that if you had said the words that day, I would have happily throttled him. And if you would like, I still can."

"There is no need." She glanced up at him, then smiled ever so slightly. "I stabbed him in the neck."

He stared at her. "You stabbed Harlan Stoke in the *neck?*"

"Yes. With a very pretty silver fan." She smirked, clearly pleased with herself. "I shall always treasure the memory."

He bit his thumb and closed his eyes to try to keep from laughing.

"Sometimes, Lady Constance, you really are the woman of my dreams."

"Thank you for finally realizing it," she said primly. "I do have my attractions when I am not being cruel and monstrous."

He sighed. "I'm so sorry that I made you feel that way. It's beginning to be clear to me that I have been acting like an arse for far longer than I realized."

She smiled tightly. Not in such a way that invited further conversation, but in such a way that made him feel she did not disagree with him.

Christ, if only he'd realized.

Could he have simply said what he'd wanted from the start? It was almost too painful to consider, but he couldn't stop himself. "Constance, may I ask you a question?"

"Yes."

"What did you hope would happen if you had succeeded in getting my attention? What did you want?"

"Oh, I don't know," she said lightly. "What do silly young maidens ever want when they develop brief infatuations with unsuitable young men? Fond words? A poem?"

She looked away and spoke less archly. "Perhaps a correction to our encounter in the garden maze?"

Of course. He'd been so stupid.

"I wonder if it's too late to make it up to you." Impulsively, he reached over and tipped her head toward him, and kissed her on the lips.

Just lightly. Chastely.

The way he might have when she was seventeen.

She sighed and closed her eyes.

"I'm sorry that it took me so many years to get around to that," he murmured, rubbing her slightly parted lower lip with his thumb. "It seems I'm not as perceptive as I ought to be. Next time, just tell me what it is you want."

"All right, children," Rosecroft's voice boomed from the terrace doors behind them. "That's enough. Lovers' quarrel is officially over."

Reluctantly, he moved away from Constance.

She stood up. She was smiling.

"Thank you for the unsightly flowers, Lord Apthorp," she said, formally executing an exaggerated curtsy for the benefit of Rose-croft, who was now observing with his arms folded over his chest. "I shall cherish them."

She leaned in and dropped her voice so his cousin couldn't overhear. "And what I want, Julian, my dear friend, is for you to kiss me again the way you did in the powdering closet."

With that, she winked, took her flowers under her arm, and flounced out of the room.

"Seems she forgives you," Rosecroft drawled. "Now we can all live happily ever after."

Apthorp winced, trying to pretend that it was that simple, and knowing that it wasn't.

And yet, as he walked back along the dark streets to the Strand, he could not help but wonder what might happen if he did the wild, illogical, wrongheaded thing he now suddenly could not stop imagining.

Simply asking her for what he'd always wanted.

CHAPTER 10

"*E*ntrez," Valeria Parc commanded, ushering Constance inside the door of her small boutique in a swirl of scarlet silk. "And stop slouching."

Most mantua-makers were known for flattering their customers. Valeria Parc was not like most mantua-makers.

Constance followed her inside, inhaling the fragrance of fresh violets that always wafted from Valeria's pile of glossy black hair. The floral note was in striking contrast to her air of menace.

Valeria led her to a cloth-covered platform in front of a floor-to-ceiling mirror, positioning her just so until she stood in a shaft of sunlight. "Stand here." Her green eyes flashed in the mirror as she flicked them over every nook of Constance's figure, taking measurements with her eyes.

"You've lost at least an inch of bosom."

This was not a compliment. Valeria was a great proponent of bosoms.

"Oh, what's a bit of bosom?" Constance said, turning away from the sight of her own reflection. In truth, her figure *was* reduced. Her appetite tended to fluctuate with her mood. When she was happy, she celebrated with cake and cream teas from morning till night; when she was unnerved, she ate nothing.

She had not had a proper meal in a week.

Valeria took her chin in her hand, examining her face.

"You lack verve. Are you ill?"

She was not ill, only exhausted. Her custom of sleeping until luncheon had given way to restless predawn dreams that left her feeling hot and incomplete and unable to fall back to sleep. *Distressed.*

Distressed about the most unlikely thing in history: *kissing the Earl of Apthorp.*

She tried for a breezy smile. "I am only tired from the excitement of preparing for my wedding. I trust in your abilities to restore me to beauty. I shall convert my brother's entire fortune into gowns if that's what it takes."

Valeria gave her a grim smile, for she enjoyed discussion of material enrichment nearly as much as she enjoyed probing Constance's spine with her hard, pointy fingers.

"And how is your Lord Apthorp?"

Constance winced as the dressmaker tugged at her stays. "Very well. I think."

In truth she'd barely seen him since he'd shown up bearing a sad expression and a deformed bouquet in a gesture so touching and romantic she could not believe she had not concocted it herself. He and Westmead had spent the week furiously crisscrossing town to secure votes for the bill; on the few occasions she had seen him, it had been in public, and they'd done little except perform fondness at each other from across dining tables and crowded rooms.

Yet whenever she caught sight of him, her breath hitched in a way that was difficult to cover up. It felt as though she risked propriety by merely looking at him from afar, because whenever she did so, she could not stop imagining him touching her.

Next time just tell me what you want.

But what if I don't know?

Ever since that humbling disaster in the portrait gallery, she'd distanced herself from any man who'd seemed even slightly interested in seducing her. She'd told herself she'd been unpersuaded by her suitors—that they were unattractive, or indiscreet, or too flirtatious, or too dull. But perhaps the problem had been not with the gentlemen who wished to woo her, but with her own unhappy history with amorous solicitation.

Perhaps she'd simply been afraid.

Well. She was *not* afraid of Apthorp.

And now that she'd had proper tutelage in such things that could transpire in a powdering closet, she wanted to advance her studies.

For when Apthorp had shown up with those roses, she'd begun to feel acutely that she'd missed an opportunity.

The next time a man studiously ignored her, and was faultlessly well-mannered and appeared blander than blancmange— she wanted to be ready.

She now understood that men like that had hidden depths.

"*Voilà*," Valeria said, stepping away to show her her reflection in the mirror.

The shimmering pink gown was perfect for her engagement ball—a ludicrous confection of silk and whalebone and intricate golden Arras lace that made her more spectacle than woman. It was the kind of gown that cried out to be looked at.

It was not the kind of gown that cried to be taken off.

"You don't like it?" Valeria asked.

"I love it. But I wonder. Do you have any designs that might be more appropriate for ... after the wedding? To be worn in private?"

Valeria raised one exquisitely arched black brow at Constance. "Ondine, bring my designs for the nuns." She winked.

Ondine returned with a portfolio of sketches. She was blushing.

Valeria dropped her voice. "Usually I reserve these for ladies of pleasure. But you have never done the usual thing. Care to have a look?"

Constance opened the book to the first page, and immediately realized why Ondine was the shade of a plum. The sketch was of a woman draped in a diaphanous fabric, her figure limned in cutouts lined with lace. It was not so much a gown as the absence of one.

Constance smiled. "I think I might be ruined just from *seeing* this."

"Imagine how your Lord Apthorp will feel."

Yes. *Imagine.*

He was used to her in elaborate court gowns that made her silhouette twice its natural size. Such gowns made her feel dramatic and powerful and safe.

Not … like this.

She knew he was not eager to share his secret life with her.

She knew he valued propriety and honor.

She knew he did not trust her.

But perhaps if he saw her in something like this …

Perhaps he might be inclined to take a risk.

"Two of these," she said decisively, pointing at the sketch. "One in crimson and one in cream."

"Very well," Valeria said with a smile.

As the seamstress helped her dress, Valeria whispered in her ear.

"I'm meeting with the costumer at the Theatre Royal today about the matter we discussed. I'll write to you should I learn anything pertinent. Unless you'd like to come along?"

"Thank you, but I can't. I am planning a surprise for Lord Apthorp this afternoon. Do keep me apprised."

∾

APTHORP ARRIVED HOME FROM A MEETING WITH WESTMEAD AS weary as he'd been in years. He was hoarse from making promises to scheming politicians. His bones hurt from rattling across London in ill-sprung carriages. His heart ached from gazing at Constance over candlelit dance floors, making a show of how much he looked forward to a wedding that would never happen.

And fighting back the gnawing feeling that it should.

For if she had longed for his attention as a girl, if she trembled when he touched her, if he could not look upon her without smiling in a way that hurt his jaw—was it not within the realm of possibility that this thing between them might be salvaged? Was it possible that he had not *imagined* a connection all those years?

He couldn't sleep for debating in his mind which was the greater risk: to throw away the only thing he'd ever really wanted, or to admit to Constance that he wanted it.

For if he did, he would need to explain to the woman he least trusted with his secrets the full truth about his past. A truth that could ruin him a third time over.

He wanted to. It was dishonest to pretend he didn't, and since his every waking hour had devolved into a pretense, the least he could do was stop lying to himself.

But he could not quiet the part of himself that was equally convinced that doing what he wanted would, as usual, only make things worse.

He needed a night alone to mull it over before they attended church tomorrow with the Spences, when he'd have a chance to talk to her in private.

But something in his house was off.

The air inside the vestibule smelled like lemons and vinegar, rather than its customary redolence of must, and Tremont was not at his usual post downstairs. He lit a candle to investigate, but oddly, it did not flare and give off the stink of barnyard fat, for someone had swapped his inexpensive tallow tapers with pleasant-scented beeswax ones.

He held the flame up to the wall. In the dim light it was not just the air that was different. It was his entire house.

Tapestries had been hung over the worst of the damp stains and peeling plaster.

His worn parlor chairs had been replaced by homely, well-stuffed sofas. Someone had arranged fresh flowers on the table in a silver bowl he did not own, and laid a soft, plush India carpet on the floor.

What the devil? If he was the victim of a burglary, the intruders had rather missed the point of thieving.

He heard footsteps from upstairs.

"Tremont," he called, "is that you?"

He was answered by the muffled sound of furnishings being dragged across the floor. He snatched an iron fire pike from beside the hearth and marched upstairs, wielding it before him.

In the hallway two footmen and three housemaids paused their various acts of domestic improvement—hanging paintings, sweeping floorboards, polishing woodwork— and stared at him, alarmed.

Constance stood behind them, conferring with Tremont over a list.

"What are you doing here?" he cried.

Constance jumped, and turned around. "Lord Apthorp! You've returned! But why are you armed?"

He realized he was wielding the iron poker with a greater degree of animation than was strictly safe when one held a metal hook. He put it to his side.

"What is all this?"

Constance smiled. "You're early. We were hoping to finish before you returned. I wanted to surprise you."

"You have certainly succeeded."

She gestured up at the walls, which were remarkably absent of spiderwebs, and waved her hand through the air, which had the tang of freshly burned cedar. "Tremont and I have been working like two bandits to get your home in order. With the help of these lovely people of course."

She smiled at the assembled servants, most of whom were still eyeing his poking stick nervously.

He put it behind his back. "And they might be ...?"

"Your new staff. I brought anyone Westmead House could spare. Miss Pip here has agreed to run your kitchen. Miss Smith, Mr. Carmody, and Mr. Fine will make up the rest of the house. And this is Mrs. Haslet. She's head maid at Westmead House and will make you a fine housekeeper. Once she has assessed how much work needs to be done, we'll hire additional servants."

Constance beamed at him.

All he felt was shame.

"May I have a word with you?"

"Of course."

He stepped into his study, waited for her to follow him, and pulled the door shut tight so as not to be overheard. "Constance ... I see you mean well by this—"

"I do!" She nodded vigorously. "Don't you like it?"

It was impossibly sweet of her. So sweet it produced a heavy feeling in his chest. Nevertheless ...

"I can't accept it," he said quietly.

She cocked her head like a parrot who understood his words but not their meaning. "Can't accept it? Whyever not?"

He closed his eyes. Would there be no end to his leveling this month?

"I see you mean this as a kindness, and I'm touched. But surely you must not think I live this way out of a personal taste for filth? I don't employ more servants here because at present I cannot *afford* them."

With his creditors calling in his debts and his usual means of supplementing his coffers with small coin decidedly unavailable, he had less than four guineas of ready money at his disposal to spread between his needs in town and his estate. He'd withdrawn from his clubs, given up his horse, sold off his silver. Even with those economies, when wages came due in Cheshire next quarter day, he had no earthly idea how he would pay them. And the small comforts he had always been able to provide his mother and sister would not be forthcoming.

It was humiliating to admit how bad things actually were, even to himself.

Admitting it to Constance, who exuded money like her strange perfume, was a special form of torture.

"I can't pay them. Please see them reinstated at Westmead House."

Her face softened, in that way nice people had of pretending that something that was humiliating wasn't. "No need. I will continue to pay their wages out of my household budget. It's a gift."

His pride dripped to somewhere beneath the well-scrubbed floorboards.

"That's kind of you, but there is no need for it. I'm not home to visitors, and the season will be over soon in any case. And once I have the money, I'll sell this place and buy a proper house in Mayfair."

She rolled her eyes. "Ah, Mayfair, where the houses are as alike as the people. Why move there when this place has so much history and character? If you kept it and improved it, it could be a jewel. Besides, what's the appeal of doing what all the boring people do when one could stand out?"

Because standing out was not an advantage when one had things to hide. Dullness was a form of self-protection. But saying as much would only invite questions he did not wish to answer.

"Constance, I simply cannot accept your charity."

She continued to smile at him, as if by not acknowledging his obvious humiliation, she could erase it. "It's not charity; it's *strategy*. You must make a point to entertain here. When your creditors hear that your home is full of valuables, servants, and fine food, they will glean you have regained access to funds. After all, you are now living in anticipation of my very considerable dowry. And Lady Spence has expressed a desire to visit us at our future home. If it is not in order, she will know that something is amiss."

She gave him a winning smile.

His head pounded. "Would you please just do as I ask one *bloody* time?"

She narrowed her eyes at him. "I'm afraid that cursing will not change the fact that I am not known for doing things I disagree with. Besides, I can't bear to see *a friend* live in such disorder." She gestured at a number of trunks shoved up against a wall. "It's a wonder you're always so elegantly attired when you live amidst this squalor."

She lifted the lid of one trunk distastefully and grimaced at the mess of papers it held. "Have you unpacked nothing since you left the Rosecrofts?"

"Leave that. Please inform the servants they will not be required here."

"I'm afraid it won't be that easy," she said, busying herself by prying off the lid of another crate. "I've already begun issuing invitations and no one will believe I intend to live in a crumbling rathole. You must be seen to be preparing your home for my arrival."

She paused to peer inside the trunk. "Ah, look, here are your riding effects." She pulled out a whip. "I'll have these sent down to the stables. Or, rather …" Her voice trailed off.

From deeper in the box, she extracted an iron key on a long leather cord.

What was *that* doing with his riding gear?

"What's this?" she asked, fingering the intricately wrought key. "It's very pretty."

He quickly snatched it from her hands. "I've been looking for that," he said, putting it into his coat pocket.

She plunged her hands back inside the trunk.

"Constance, could you please—"

She yelped, producing a pistol, which she gingerly held up in the air with two fingers.

"Good holy God, Apthorp. You should not store firearms so haphazardly. What if some unsuspecting young lady accidentally shoots off her own hand?"

Fuck. These were most certainly not his riding effects.

He stepped forward and removed the weapon from her hand. "It's not real. But let that be a lesson to young ladies not to nose about in other people's private things. You've made your point. Go downstairs."

She shot him a challenging smile, evidently enjoying teasing him. "I wasn't nosing. I was *cleaning*. You should try it. Why do you have a fake pistol?"

He pointed at the door. "Out."

"Oh no, I don't think so. This is far too intriguing." With a teasing look at him, she plunged her hand back in the crate and produced a cord of rope, a blindfold, and a pair of leather cuffs with silver hooks.

"Oh dear," she said, suddenly less amused.

He could only agree with the sentiment.

"So that's how you've been paying your bills. You're a *highwayman.*"

Her game was growing tiresome, and he was increasingly concerned by what else might be lurking in that trunk. "I assure you I'm not a highwayman." He reached out for the cuffs. "Give me those and go downstairs. If you must paw through my things, you can do it in the kitchen."

She chuckled, in a flirtatious way that would be attractive were it not that he desperately, desperately wanted to prevent her from reaching back into the box. "So secretive, my lord. *Exactly* like an outlaw. Tell me, *why* would an elegant gentleman like yourself possess a box of blindfolds and fake pistols if he was not using them to rob coaches?"

She plunged her hand back into the box, rummaged deeper, and extracted a long, carved marble phallus. Seeing what she had retrieved, she froze, her jaw agape, holding it out in front of her. Her eyes roved over his face, and her mouth formed a perfect O as realization dawned in her eyes.

He lunged, snatched the object from her hands, and threw it in the box.

"Stop this! It is not appropriate for you to see these things."

She leaned back against the wall and looked up at him in wonder. "*Wednesdays*. These are for Wednesdays."

"Go downstairs, Constance," he muttered. "You shouldn't have seen this."

"It's all right," she said softly. "I see that you're ashamed. I shan't antagonize you further."

"Oh, I'm not *ashamed*," he snapped, for a man could handle only so much raillery from a girl too innocent to realize she was baldly slinging accoutrements of erotic play all about the room before he lost his patience. "Far from it. I'm *annoyed* that you keep *prying*."

She glanced at the crate, from which the priapic head of the large, extremely suggestive plaything she had discovered glinted in the light.

"But I'm confused. You told me I was wrong about your ... desires. But if you have all this, you must ..." She trailed off, not quite accusing him of lying to her, but looking as though she did not intend to let the matter drop.

He rubbed his temple. None of this was in any way proper to discuss, but if the choice was between being thought a sanctimonious liar ... he'd rather have out with the truth. He *wasn't* ashamed of what he did with these objects, and he was tired of the implication that he should be.

"I didn't lie to you, if that's what you're suggesting. These things are not for use *on me*, though I would not be embarrassed if they were. I use them to pleasure lovers who happen to enjoy such things." He shot her a mordant glance, to be sure she would not miss his meaning. "In *private*."

"You couldn't possibly mean ..." Her eyes widened. No doubt, she was recalling the entries in his diary in a new light. The correct light. "You *injure* people?"

Alas, no. *Not* the correct light.

"No, Constance, I don't *injure* people. I sometimes elicit a bit of pain, but only if they very specifically ask for it."

"But why would anyone ask for such a thing?"

"Must there always be a reason for what we want?"

She looked uncertain. "I just don't see what could be appealing about being whipped or tied up or—" She again glanced at the trunk.

"Care for a demonstration?" he shot back.

He regretted saying it even as it left his mouth. He needed to end this conversation.

But it *irked him* that a girl who did not know kissing from mauling felt entitled to mock his—or anyone's—tastes in bedsport.

"Why, yes," she said. She tossed her head back like a helpless maiden and brandished two limp wrists. "Ravish me, Lord Apthorp, I am *most* curious."

Her mockery irritated him.

"Don't ask for what you don't want," he said in a low voice.

She fluttered her lashes at him. "I think you want me to believe you are more intriguing than you really are, Lord Bore."

Without a second thought, he snapped up her wrists in his hands and whirled her around so that she faced the wall. She breathed in, startled.

"Do not call me Lord Bore," he whispered in her ear.

"Why not?" she whispered back. He felt her breath quicken at the light pressure of his fingers on her wrists.

He smoothed her pulse points with his thumb. "Because it hurts my feelings."

For a moment, they were both completely still. His hands on her wrists, her back to his chest, the room silent except for the slight intake of her breath.

"Are you nervous, Constance?" he asked.

"No, I'm patiently awaiting my demonstration."

He lifted her wrists above her head and pressed them against the wall. "Stay just like that."

"Why?"

"Because it pleases me."

He moved a hard-backed wooden chair from behind his desk and placed it in the center of the room, turning it so it faced the wall.

"Sit," he instructed her.

She scoffed at him. But, curiously, she did exactly as he asked.

He reached inside the crate and rummaged until he found what he was looking for: a long silk scarf. He came behind her and brought her wrists behind her back, tying them together with the scarf, and then securing them to the chair.

He stepped back to appraise his handiwork.

The black silk against the white of her wrists made for a lovely contrast.

"Well. I am your captive," she said. "What now?"

He smiled to himself. *Now, Lady Constance, I will let you wait while I stare at the sight of you like this and memorize it.*

A few seconds passed in silence.

"Apthorp?" Her voice was less confident now. "You wouldn't … leave me like this?"

He chuckled. "Not unless you wanted me to."

"Why would I want you to?"

At the rising uncertainty in her tone, he came to his senses. This was inexcusable.

"That's as much as I can say without imperiling your virtue."

"I'm not at all sure my virtue survived the sight of your ridiculous Priapus," she said, clearly annoyed at him for avoiding her question.

"It's called a dildo," he said, reaching for the ties at her wrists and beginning to unknot them. "If you must belittle it at least use its correct nomenclature."

She huffed. "I'm not sure I believe that this is something people like."

He was not sure he believed she *didn't* like it. He had heard the change in her breathing sure as anything. But in matters such as this, one took a lady at her word.

"You're welcome to draw your own conclusions. Hold still while I untie you."

"This is a rather unconvincing demonstration," she pronounced, like that settled it. "*Most* disappointing."

"I know," he said in a low voice, unwinding the silk. "Ideally, I'd keep you tied up for much, much longer."

She was quiet for a moment. Which pleased him.

"Oh?" she finally asked. "And then what?"

He released the silk and dropped it over her shoulder, letting it fall into her lap. He gripped the back of the chair, letting his fingertips brush against her hair. "I'd stand behind you and kiss a trail from the back of your neck to your shoulder."

"Why?"

"Because I *wish* to."

She turned to look at him, chewing on her lip.

Gently, he took her head in both hands and repositioned it to face the wall.

"No. I wouldn't let you watch."

"Why not?"

"Because without being able to see me, you would never quite know what to expect. And I think, Constance, that you might like that *very* much."

She let out a sigh so shaky that he felt it in his palms.

He smiled.

He'd thought so.

He'd always thought so.

He knew her type.

He *adored* her type.

He put his hands lightly on her shoulders. "You'd be impatient. And that would only inspire me to prolong the waiting."

The pale skin along her neck was pink and flushed. It pleased him immensely.

He took a single finger and rubbed it along the nape of her neck.

He leaned down so that his lips were flush with her ear. "You'd be in agony, Constance, by the time I let you up. In *agony*."

He smoothed his hand from her neck to her jaw, letting a thumb graze over her bottom lip. "You know what I mean, of course," he whispered. "You're aware of the condition."

She was so utterly still that he could feel her breath on his skin when she finally whispered:

"*Yes.*"

CHAPTER 11

*N*ever, in her most private moments, among her most wicked thoughts, had Constance ever wanted something like she wanted Apthorp to touch her.

It was undignified, and she didn't care.

The servants were noisily cleaning the hall outside, and she didn't care.

He was no doubt making her feel this way out of pure spite—enjoying her discomfort—and she *didn't care.*

Her whole body was one long ache. She wanted to take his thumb into her mouth.

She wanted him to move his hands down to her breasts.

Next time, just tell me what you want.

"Perhaps you might—" she whispered.

A sharp rap sounded at the door.

She froze. So did he.

He cleared his throat. "Yes?" he said pleasantly.

"The countess has arrived, my lord," Tremont said.

Curses. She had become so wrapped up in his demonstration she had forgotten to tell him the rest of her surprise.

"What countess?" he asked, stepping away from her.

There was a pause. "The Countess of Apthorp, my lord?"

He shucked the silk scarf off her lap, threw it into the nearest box, and stormed out into the hall. "My *mother?*"

"Yes, with Lady Margaret. Lady Constance said you were expecting them. Mrs. Haslet is laying out tea and refreshments in the parlor."

"Ah. Of course," Apthorp said smoothly. "The date slipped my mind. Thank you, Tremont. I shall be with them momentarily."

He closed the door and whirled around and he really *did* look like a highwayman, with that expression in his eyes. Not the kind who would tie you up for your enjoyment; the kind who would cheerfully kill you for your jewels.

"Explain yourself," he barked.

"I arranged for your family to visit. As a surprise. Aren't you pleased?"

She tried for an infectious smile. Perhaps if she evinced enough happiness for both of them, he would simply absorb it and stop glowering at her.

"*Pleased?* I'm the very furthest thing from pleased."

This was not the reaction she'd hoped for.

"But you heard Lady Spence. Inviting your mother here will show her we are seeking to follow her advice. Besides, I've arranged for a fabulous visit—balls and the theater and a trip to the *Ridotto al Fresco* and new gowns from Valeria Parc. At my expense, of course. Don't you want them to have a little merriment?"

He was staring at her like she had replaced his fake pistol with a real one and shot him in the stomach without warning.

"I don't know how I continue to let myself be shocked by you," he whispered. "What was I *thinking?*"

"Why are you so upset?"

He didn't answer. Instead, he threaded his hands through his hair like he wanted to rip it from his skull and marched out of the room without another word.

"Wait," she hissed, following him. "Can we just—"

But she stopped, because a small child came toddling down the hall and nearly collided with her shins.

"Why, good evening … ," she said to the little, golden-haired moppet, perplexed. "Who might you be?"

The little girl smiled up at her, flashing dimples and an angelic smile exactly like Apthorp's. He turned around at the sound of her voice and, taking in the sight of the child, whispered something that sounded very much like *fucking Christ*.

The little girl launched herself down the corridor, landing in a pile at his ankles.

He removed the tortured expression from his face with visible effort, like he had to peel it off, and bent down to scoop her up.

"Annie, my love," he said, placing a kiss on her cheek. The little girl wriggled delightedly in his arms.

"Anne?" A thin young woman came dashing up the stairs.

"Up here," Apthorp said, turning toward the voice.

Lady Margaret rushed in and her face broke into a smile. "Julian!"

Without setting the child down, he held an arm out to embrace his sister. "Margaret. It's been too long." He glanced at Constance. "Lady Constance, you recall my sister?"

"Of course I remember Lady Margaret. I'm so pleased you were able to visit."

Lady Margaret curtsied. "You were *so* kind to suggest it. We had no idea Julian had taken up residence in this old place." Her smile turned wry. "My brother can be such a sparing correspondent."

Constance knew that feeling well.

"And who is this charming creature?" Constance asked, gesturing to the child, who was now playing with Apthorp's hair, obviously thrilled to be near him. Her joy reminded Constance of herself on the rare occasions her brother had allowed her to visit him as a little girl.

"This is Miss Anne Haywood," he said, handing the girl to his sister. "My ward."

Constance glanced up at him. "I was not aware you had a child in your care," she said lightly.

"Miss Haywood is the daughter of our late cousin," Lady Margaret explained quickly. "She lost her parents to illness and Julian offered to serve as her guardian. Mama and I look after her."

Margaret's face had a strained, apologetic kind of look. The kind of expression one might wear were one in the position of having to pass off one's brother's child to his betrothed.

"How kind," she said to Margaret. But how *scandalous* of Apthorp, who was always so long-winded on the subject of masculine honor.

Was this why he had not wanted his family to visit? Because she'd find out he had a by-blow? Was there no end to the scandalous things that he'd managed to keep hidden?

The countess came into the hallway, following the commotion. "Oh, my dear child," she said, setting her eyes upon Constance. "Julian, how beautiful she is."

She folded Constance into a hug. Her bones felt frail beneath Constance's grip. Both the countess and her daughter were painfully thin, and she could not help but notice that the lace of their gowns was dingy from frequent laundering, and looked mended many times.

She had known Apthorp's coffers were not full, but this was far worse than she'd expected.

"I hope your journey was not too uncomfortable?" she asked the countess, trying not to stare at the pilling edges of her woven shawl.

"No, dear, the carriage you sent was positively decadent." The countess beamed at her. "My son is blessed to have a woman as considerate as yourself as his future countess. How blessed we *all* are to welcome you into our family."

"I'm so happy to be part of it," she said, swallowing around an uncomfortable pang of guilt at her dishonesty. "I hope I will be a good—"

From behind his mother's shoulder, Apthorp's eyes shot daggers at her.

"A good friend to you," she finished wanly.

"Let's become better acquainted," Lady Apthorp said, taking her hand and squeezing it. "I can't wait to know everything about the woman who has so utterly charmed my son."

APTHORP NOTICED A SMALL SMILE PLAYING ON HIS SISTER'S LIPS THE next day as they sat in the parlor of his town house drinking tea with Constance.

He had watched her laugh more in the last five hours than he could remember her laughing in the entirety of the last five years.

It made him want to go outside and bury himself in the garden, or lie in the road and let himself be trampled by horses.

The whole painstaking day had left him unutterably depressed.

Constance had prepared for his family like they were royal princesses. New feather mattresses and soft quilts had been awaiting in their bedchambers, along with French *eau de toilette*, books to amuse them, and new stationery embossed with their initials. His larder had been filled with fruits and cakes and delicacies and the fine teas his mother liked. A dressmaker had arrived with new gowns and gloves and hats. A nurse had followed, borrowed from the Westmeads to look after Anne. By the time Constance came to drive his family to the church service at Lady Spence's congregation, his mother and sister were so happy they were radiant. And the day had only improved in her company. Following the service, Constance had arranged a lavish family lunch at Westmead House, attended by a group of friends hand-picked to welcome his mother and sister back to London. She'd set out a slew of desirable invitations for them to choose from over the coming weeks. She'd showered them with compliments and hugs.

They had reacted the way people typically did when confronted with Lady Constance Stonewell's powers of seduction: they'd fallen instantly, rapturously in love with her.

As they sat in his freshly redecorated parlor drinking her exquisite tea and laughing at her musical recounting of the season's most delicious gossip, he could see them imagining her as the center of their family. He could see them picturing a more permanent return to town and the busy, privileged life they'd once enjoyed. He could see them delighting in the effect Constance's charm and energy would have on life at home in Cheshire—Christmas musicales and quarter day feasts and pageants for the tenants.

She was like the miracle they had not dared be optimistic enough to hope for. And he *knew* what hoping for it felt like. Just as he knew how it felt to give it up.

She would be the next thing they would lose in a long string of wrenching disappointments he had caused them.

Because in ten days' time she would break off their engagement and disappear into the night.

And he wouldn't try to stop her.

That misty idea he'd been entertaining—confessing his true feelings, asking for her hand, convincing her to stay—had been the product of foolish, sentimental self-delusion. There was simply no way around the truth: he could not marry a woman he could not trust.

He wanted to pound his fists against the wall with irritation for wasting a week letting himself hope. Instead, he rose abruptly. He'd allowed this to go on for far too long.

"Tremont?" he called into the hallway. His valet appeared.

"Summon Lady Constance's carriage." The man nodded and disappeared.

The ladies looked up at him in surprise. "What's the matter, dear?" his mother asked.

"The weather is turning nasty. Lady Constance should return home before the storm sets in."

"Oh, yes indeed," Constance said, smiling to cover up his rudeness. "I was so enjoying our chat I hadn't noticed the change in the air."

"I'll see you out," he said. "I need a word before you leave."

USUALLY IT WAS GRATIFYING TO BE PROVED RIGHT ABOUT something others had insisted you were wrong about. Constance was well versed in the satisfaction that came with defying the prevailing view and winning anyway. She had never met a rule she hadn't enjoyed breaking, and considered shattered precepts the glitter that lit the pathways to personal contentment.

But today she was *not* content, and not because she had been wrong in her defiance.

Inviting the countess and Lady Margaret to London was an *obvious* success. They were delighted to be here. Their presence conferred an immediate wholesomeness upon Lord Apthorp that made the rumors about him seem distant and preposterous. And most critically, Lady Spence had been so pleased that Apthorp had taken her advice, she had agreed to bring Lord Spence to the Strand to dine with them the following week.

And yet, rather than apologize to her for his foul mood the night before, or at the very least allow that her judgment had been wise, Apthorp was regarding her like she was an abscess that had lamed his horse. She had consequently spent the day dizzying herself performing such raptures of charm and happiness that no one might notice his ill temper, and now she was exhausted.

"That was rude," she whispered as she followed him into the hall into which he had so suddenly dismissed her. "I hope you intend to apologize."

"*Me* apologize," he repeated. He removed her cloak from a peg on the wall and pointedly handed it to her. "I was thinking that the opposite was in order."

"You wish for me to apologize for possessing the audacity to plan a day of pleasure for your mother and sister while also securing an audience with Lord Spence? Very well. I *am* sorry. I can't imagine what came over me, wasting my efforts on an ungrateful *child* like yourself."

He took a deep breath. Wind rattled through the stained-glass windows of the ancient door, making his dark expression seem positively menacing. Outside a curious April storm was brewing, the kind that brought hailstones the size of pebbles and icy flecks of rain.

"There is to be no more of this," he said evenly. "No more outings. No more church. No more teas. You've used my family for your purposes like props. Now you are to leave them bloody well alone."

"Don't be ridiculous. There are ten more days before the vote, and we'll need to be seen everywhere—"

"*Not* with my family."

She lowered her voice, not wanting them to overhear her through the door. "Why are you so determined to keep them away? Can't you see the effect it's having? They're gaunt and gray as carrier pigeons. You'd think a trip to church was the most amusement they've had in years."

He clenched his teeth. "Because in a fortnight we are going to call off this engagement. And it will be the latest thing in eight years of misery to *devastate* them. I *told you* that. And you gave me your *worthless* word."

Her pulse began to beat intently in her throat. It was true that he had said these things, but she had dismissed them, inferring the real reason he would not permit the visit was that he could not afford the expense of hosting his family in a comfortable manner. Making the trip a gift had seemed like a gracious solution.

"I see," she said softly. "I'm sorry. Truly. I misunderstood. I thought you were concerned about your finances."

His face went even darker. She closed her eyes, remembering belatedly that acknowledging her awareness of his poverty only ever made things worse.

"I *am* sorry that I ignored your wishes," she said quickly. "But now that they are here, you must at least admit that their presence is helpful to our cause. And their future, after all, depends on our success."

"I never stop considering their future, Constance," he hissed. "I have not spent a day of my life in which it did not weigh on my mind since I was seventeen years of age. Do not lecture me on what they need. You know nothing of it. This will *hurt* them. Losing *you* will hurt them. And then they will return to Cheshire with nothing but their loneliness and disappointment and the stench of a fresh scandal coming off their family name. Can you understand how that might feel?"

She huddled back into the corner of the vestibule, realizing she had made a terrible mistake. After their moment in her cousin's parlor with the roses, she had somehow allowed herself to think of Apthorp not as a man she had wronged, but as her ally. A man whose fortunes were entwined with her own.

He wasn't.

What he felt for her was a loathing so thick it made him hoarse.

Suddenly, she hated him. "Can I understand what it feels like to be scandalous and unwanted and *alone?*" she repeated. "Actually, I know quite well what it is like to live in exile because one's relatives believe it is in one's best interest. It's so lonesome that I would do nearly anything to avoid experiencing it again. And yet I'm welcoming that very thing for *you* and still you reproach me."

"Constance—" he said quietly, his eyes hooded, but she did not care to hear his opinion on this matter. She'd heard quite enough of his opinions.

"You have always believed I am an overindulged, frivolous creature who could never fathom pain or sadness. You persist in believing this even as *I give up everything I care about to save your reputation.*"

She was so upset her voice shook, and she hated it.

"Malign me all you like but don't forget our success has not come about by accident, Julian. I spend my nights plotting your social engagements and writing letters to hacks eliciting support for your bill. I have planned your political dinners, your engagement ball, your bloody *wedding.* I'm exhausted, because I can't sleep for dreaming about you and—"

He put two hands on her shoulders. "Constance."

"Do not touch me," she rasped. She wrenched around his body to the heavy doors and stepped out into the storm. Her coachman, seeing her, leapt out into the hailstorm to retrieve her.

"Wait," Julian called raggedly, following her onto the street.

But she had had enough of repeating the same story over and over, expecting a different ending.

Their story would end like this. Without a backward glance.

CHAPTER 12

I *want you to touch me.*

The hands that were always just out of reach of the place she so fervently wanted them to go swept over her. Soft and masculine and knowing, brushing down over her stomach to her hip bone, teasing her skin. She lifted herself toward him, into the heat that was never as close as she wanted it.

I want you to touch me.

Softly, softly, his hands slid lower. *Yes. Please. There.*

Thump.

Someone at the door. The hands retreated. *No, don't go, let them knock. Come back.*

Constance opened her eyes, as usual, to darkness and the feeling of wanting.

Thump.

She groaned. The insistent knocking was coming not from her door but from her window, like a branch had fallen from the tree in last night's storm and decided to amuse itself by beating her awake from a dream that had seemed so, so close to finally delivering some blessed relief.

Which was appropriate, given the whole world seemed to be conspiring to make her as wretched as a cat in a river.

Thump.

She dragged herself out of bed and stomped to the window, prepared to give the insolent branch a beating of her own. She yanked open the curtains to find that the window was being assaulted not by a tree but by a man.

An unusually handsome one, who was rain-soaked and bedraggled, as though he had tromped halfway across the city in the drizzle at an hour that barely qualified as dawn to creep into the Rosecrofts' garden and thrash at her shutters while she dreamt about him.

"Apthorp?" she hissed. "What are you doing here?"

"I have a key to the mews."

"Yes, but *why* are you attempting to break into my room in the middle of the night?"

He looked at her from below his lashes. "I need to apologize. For what I said to you."

Her heart constricted more than she liked at the sadness in his eyes, so she crossed her arms and took an insolent tone. "I prefer my apologies to occur *after* sunrise."

"I couldn't wait. I've been up all night, turning it around in my head. May I please come in?"

"*No.* If you are caught in my rooms, you will be forced to marry me at once, which will make ending our engagement impossible."

"That's why I'm here. I don't want to end it. I want to marry you."

He said this with all the enthusiasm with which he might announce he wished to be buried at sea when he died young of plague.

"Oh, dear God," she muttered. She turned, walked directly back to her bed, threw herself upon it, and drew the bed-curtains around her for good measure.

She heard him clambering through the window and laughed bitterly to herself, for making hysterical scenes before dawn was really more in line with her sensibilities than his. Her love for theater must be rubbing off on him.

"Constance?" he said in a low, ragged voice. "Would you please come out? I've been up half the night thinking this over, and I can't do this anymore."

He pulled the bed-curtains open and sank to his knees. He took her hands in his, and looked into her eyes with an impossibly tragic expression. "Please marry me."

To think that mere minutes before, she had imagined those same hands doing all sorts of unspeakable things to her. She would, in fact, prefer that they do unspeakable things to her than clutch at her while he performed a guilt-induced offer of marriage.

"Why are you asking me this now?"

"Because of what you said. What you're giving up. What my family will suffer. I'm asking far too much of all of you when there's a simpler solution."

"There is nothing simple about marriage."

He leaned forward. "Constance," he said, looking at her pitifully. "If we marry, you won't have to *leave*. You won't have to be alone."

Her heart shriveled like a leech in salt. *Of course* that was why he was here.

In her moment of frustration she'd been weak. She should *never* have spoken of her loneliness to him. For now not only would he look at her like she was pathetic, as he was currently doing, but he would feel like a villain for letting her sacrifice her happiness for his. Given his need to regard himself as the most exemplary man who'd ever lived, he could not stand to think himself a villain. He would prefer to consign them both to a lifetime of misery and resentment.

She had accidentally built a trap. She had to set him free, lest he spend the rest of their lives torturing them both.

"Don't be ridiculous, Apthorp," she said in her coldest voice. "I would never marry if it were not for love. I don't love you. And God *knows* you don't love me."

His face performed a series of somersaults, as though this assertion was somehow surprising or debatable.

"But, Constance," he said quietly. "What if I *did*?"

HE HAD NEVER INTENDED TO SAY THESE WORDS TO HER, BUT HE WAS wet and tired and sad and now he couldn't seem to stop them. "Constance, what if I told you that I've loved you all along? For years."

It felt so good to finally say it, to admit it, after so long of hoarding it away that he couldn't help but smile. He couldn't stifle a small laugh. He felt such a pang of lightness and pleasure in *finally* saying the words aloud—in admitting, *finally*, the wrongheaded thing he wanted, even though it made no sense—that he half expected the sun to rise and the rain to clear and the room to fill with birdsong and pots of gold and unicorns and a fairy who might play a lute in the corner as they danced.

Instead, Constance's eyes went a shade of icy blue akin to a winter's frost.

"How dare you say such a thing to me?"

The birds and unicorns disappeared as abruptly as they'd descended. Of course she would not respond romantically to such a declaration. He'd gone so far out of his way to hide the truth that it could not seem anything but insincere to her.

He reached out and smoothed her pretty hair, all mussed from sleep. "I know it may seem unlikely, but it's true."

She laughed in a glacial way that matched the coldness in her eyes and tossed her head out of the reach of his outstretched fingers. "I may be young and foolish, Julian, but I know that love is not something you declare at someone when it happens to suit your motivations. Nor does it manifest overnight in a fit of guilt. In the future I'd suggest you allow me to be the cynical, conniving one between us; I'm much better at it."

The cold in her voice began to seep into his bones. "I'm not saying this to assuage my guilt," he said quietly. "I'm saying this because it's true."

"It could not possibly be true, because love is not a declaration. It is a system of behavior. If the treatment I have enjoyed from you over the last five years amounts to your way of showing love, I'd do anything to avoid such adoration for the rest of my life."

He flinched, because the pain in her voice was unmistakably real. If he'd learned one lesson in the last two weeks, it was that his efforts to protect his heart had bruised hers.

"Oh, don't look so distraught," she said coldly. "I know I made you feel terrible earlier, but I was only manipulating you to win an argument. The truth is I've let a gorgeous villa on the sea near Santa Margherita, and I'm going to write plays and take handsome lovers and eat myself plump on *pistou*. You needn't worry I shall die of unhappiness deprived of the chance to expire from boredom sewing doilies and making charity boxes in some freezing Tudor hovel with your sister."

He closed his eyes. "You don't need to be so contemptuous of my life."

"And you don't need to save mine," she said firmly.

He stared at her, and she was so absolutely certain of herself that he could only admire her even as the truth crushed down on him: he had lost her.

Not a month ago, when he'd asked about proposal gifts.

Not weeks ago, when he'd learned that she'd exposed him.

He'd lost her years and years and years ago.

And he was not going to get her back.

She sat up in bed, staring at him with an appraising glint in her eye. "But you're right. We can't go on like this."

"Like what?" he asked, utterly defeated.

She waved her hand between them. "All this fawning over each other in public and then quarreling in private and then having to pretend to be in love ten minutes later. It's just too difficult. It's confusing us both, and if we slip, this entire ordeal will be for nothing. We must do a better job. I propose a truce."

"What kind of truce?"

She met his eye and smiled. "For the rest of our time together, let's pretend to be in love."

He groaned. "Isn't that what we have been doing?"

"I don't mean just in public. In private too."

She smiled angelically. "I will not bedevil you nor meddle in your affairs. You will not accuse me of treachery nor lecture me on my behavior. For nine days we will simply help one another, and be infatuated and sweet. And then, when it's over, we need never set eyes on each other again. Do you agree?"

He looked at her sadly. "Yes, Constance. For nine days, we will simply be in love."

And what he meant, he knew, is that they never would be.

She took his hands in both of hers, and looked up at him with an expression so guileless he'd be powerless to deny her anything.

"Julian, my dear friend, I am going to insist that you prove it."

She reached out with both arms and pulled him into her bed.

CHAPTER 13

*I*n his surprise he collapsed down on her rather inelegantly, and she liked the way his weight crushed her, and his rain-dampened clothes brushed her skin, and the scent of his woody hair oil mingled with the smell of her freshly laundered sheets.

Despite her anger, the remnants of her dream had not yet faded, and his body beside hers brought back that urgent feeling that if he would only touch her, she would feel so much better.

She scrambled for his hands and put them on her breasts over her nightdress.

"Prove it," she whispered again, reaching up and finding his lips with hers and nibbling him the way she knew he liked. The way she could not stop thinking about ever since the wig closet.

His hands moved down to cup her back, and his body turned in toward hers, and she kissed him more deeply, shocked and pleased that he was doing exactly what she wanted.

But when she dared to put her tongue against his, he suddenly pulled away.

"What are we doing?" he gasped.

"Pretending to be lovers. Come back."

"No, Constance."

"Why not?"

He was scrambling for distance. "Because it isn't right. This isn't *real*. You just explained in very vivid detail why you do not wish to make it real."

"That's the *point*, Julian. We're pretending."

"This is not pretend. I should leave."

Next time, just tell me what you want.

She knew what she wanted. And this might be her only chance to get it.

She wished she had her courtesan costumes from Valeria, because he was looking at her like she was a child.

"Julian, I can't stop thinking about you. About that day, in your house, with the ties. I can't stop imagining—"

"I should *never* have done that."

"I wish you had done *more*. Don't play innocent with me. I've read your journals and seen what's in your trunks. I know that you can teach me and I *want to know*. When I leave, I want to be a woman of the world, not some frightened virgin who has to be lectured on how to kiss. If you care about me at all, give me this."

He closed his eyes and was silent.

"Someone will teach you, eventually," he finally said. "Someone you *like*."

"I don't want someone I like—I want *you*. I *dream* about you. You kissing me and … other things. I awaken and I feel uncomfortably *distressed*. In my body."

He swallowed.

"What is it exactly that you want?"

"I want you to make love to me."

H<small>E HELD HIMSELF VERY STILL, NOT TRUSTING HIMSELF TO RESPOND</small> until he controlled his racing heart. And other body parts that were behaving in a way that was not in keeping with his private code of conduct. Which did not extend itself to corrupting gently bred virgins, no matter how strongly they claimed to desire corruption.

Were they to be married, he would toss her over his shoulder and corrupt her to her heart's content. Were they on Charlotte Street, he would give her whatever she desired without a second thought.

But they were in Mayfair, where he despised the kind of men who did what she was asking. Joining their ranks would make him the worst kind of hypocrite.

"Julian," she whispered. "Please. If this *distress* persists, I shall go mad. And since you caused it, you must make it stop. If you want to do one kindness for me, do this."

She gestured at herself. Her lips were swollen from his kisses, pink from abrading against his unshaven skin. Her nipples were hard beneath the thin fabric of her girlish nightdress. Her arms and chest were flushed.

She was, indeed, the picture of *distress*.

Exactly the kind of distress he was, quite literally, an expert at relieving.

Would it be so wrong to offer her a kind of … lesson? Like he might teach her how to string a bow if she'd expressed interest in learning archery?

"I'm sorry, but I can't do what you ask," he said slowly.

Her lovely brazen confidence seemed to deflate all at once.

She buried her head beneath a pillow. "Of course," she muttered. "I don't know why I ever expect anything from you beyond dejection. I'm sorry I asked. I'm sure it's perverse of me to even want it."

Fuck.

He'd already bruised her so many times. The last thing he wanted was to embarrass her for making such a vulnerable, intimate admission. For years it had been a kind of calling to make his lovers feel safe expressing their desires, no matter how unusual. He would not fail on this count with the woman he treasured above any of them.

For someone who was so candid on other matters, Constance rarely spoke about her feelings. He realized he knew little of her private dreams, her secret heart.

He'd never asked.

Damn him, *he'd never asked.*

Perhaps if he had, he would not have ruined things before they'd ever started.

He put his hand gently on hers, until she peered out at him from beneath the pillow's edge.

"Constance, there is *nothing* about you that is perverse. But I can't … touch you. And not because I don't want to, or because it's wrong for you to wish for it, but because it isn't right for me to take such liberties if there is to be no future between us."

She groaned.

"But I could offer you some guidance in soothing the … *distress* … if you would like."

She played with the corner of a lacy sham. "Oh?"

He was speaking with exactly the same tortured vagueness she had used, and he rolled his eyes at himself. He was a grown man with a history of having far more frank and detailed conversations on such matters with women he'd known for as many minutes as he had fingers. "What I mean is, if you don't know how, I can help to teach you how to come."

Constance blinked. "To *come?*"

"To experience a relief from distress … a sort of climax of pleasure. You don't need a lover for that. You can do it yourself, whenever you like."

She widened her eyes at him in a way that suggested she had not discovered this on her own.

"To come," she said. "What a strange expression."

"The French call it *la petite mort*. You can call it whatever you like. The important thing is not what you call it, but how it feels."

"And how does it feel?"

He could not even begin to answer that question.

"There is really only one way to find out."

WHAT HAD SHE JUST CONVINCED HIM TO DO?

Surely, judging by the way Apthorp's voice had grown low and gravelly, he thought that whatever it was would land him very thoroughly in hell.

Which did nothing to change the fact that she very much wanted whatever this death was, particularly now that Apthorp was perched beside her in her bed. One could not be held responsible for the effect that such a sight engendered in one's most private places. The sticky heat between her legs that had plagued her whenever she spent too much time recalling their encounter in the powdering room was more insistent than ever, and the nagging pulse of it went straight to her brain.

If there was a cure for this restlessness, by God or by Beelzebub, she must have it. Her mortal soul was no doubt intended for the inferno anyway, if Mrs. Mountebank had anything to say about it.

"What do I do?" she asked.

Apthorp—no. *Julian,* for she could not think of him as stiff Lord Apthorp when he looked at her that way, his eyes banked fire, the heat of his body making her bedsheets so warm her skin was prickly to the touch—swallowed a breathy noise. Half laugh, half sigh. Like a man who longed for something that he didn't want to want.

"Lean back on your pillows," he said huskily. "Try to relax."

She could not imagine being *relaxed* with *Julian* in her bed.

Nevertheless she arranged herself as he instructed. But now that she had asked for this, she felt very, very shy.

"I am not relaxed. Quite the opposite. I'm terribly nervous."

He nodded. "That's all right. It can be hard to let go in the presence of another person. Try closing your eyes."

"Perhaps if you kissed me, I would be less nervous. Is that not how this works?"

"I told you. *I* won't touch you. But that doesn't mean that you can't touch yourself."

"Being rejected does not induce in one the desire to be witnessed touching oneself by the very person who finds one undesirable," she said, taking a prim tone because if she said it any differently, she might burst into tears. Tortured elocutions were the only comfort she had left.

He closed his eyes. When he opened them, he was smiling at her.

"Is that what you think I am doing? Rejecting you? My God, Constance. I … Look at me."

She did so, reluctantly. His eyes were dark, the way they had been when he kissed her.

"Not there," he whispered.

He looked down to his lap, and dragged a hand across his breeches, which strained with the evidence of male excitement.

"Do you see how hard I am?" he asked in a low voice. "I would *love* to do what you ask. But I can't. So instead, know how badly I want to, and close your eyes."

She did. And knowing that she was not alone in this bloody state of wanting made the wanting so much worse. She felt frantic with it. Like she'd do anything to make it go away.

"Good," he murmured. "Now focus on how your body feels. Where you might want to be touched."

Breasts. I want your hands on them again.

"I can't say," she whispered. "I feel so bashful."

"You don't have to *say* anything, sweet girl. Just touch yourself. Pretend I'm not here."

She shook her head. This was absurd. He was beside her like the golden dawn itself with his tousled damp hair and glinting amber eyes, swollen in his most intimate places because he *wanted* her, and what *she* wanted was for him to take her in his arms and make her feel better. Not to observe her performing some scientific inquiry into lust.

She opened one eye and peeked out at him. "I can't. It's too odd. It won't work."

He reached for his cravat and began to unwind it from his neck.

"Perhaps it would help if you couldn't see me," he said softly. "Lift up your head, and I'll make it a little easier."

She obeyed, if only because it was an excuse to let him touch her.

Gently, he lowered the linen around her eyes and wrapped it snugly, tying it behind her head.

It smelled like him. Oh God, it *smelled* like him.

A bit of light flooded through the soft cloth, but she could not make out any shapes. It was not like he wasn't there, but it at least saved her from having to look at him in her state of infernal bloody *wanting*.

"Is that better?"

"Maybe," she whispered.

She felt him sit down at the end of the mattress, near her feet.

"I can't tell you how to find pleasure. Every woman is different. But I'll tell you what I'd do if we were lovers. And if you'd like to try yourself, you may. And we can stop at any time, and forget this ever happened."

Sneakily, very sneakily, she shifted so that her heel touched against his hip. The contact with him sent a jolt up through her leg.

"Tell me what you would do," she whispered, because she

suspected whatever he would do, she would like. She brushed her arch against his thigh, as if by accident, and tried not to exhale at the pleasure of touching him. God, how she wanted to touch him.

"Hmm," he said softly. His tone was not at all playful. "First I think I would touch your breasts."

Could he read her mind?

She closed her eyes beneath his cravat and inhaled his cedary smell, and, summoning every last filament of courage in her body, actually did it. She pretended it was his hands that grazed her as she reached up over her breasts and pulled the fabric taut. "Like this?" she asked him.

"Yes," he said, except it sounded more like *Mmm.* "Just like that. And then I might squeeze your nipples through your nightdress, so I could just make out the pink."

Her nipples grew firmer beneath the linen, and when she rubbed them through the cloth, it felt so tight and good that for a moment she forgot that he was watching.

She heard a heavy sigh, and felt him shift, making the slightest, slightest contact with her toe. *Almost* like he wanted to touch her too.

"Oh yes, just like that," he said raggedly. "Rub them between your fingers."

She did, and the friction of the smooth linen gown over her puckered flesh felt achy and lovely and made feelings in her stomach spark. Her breath quickened. Normally she would be horrified that he might notice and try to hide it, but with the fabric draped over her eyes, she felt strangely free. Almost like she *wanted* him to notice. She bit her tongue and flexed her leg, so that her heel pressed against the muscle of his thigh.

He didn't move away.

"Yes," he said in a voice that was not quite a sigh. And when she heard the hitch in his breathing, and knew he liked it too, a flood of *distress* shot down to her belly.

"Does that feel good?" he inquired.

"Yes," she admitted. An understatement. "But I have yet to experience the death."

He chuckled. "Sweetheart, sadly you are nowhere near the death. But don't worry. We'll see if we can kill you yet."

"How?" she whispered.

"Well, what I would do is get that gown off you entirely, because I would be dying to run my hands over your skin."

She smiled at this admission that he liked her skin. And then she imagined him actually looking at it—here, right now, in this bed—and got very, very hot. "Yes," she agreed, "that sounds like just the thing."

She could not imagine letting him see her nude under normal circumstances. But at this moment it seemed rather necessary and urgent that she no longer be clothed.

She shimmied her nightdress up over her thighs and pulled it over her head, careful not to let her impatience disturb the ties of the cravat. She had no desire to see him watching her. She just wanted to imagine it. She leaned back against her pillows and ran her hands along her naked breasts and belly and heard him breathing as he watched her.

"Oh, you're a beautiful creature, Constance."

"No, I'm not," she objected. But it was disingenuous, because in this moment she did feel beautiful. Especially when he said:

"Show me where else you want to be touched. Pretend you're guiding my hands wherever you want them."

Lower.

She traced her hands over her belly, which provoked a sharp reaction between her legs—a pang. *Did she dare follow it? In front of him?*

Yes. Now was not the time for hesitation. She brought her fingers down to trace the path of the *distress*. But there she lost the thread, for it was somewhere deep inside her, and every time she'd ventured to locate the source of it alone, she'd only left herself sweaty and frustrated and irritable, unable to produce the relief that she desired.

Her fingers paused at the hair between her legs.

"Yes, that's exactly where I'd want to touch you," Julian whispered.

Tentatively she ran her fingers lower, but stopped at the shock of what was happening there.

"You're so wet," he murmured, and the tone was not confusion or disgust but something more like ... hunger.

"That's good?"

He groaned. "Very good."

She ran her fingers over her flesh, exploring, though feeling rather aware that he was watching her and she had no idea what to do next.

"What now?" she asked.

"I'd spread your thighs a little wider and stroke you right there, at that lovely swollen bit, below your middle finger."

She moved her fingers slightly. *Oh.*

"I might stop there and linger for a while. Stroke you. Just to see what makes you feel the best."

It all felt good. It felt *acutely* good. It made her jam her heel even deeper into his thigh, not even bothering to pretend it was an accident. But he didn't move away. Only kept talking in that low, intimate voice.

"But I would also want to make sure you felt good all over, so I might explore a bit to see what other places make you shiver. Deeper, between your legs, where you are very, very wet. Just slowly. Just to make sure we're being very thorough."

She did as he suggested, and more of her seemed to awaken in response. But the "lovely bit," as he had called it, seemed to cry out for more focused attention. She kept finding her way back to it.

She heard herself make a little noise and froze, worried he would laugh at her.

"Oh, sweetheart," he breathed. "Yes, just like that. Let me hear how good it feels. Stroke yourself there. A bit faster if you like, in little circles, until you just can't stop and go right over the edge."

She rubbed her fingers rhythmically. "Julian, the distress is getting *worse*," she gasped, curling her toes into his leg.

"I know, sweetheart." She heard a smile in his voice. "It gets worse before it gets better. But it's worth it, I promise."

His low, rumbling voice made her feel woozy and she pressed her fingers to her *fleur* a bit harder, and was rewarded with a shock of pleasure. She gasped.

"I might slip a few fingers inside you, Constance, now that you are close. Feel how hot and slick and tight you are."

His voice was heavy, thick, and he had moved closer, so his thigh was flush against the bottom of her foot. Close enough that she could feel the heat from his body radiating through his clothes into her instep.

"I'd want to take care of you so you feel full and needy, like you have every possible sensation that you want. All at once."

She *did*. Oh God she *did*.

"I'd do it just like that until you were in agony. Until I was in agony with you."

A little cry escaped from her involuntarily, shocking her. In response, she heard him emit a low, painful-sounding groan.

"Oh, sweetheart, I would be so happy to hear how good it feels. It makes me so hard to think about it. To watch you."

Hard. She remembered how it had felt when his manhood had pressed against her in the butler's pantry, and that memory made her feel empty in a way that was unbearable.

"I want to feel it. *You*," she said. "Please, it's not enough."

"I can't, Constance. I want to, but I can't."

She continued to touch herself, trying to get past the edge of intensity that promised something better, but she couldn't.

"It's not *enough*," she said again. It was never enough. She had tried so many times to bring whatever it was she wanted, and this was better, certainly, but still left her agitated, and she knew she would be distressed *forever*. She closed her legs, wanting almost to cry in pure frustration.

Suddenly the mattress shifted and her foot lost the contact with his thigh. She heard him walk across the room and fumble through her things.

"Oh God, don't leave me like this."

The mattress shifted once again, and she felt him back beside her. "I have an idea. Give me your hand."

She did so, and he placed something firm and round in her palm.

It was … an apple. An apple from the basket she kept on her desk.

"What … Julian … Your solution to my misery is to offer me a piece of fruit?"

His voice was amused. "Constance, I am going to tell you a secret. On *Wednesdays*, when a lady visits the club wishing for satisfaction in a way that will not compromise her virginity … certain items can be used to help her find her pleasure. Like the one you found in my trunk. I can bring you a more permanent solution, but in the meantime you might find this feels a bit like the hardness of a man."

She was, quite literally, speechless. She remembered the pang of arousal she had felt upon pulling the obscene marble carving from his chest and realizing what it was—the frank rudeness of it was unlike anything she'd ever seen—but this was not a phallus. It was a food.

"What would you have me do with it?"

His voice was low, and seductive, and not at all shy. "Put it between your legs and pretend what you're feeling is my cock."

His cock.

The sultry, frank way he said it made her want to try, even though what he suggested struck her as absurd.

"Like this?" She took the apple and placed it at the juncture of her thighs.

It felt … round. And hard. And smooth. And not unpleasant.

"Lower, so it rocks against your quim."

She slid the apple between her legs. At first the strangeness overwhelmed the pleasure. But as her warmth and wetness met the fruit, suddenly it felt … rather lovely. Full. It hit her in all the right places at once.

"Oh my," she whispered.

"Oh, sweet girl, yes," he said. "Make it nice and slick and wet, like it's my cock, straining to be inside you."

She arched back and extended her foot until she felt it, again, the hardness of his cock beneath her toes. She grazed it as she stroked her flesh and moved against the fullness of the apple, pretending it was him.

Something broke apart inside her.

She could feel it. She could feel the death rising up, taking hold of her.

She ground her heel into his thigh and gave herself over to the rhythm of her hips as her fingers performed a miracle she wished she had known about before.

She cried his name out as it took her.

And when she came back to herself, she decided he was wrong.

This feeling was not a *death*.

It was more like waking up.

APTHORP WATCHED HER SHUDDER. HE WATCHED HER SLOWLY, sweetly recover, her blond hair spread beneath her like the moonlight, her face half-hidden by his neckcloth, pale skin flushed, her body limpid, the glistening red apple tossed aside in her damp and twisted sheets.

He watched her smile. The way the corners of that lovely,

lovely mouth twisted up in satisfaction squeezed his chest. He would not forget that smile for the rest of his natural life.

"Thank you," she whispered.

He breathed out through his mouth. "The pleasure was all mine."

"No." She grinned, reaching up and unwrapping his cravat from around her eyes. She met his gaze shyly and wiggled her foot —her erotic fucking foot, the memory of whose roamings he would carry to his grave—against his straining cock. "It wasn't."

God, he wanted her in that moment. All flushed and saucy, the knowledge of a newfound private power shining from her eyes.

She rolled over on her side and looked up at him brazenly. "But it could be."

Her eyes traveled from his face down to his lap, where his erection was making its interest known quite obnoxiously beneath her toes.

She stared at the bulge it made with open interest.

"Is it the same for you?"

"Not quite."

Her foot ventured nearer and it took everything he had not to press her toes on top of him just for sheer relief.

Damn him, he had let this go on too long. It had been one thing when they could both pretend she touched him accidentally, lost in the throes of passion. This was beyond his private contract with himself.

He shifted away.

"You don't have to move," she said thickly. "I'd be curious to learn. If you wanted to provide a demonstration."

To want something so badly was pure torture.

It would be so easy to undo his falls and bring himself off here while she watched, narrating the experience of his pleasure. Telling her how badly he wanted her, how hard she made him. How the memory of binding her hands had left him … *distressed* … many times. How he was jealous of a piece of fucking *fruit*.

She must have noticed his erection straining at the thought, for she scooted forward and placed her hand beside it, on his thigh.

"Oh my," she said. "May I touch it?"

The entire Renaissance had not produced a more appealing vision in all its attempts to capture heaven.

Please, I beg you.

He was so tempted. And not just bodily.

It was hard to put aside the desire to plead, once again, *Only if you'll marry me for real.*

But she didn't want that.

So making love to her would not make the situation better. It would merely make him unable to live with himself, and lose her anyway.

He stood.

The effort nearly killed him.

And as he did, he told her the truth. "I just can't, Constance. I couldn't bear it."

CHAPTER 14

*C*onstance counted the hours that stood between herself and freedom. One hundred and sixteen and three-quarters.

She longed for it. Perhaps then, finally, she could rest.

Pretending to be in love had become excruciating.

It had been far more amusing to pretend before her edict that she and Apthorp behave the same in private as in public. Now every single day was an agonizing exercise in tender, sweet dishonesty.

He'd not renewed his suit to marry her. He'd not repeated his claim he was in love with her. He'd not acknowledged the moments they'd spent together in her bedchamber.

No one observing them would perceive that anything had changed.

And yet, somehow, everything was different.

He was different.

His mouth, which had always been so resolutely stern, rested in a smile when he was with her. He laughed more easily and stood more languidly and talked more freely. He found reasons to touch her—adjusting her cloak around her shoulders, brushing a strand of hair out of her eyes. He began to call her *my love.*

In *private.*

Without a *touch* of irony.

But the true difference was in his eyes. There was a softness to them, as though a veil had been lifted and he was letting her see him for the first time. And when she looked into them, some emotion blazed back at her that looked immoderate and unsettling and naked.

It looked like adoration.

It was the way she'd always wanted to be looked upon by someone, and yet when she saw it in his eyes, it made her so nervous that she had to look away.

And so each day she retreated, not sure what to think or how to feel.

Her mood did not lend itself to entertaining. She did not wish to perform; she wished to go into her bedchamber and lock the door and be alone and think. She wished to write in her journal for hours and hours, for days and days, until her hands cramped and she was up to her elbows in spilled ink and she knew, somehow, what to do.

But hours and days were not a commodity she had to spare. Every waking moment between now and the morning she would climb out her window and depart for the coast was consumed by the production of The Courtship of the Century, the theatrical masterpiece in which she served as star and playwright.

And tonight was the most climactic scene: she must so impress the Spences with her homespun, pious manners and infectious matrimonial joy that they agreed to support her fake fiancé's bill once and for all.

I'd rather be stabbed in the eye.

Stop it. Blindness would stand in the way of your writing and you would look very odd with an eye patch.

She smoothed a woven cloth she'd personally secured from the servants' kitchen at Westmead House over the old oak table in Julian's dining room, for she'd learned Lord Spence enjoyed a humble home. She'd spent weeks subtly seeking clues on how best to win him over and staged the night accordingly. The family Bible was prominently displayed on the mantelpiece, for Lord Spence was pious. The house smelled deliciously of roasted beef, nutty bread, and stewed apples, for Lord Spence had a weak stomach and preferred plain foods. The table was laid without wine, for the Spences eschewed spirits. Tulips were arranged in glass vases, for Lord Spence invested in the tulip trade.

When Lord Spence arrived, he visibly relaxed. As did his wife, who commented on Constance's seeming knack for cultivating a domestic atmosphere.

The only person in the room who did not seem charmed by the small meal was herself. She hoped her grim demeanor might be mistaken for an air of spiritual devotion.

"Countess, I am so pleased you were able to visit," Lady Spence said to Apthorp's mother. "I can already see the effect you are having on my goddaughter. She is quite mollified."

Constance did her best imitation of a demure smile. "I'm delighted that you think so."

Apthorp paused and glanced up at her across the table, as if wondering if this was true.

"You know, it seems to me she is unusually doleful," he said in a low voice that she could tell was pitched mostly to her ears.

He said it lightly, but the comment held a question. Something like, *Are you quite all right?*

She was *fine*. Was this subdued manner not what he—and everyone else—had always wanted from her?

She darted her eyes away from him and smiled apologetically at Lady Spence. "Lord Apthorp jests. He was just commenting last night that I have benefited immeasurably from your steady guidance."

"No, he's right. You *are* far less lively. I scarcely recognize you," her brother said, glancing at her with an unusual amount of concern. "Are you ill?"

The troubled look in Archer's eyes made her want to pull him into the hallway and confess all her secrets and wait for him to sort it out until there could be some happy ending.

But telling him any part of it would mean confessing the whole sordid mess of lies, which was impossible, as he was the primary person the lies were constructed to protect.

She was in a prison she had designed and built herself.

Alone.

As she always had been.

And soon would be forevermore.

Do. Not. Cry. Into. The. Roast. Beef.

"I am quite well. The excitement of planning for the ball has only left me tired. From joy."

Lady Spence smiled. "Of course, dear. Besides, our aim is to make Lady Constance less lively, Westmead, and more godly. As I'm sure Lord Apthorp agrees."

"Actually, I adore it when Lady Constance is lively," Julian said, once again looking at her with that tenderness he'd displayed all week. "I've always thought it's what makes her so remarkable," he added softly.

Lady Margaret put her hands to her lips, to hide a smile.

Even Constance's frigid-hearted brother shook his head, looking faintly moved. Moved *on her behalf.* Because he thought that Apthorp was telling the truth.

Because she had created a monster.

He was so touching and solicitous it made her *distraught.* He was so good at behaving like he loved her, she was beginning to believe that it was true. That all the cynical things he'd said to her that night in her bedchamber had been real.

And if they *were*, why was she in the process of dismantling her life to escape him?

Did she really want to leave? Or did she want him? And if she did, would he not just do what he had always done: remember all the reasons he found her lacking and dismiss her as soon as she betrayed the slightest interest?

Was she to believe a week of loving looks and gentle touches over a near decade of being rejected, ignored, and chastised as unfit?

She resumed the task of sawing at her beef, but her hand trembled, and she had to put her knife aside.

"Are you quite all right, my love?" Julian asked, no longer hiding his concern.

She smiled at him brightly. "Yes, of course, darling."

"Lady Margaret, how are you enjoying your sojourn in London?" Cornish Lane Day asked brightly, no doubt in an effort to reorient the conversation around some subject more charming to the Spences than Constance's emotional unraveling.

Constance had noticed him sneaking glances at Margaret all night.

Margaret blushed prettily. "'Tis far more excitement than I am accustomed to. I can scarcely sleep at night for the noise, though my bedchamber overlooks the gardens."

Lady Margaret blushed deeper, no doubt shocked at herself for having inadvertently mentioned her bedchamber in front of a gentleman.

Constance dug her nails into her palm beneath the table. She did not want to think about bedchambers. She could scarcely eat or sleep from her constant, never-ending, *godforsaken* thoughts about bedchambers.

Mr. Lane Day smiled at Lady Margaret, clearly charmed by her. "I am the same, for all my years here. I find that the longer I'm in town, the more the quiet of the country beckons."

"But your work here must sustain you," Margaret said. "I love to read about politics in the paper. I saw with keen interest your essay concerning Lord Hardwicke's marriage bill last year. The parallel you drew between unsuitable gentlemen and the advantages of wolves in the forest was very apt—I smiled when I read it."

Lord and Lady Spence nodded. "Yes, a very virtuous bill, that," Lord Spence said. "Marriage should be performed in a church."

Constance plunged her nails deeper into her hand. No recent piece of legislation made her angrier than Lord Hardwicke's bill, which had replaced the practice of marriage by vow with a system in which banns must be issued weeks in advance, parental permission secured for anyone beneath the age of majority, and the ceremony performed in a church. It was purported to protect women from men who would abuse them with false promises of marriage under the old codes. But in her opinion, its primary effect was to put barriers between women and what modest control they had over their own lives.

"Indeed," Lady Spence sniffed. "We are not pagans."

"But as a Christian woman, Lady Spence," Constance found herself saying, despite the fact that it was not at all a good idea to speak, "have you no concern that the law makes the sacrament of marriage a transaction, based more in coin than in religious principle or love?"

Lord Spence raised a furry brow. "What do you mean?"

"Well, take the clause on marriage prior to the age of majority. By requiring a father's permission, the law allows him to treat his offspring as chits to amplify his fortune, with no concern for what they might wish for their own futures."

"No one chooses his fate," Lord Spence said severely. "That is in the hands of the Lord."

Apthorp caught Constance's eye across the table and subtly shook his head, warning her not to pursue the debate. He cleared his throat. "The law is intended to protect women from bigamy and false promises, is it not? That can only strengthen our society."

"Ladies don't need gentlemen limiting their choices for their supposed protection," Constance said, in a louder voice than she meant to. "They need the ability to protect themselves. They need information. They need *rights.*"

Everyone stared at her.

Lord Spence laughed. "Indeed. Rights!" He merrily sawed into his beef. "You've raised a proper hellion, Westmead."

"Thank you," her brother said, continuing to look at her as though trying to diagnose an ailment of the mind.

Lord Spence continued to chuckle. "Apthorp, you'll have to take her firmly in line."

Apthorp arranged his face into an exquisitely neutral expression. "I cherish Lady Constance in no small part for her independent mind. It is, in fact, the reason that I fell in love with her."

She retreated to the farthest recesses of her uncomfortable wooden chair, not wanting anyone to observe that she was touched by the sentiment to the point of wanting to weep. Touched by the *performance* of the *fake* sentiment she herself had *insisted* he demonstrate at all times.

Unless it was *true.*

What if it was true?

She could feel everyone looking at her, wondering why she was so fractious.

She should be happy in this moment, with victory so close at hand.

She should be seizing it, spearing it on her fork, and savoring its sweetness.

But she didn't want sweetness. She felt like if she ate a single pea, she would choke.

Because if she seized this success that sat before her at the table, so easily in reach, it was well and truly over. The family environment, the hum of purpose, the comforting patter of the ladies, her brother's solicitude. Even the dreadful sewing.

And, of course, her kind and handsome and altogether lovely fake fiancé, Julian.

She had arranged it to work out exactly as it had. She had simply not expected it to *hurt* so much.

"My dear Lord Apthorp," she said, finally finding the soothing tone that was required, "you are kind. But Lord Spence is right. I *can* be quick to temper. I am blessed that my future husband is possessed of so much patience."

"Patience is about all he is possessed of by the sound of it," Lord Spence cackled. "You'll certainly need your waterway to afford the likes of this one for a wife. Westmead's ruined her for anything but lavish rot."

"You *are* a direct fellow, aren't you?" her brother whistled, warning in his tone.

"Well, that's why I'm here, is it not?" Spence intoned. His great, thunderous voice was giving her a headache. "The ladies may be fooled by your sudden interest in our congregation, Apthorp, but let's be frank. I am here not because my wife has saved your soul but because you require my votes to save your bill."

"Your support would indeed do much for the welfare of my tenants, who suffer from the high price of coal," Apthorp said. "These canals will open up the entire region to fair trade."

Lord Spence tapped his hands on the table. "My wife tells me you're a decent man. Increasingly devout. That the trap in the papers is all slander. Is that right?"

"It is," Julian said.

"Well, my secretary tells me a bloc is fomenting to oppose Henry Evesham's appointment to lord lieutenant."

Apthorp coughed on his elderflower cordial. "Pardon?"

"I've put a proposal before the Lords to convene a special committee to investigate vice, naming Henry Evesham as lord lieutenant, with broad powers to wrest this infernal city out of bedlam."

Apthorp looked taken aback. "I'm afraid I've been preoccupied with the coming vote. I was not aware."

"Nor was I," her brother added, looking most displeased.

"It is very important to me that it passes, gentlemen. And, if you are indeed so *reformed*, Apthorp, I imagine you share this impulse."

"No one is a greater supporter of Mr. Evesham's aims than we are," Constance said quickly, for Julian looked like he might be inclined to disagree.

"Yes," he echoed, looking somewhat pained. "Of course you have my support."

"If you can assure me of your votes, I will grant you mine in favor of building the canals."

"I'm so very glad to hear it," Julian said. "Thank you for your consideration, Lord Spence. I know we are all very grateful."

Lord Spence stood, rubbing his prodigious belly. "Well, no need to dally over pudding. Eugenia, I'm feeling most dyspeptic. Apthorp, tell your man to call my carriage."

As soon as the Spences departed, Constance leaned back in her chair. "I thought they would never leave."

"They only stayed for two courses," Lady Apthorp noted.

"Only? It seemed to last forever. I feel like I have aged into a wizened old crone since they arrived."

"You're ill-tempered as a crone, if not precisely wizened," her brother observed. "*Yet.* Apthorp, where's your Armagnac? My sister clearly needs a drink."

Julian poured them all a round. "I believe a toast is in order," he said. "To our canals. And our immortal souls."

He winked at Constance.

Everyone cheered, except her.

Her brother raised a brow at her. "You are not pleased?"

"I am overjoyed," she said. "But I am also exhausted. It must be my nerves. I was so worried I would say the wrong thing that, well, I nearly did. Would you escort me home, Archer?"

Julian stood and touched her arm. "I had hoped for a word before you left. I have something for you. Would you mind?"

His eyes locked onto hers. Implying what he wished to give her must be exchanged in private.

But tonight, if she was with him in private, she would break her own oath. She could not pretend to be in love when her heart hurt so much that looking at a dingy room full of homespun cloth and hymnbooks had her on the verge of tears.

She yawned. "Oh, I'm so very tired. Can it wait until tomorrow?"

He looked like he wanted to protest, but she could not stand to be in this room with him and her emotions a moment longer. She took her brother's arm and all but dragged him to the hall.

ROSECROFT PULLED OPEN THE DOOR OF HIS TOWN HOUSE AT HALF past eleven with an expression of sheer disbelief.

"Apthorp, I consider myself a progressive man, but even I must draw the line at midnight callers. You can see her in the morning."

Apthorp held up the wicker basket he'd brought. "I'm sorry. It can't wait. Is she awake?"

"I doubt it."

He didn't. He knew from the pallor of her face she had not been sleeping.

He would have preferred to simply sneak back to her window, dispensing with his cousin entirely, but she would have trouble explaining how his gift had appeared in her room overnight.

"James, I'm in agony. I *have* to see her tonight. Please."

His cousin sighed. "Another lovers' quarrel?"

"No. But she was upset tonight, and I don't know why, and I have something for her, and I can't stand imagining her—"

His cousin lifted up his hands and stepped back, making room for him to come inside. "Very well, very well. Come in, you poor sop. Wait in the parlor. Westmead's here, having a drink. I'll see if she's awake."

He disappeared up the stairs, chuckling.

The duke was sipping a brandy by the fire. He raised a brow at the sight of Apthorp. "Well, don't you look *aflutter*," he said in an amused tone. "What has my sister done to you?"

"Nothing, Your Grace. I have a gift for her that won't keep overnight, and she rushed away before I had a chance to give it to her."

"What an inspired excuse to come calling in the dead of night," he drawled. "But don't mind me. I know young love can be a trial."

"It's no trial to be in love with your sister, Your Grace. Not at all."

Being in love with Constance Stonewell, and not pretending that he wasn't, was like breathing fresh air after a decade in a cave under the ocean. It was like feeling the heat of fire on your skin after a long, cold march through the snow without a coat.

He did not have to feign enjoyment of her wit, nor appreciation of that delicate way she bit her lip when she was thinking. He did not need to pretend that his eyes drifted toward her whenever she was near him, nor affect an appearance of longing for her company when she was not. He was left with the task of doing what many men never had the chance to do in all their lives: carry out a lovely springtime romance with the woman of his dreams.

Watching her conduct the symphony of their final days was like watching Bernini sketch the pietà, or listening to Vivaldi play by ear. It was all he could do not to simply gaze at her with lovesick admiration.

And yet, as the days passed by, each time they made a dashing show of courtship at a ball, or affected a tender air as they listened to a musicale, or glanced fondly at each other from across the supper table while securing their latest vote, he grew more ill at ease.

For when they were alone, her eyes were empty.

She was just as pleasant. Just as solicitous. Just as charming.

But the girl who sparred as vigorously as she danced, who

never hesitated to tease him or challenge him or tell him exactly what she thought, had disappeared.

It seemed that what she meant by pretending to be in love was to retreat behind a cloak of sweetness.

He'd never imagined he might be *wistful* for the days she'd called him Lord Bore. But tonight, when she'd seemed so dismally upset by their final victory, and so determined to run off immediately after it, he'd have given anything for her to tell him he was tedious.

Because somehow, he'd convinced the only girl he'd ever really wanted that the only future she could imagine with him was one in which she had to run away. And tonight it had felt like she was already gone. He wanted to weep at the loss.

Love is a system of behaviors, she'd declared to him.

And she was right. He'd proved to her for years and years that his sudden declaration of affection was not one to be trusted. He wouldn't press her to change her mind. Not using words.

But he was determined to *show her*, with his actions, how much he cared for her before she left. Because if she knew that, perhaps she might feel as if she had a choice.

The door opened and she entered, trailed by Rosecroft.

"Make it quick," his cousin said. "Some of us would like to sleep tonight."

Constance glanced at him like she was afraid to look at him. "Lord Apthorp."

"Constance, thank you for seeing me. I wanted to give this to you before you left, and I'm afraid it's not the kind of gift that keeps well overnight."

He pushed the basket toward her. A whine sounded from inside, like the soft cry of an infant baby.

Rosecroft raised a brow. "Constance, please tell your wayward intended that we are not a foundling house."

Apthorp ignored him. "Look inside."

Constance gingerly lifted the lid of the basket, and the head of the little spaniel emerged, all drooping ears and big brown eyes. The dog was tiny and adorable, and he happened to know that Constance had a soft spot for anything tiny and adorable. When he'd seen it on the street this afternoon, he'd simply had to get it for her.

She gasped and dropped to her knees. "Oh, a puppy!"

Laughing musically, she lifted it from the basket. "He's so small!"

The puppy yelped, as if in protest of this assessment.

She grinned and tucked the furry creature up against her face. "Oh, is he for me?"

Apthorp cleared his throat. "If you like him. I thought you might."

What he had actually thought was that he wanted her to have something that would not fail her the way he had. He wanted her to have something that adored her without condition.

"That beast shan't be staying *here*," Rosecroft drawled. "My children will persecute it mercilessly."

"I will protect him," Constance said as the puppy cuddled into her neck. "I will keep him in my bedchamber and then he will come to live with us at Apthorp Hall."

Come to live with us at Apthorp Hall.

That sliced through him—reminded him that she was acting, even now. For she had no intention of ever living at Apthorp Hall.

The puppy licked her face. "Oh, what a *forward* little shrimp you are!" she murmured, burrowing her nose into its fur.

"Don't call him a shrimp," Rosecroft objected. "He'll likely be as tall as you one day."

"He won't grow to more than two stone," Apthorp corrected.

Constance scratched the puppy behind its ear. It twitched with pleasure.

"Oh, Shrimpy, I am going to take wonderful care of you."

Westmead winced. "I forbid you to call him Shrimpy."

"Too late," she said firmly. "It's his name and now he's attached to it. Aren't you, Shrimpy, my love?"

"He's going to piss on the bloody carpets," Rosecroft grumbled.

As if on cue, a stream erupted from the puppy.

Constance yelped. "He's wet on me! Shrimpy! How could you?"

Apthorp leapt forward to take the writhing dog from her arms and put him on the floor.

"I'm covered in mess!" she cried, seeming more amused than bothered. She shrugged the soiled dressing gown from her shoulders, revealing a long, chaste muslin night rail with a lace collar that went up to her chin.

"Constance!" Westmead sputtered. "You're indecent! Even for you."

"You prefer me covered in piss?"

The outcry excited the dog, which ran about at Constance's feet.

Apthorp grabbed a blanket and rushed forward to drape it over her shoulders, pausing to tighten it just so.

"There. Now she is decent."

He could not help noticing how dainty she looked, without all her usual boning and pads. His hands wanted to linger at her slightly rounded arms. To draw down and circle the indentation of her waist with his hands.

Stop it, cretin.

She looked up at him with big, guileless eyes. "Thank you."

"You look like a little frosted cake, all wrapped up," he blurted out.

He could not believe that had just come out of his mouth in front of Rosecroft and Westmead. Both men groaned.

Constance only gaped at him. "A *cake?*"

He felt his cheeks blooming warm. "Yes, er, I mean with all the lace, like icing." He grimaced. "Forget I said it."

She raised her brow in an expression of extreme distaste. "I shall try."

"So will I," Rosecroft said. "My God, man, I should have believed Hilary when she said you were hopelessly besotted. Take that dog out to the terrace before it shits on the rugs."

"Yes," Apthorp said, taking up the leather lead, desperate to change the subject from his supposed state of sottedness. He whistled for the dog to follow him and escaped out the terrace doors.

"May I lead him?" Constance called, trailing after him.

"Stay where I can see you," Westmead called from his berth by the fire.

Apthorp handed her the leather rope and stood back by the door. He both wanted her company and did not want to have to look at her after the inanity of what he'd just said.

She led the puppy around, murmuring to him. "Ah yes, that, you see, is a fish pond, Shrimpy. Must be a good dog and not *ever* eat the fish."

The dog leapt up and splashed a paw in the shallow pool, and he heard the soft sound of Constance's indulgent laugh.

"He likes you," he called out at her.

She tossed a smile over her shoulder. "Do you think so? You know, I rather like him too."

He closed his eyes. This was what he had pictured when he'd believed himself to be on the cusp of declaring his affection. Calm nights, soft laughter. A budding friendship that he would nurture until it blossomed into something more. And then, when she was ready, he would tell her how he felt.

How had he let it go so bloody wrong?

And was there any way to fix it?

"You've seemed upset this week, Constance," he ventured, moving closer, so as not to be overheard. "And I know we said we would pretend, but since tomorrow is the vote, and we may not have a chance to be alone together, I just wanted to make sure that you—"

"I'm very well," she said, in a tone she herself would have once condemned as bland.

"Are you? Because if you need anything from me at all, you need only ask."

She looked up into his eyes. "Thank you."

She turned to the dog and began to pull his lead back in the direction of the house.

"You've had your fun, young man," Constance said to Shrimpy, moving toward the doors. As she passed, she reached out and brushed his hand.

"Thank you. It shall be nice to have a friend to take with me when I go." She paused and glanced up into his eyes. "I shall think of you whenever I am with him."

What did that mean? Did he dare ask?

"Wait," he said.

She turned, and her eyes were once again blank. He lost his nerve.

"I brought something else for you." He took the small wrapped package from his coat and slid it into her hand, placing a kiss on her knuckles. "Open it in private."

CONSTANCE PUT THE PUPPY IN HIS BASKET BESIDE HER IN BED AND stroked him as she thought of Genoa. She'd visited her friend Maria many times there, waking up to the fragrance of bitter lemon trees wafting through the windows. Gazing over the cliff tops at the white sails of passing ships on the turquoise sea. Purchasing sacks of pine nuts in dusty, quiet squares at sunset.

You're happy there. Sunshine. Salt air. Peace to decide on any future you imagine.

Any future except this one.

Someone knocked at her door.

"Yes?"

"May I come in?" her brother asked.

"Of course," she called, surprised he was still here. For a man who despised socializing, he'd lingered at the Rosecrofts' all evening for no good reason, as though he was reluctant to let her out of his sight.

He sat down at the end of the bed and looked at her like he was trying to make sense of a puzzle.

"You don't have to go through with it, you know," he said.

She looked up at him, startled. Could he somehow know what she was planning?

"With what?"

"Marrying him."

Oh. For a moment she'd thought he'd sensed she meant to run away.

"Don't be silly, Archer," she said lightly. "I *want* to marry him."

Saying the words sent a chill down her spine.

It made her realize they were *true.*

Her brother looked deeply unconvinced. "Then why have you looked so miserable all night? Hand to God, Constance, if you're having second thoughts about this, just say the word and I swear to you I'll make it right. We've overcome worse scandal."

She twisted her fingers with her hands. "You misunderstand," she said. "I don't wish to call it off. I'm only a bit misty tonight because I am so in love with Julian."

To her horror, the trick worked again. It was the truth.

She was *so in love with Julian.*

She loved him.

She did.

She bloody, bloody loved him.

Her brother stood and hesitated, then patted her awkwardly on the head.

"Then I hope you will be very happy together," he said finally.

She could barely get the words out, knowing he would look back on this moment and perceive acutely that she'd lied to him.

"I'm sure we shall."

He nodded and left.

Alone, she sank back against her pillows and wondered if she should have said something more to Julian. What would he think if she told him she was revisiting a thousand moments, regretting half her life?

She removed the wrapped package he'd given her from her drawer and stared at it, unsure if she could bear another touching gift from him.

Slowly she unwrapped the paper to find a leather box. Inside, nestled within velvet, was a smooth marble ornament, like the priapic carving she'd seen in his trunk, only daintier, prettier, and attached to an orb. A note in his script was tucked inside the box.

For your pleasure, on nights when you want someone to touch you.

I'm sorry I wasn't the man to do it. I'll never stop wishing that I could be.

All my love,

Julian

CHAPTER 15

*A*pthorp paced outside the Commons Chamber in St. Stephen's Chapel. The third reading of his bill was due to happen in a quarter hour—the series of ayes and nays that would decide the rest of his life. And yet, somehow, he didn't care about the outcome.

What had felt so vital now felt utterly beside the point.

All he could think about was Constance.

He could not shake the feeling that he was letting her go too easily. He replayed her words in his mind. *I'll think about you whenever I am with him.*

Had she been telling him she didn't want to leave? Or was he merely torturing them both by scouring her every turn of phrase for hidden shades of meaning?

He did not want to trap her in a future she would hate. But perhaps together they could create a different future from the one that she envisioned. One in which they lived primarily in London. They could renovate his house on the Strand, and she could host salons and write plays. Perhaps, once he was free, he could shed his stiff exterior and welcome her friends and her ways and show her the side he'd been so careful to hide.

The side that had existed only on Wednesday nights, wearing a mask.

"Apthorp." From around the corner, a tall figure loped into view.

Henry Evesham.

"Ah, Mr. Evesham," he said, straining for a pleasant tone. It would not do, in these halls where anyone could overhear, to imply he was anything other than friendly with the hack. "Or should I say, Lord Lieutenant. Congratulations on your new office."

"Why, thank you, Lord Apthorp." He lowered his voice. "Or perhaps *you* prefer to be called Master Damian."

Apthorp's heart ceased beating.

Feign bafflement.

"Pardon?"

Evesham gave him a long-suffering smile. "You can pretend not to know of whom I speak, but we both know that you do."

"I haven't the slightest idea what you mean."

"If that is the line you're taking, one hopes you have a strong constitution for the next story I'm reporting. London may think itself incapable of being further shocked by you, but we both know the truth is sensational."

Apthorp strove for a bored tone. "One would think, given the weight of your newfound responsibilities, you would lack time to pursue slanderous rumors."

"My newfound responsibilities enshrine in law my mission to ensure that vice and corruption are eradicated—from the top of this city to its gutters. And to those rare places, like Charlotte Street, where they so curiously intersect."

He smiled at Apthorp like he had just beaten him at chess.

"Come, now," he said. "We needn't be enemies. I will ensure your name is not among those sullied. Your peers—not to mention your future wife—will never know of your transgressions. *If* you help me."

"Why are you pursuing this? To sell newspapers?"

"On *principle*," Evesham said. "I believe the public has a right to know what their supposed betters are involved in. The same men who blame them for their gin holes and molly houses and bastards are guilty of vices that could make a madam blush. The sun shines on all men equally, my lord, as does God's forgiveness. So should earthly justice."

"I am as fond of justice as the next man, but needless persecution of those pursuing harmless pleasure does not equate to me with honor. I have nothing more to say to you."

If Evesham wanted to destroy an institution that stood out as a rare sanctuary, then he would have to do his dirty work himself. Apthorp would take his chances with ruin. Having already braved it twice, he found that he was becoming rather used to it.

"Very well," Evesham said. "But don't forget that you had your chance. I genuinely shudder to think what Lady Constance will think of you when she finds out she married a whore. And she *will* find out, Lord Apthorp. Her skill for locating inconvenient truths is well known on Grub Street."

"Bugger off, Evesham," he sighed, dropping all pretense of politeness. "I have work to do."

He leaned against the wall and watched the man retreat, feeling like he was watching his future recede with every footstep.

Whore. He preferred to think that he provided a service that was mutually enjoyable.

But it was true. For five years he had fucked for money. Fucked in ways that could probably get him hanged.

And if the truth came out, there would be no feigning Christian virtue or political blackmail to temper the force of public shame. Aristocrats were not meant to have professions. They certainly did not debase themselves by plying the oldest trade of all. He was already regarded as being less than an earl; in the eyes of society, this would make him seem less than a man.

If there was any mercy in the fact that he was going to lose

Constance, it was that it would spare her being pulled down into the muck. He knew that she would try to find an angle that might preserve his dignity. He knew that she would fight for him.

But she didn't deserve to have to try.

He knew what he must do.

He had to let her go.

For it was no longer a question of *if* the full truth would be exposed.

It was only a question of when.

"GOOD MORNING," POPPY, THE DUCHESS OF WESTMEAD, said as she greeted Constance and Lady Margaret in the towering entry of Westmead House, ushering them through air heavy with the scent of flowers.

Constance was immediately beset by an attack of sneezing. "Blasted lilies," she gasped.

"I did try to warn you," Poppy laughed, offering her a handkerchief. Behind her, the entry hall was festooned with forty feet of white flowers woven through floor-to-ceiling trellis panels that had taken the duchess's florists all month to design and days to install.

Constance had hoped the effect would be a stunning assault on the senses. The *visual* senses. She regretted ignoring her sister-in-law's warning that the primary assault would be upon her guest's ability to breathe.

"Oh, Poppy," she wailed. "What are we going to do? The papers will write I gave the entire peerage hay fever."

"We're trimming the pollen from the flowers to reduce the effect," Poppy said. She gestured at a row of footmen armed with scissors, who were going from flower to flower on step stools and ladders, carefully snipping the anthers off each lily and collecting them in glass jars. "But I daresay that if you *do* give the entire peerage hay fever, everyone will assume it was only because you wanted them to weep at the sight of you in your gown."

Constance sighed. "At least we have the acrobats. Perhaps the guests will be so overawed by Catrine Desmurier's debut performance that they will assume it is shock that has stolen their breath away rather than a heavy hand at floristry."

Margaret laughed. "Don't worry. When they see this, I don't think they will be concerned about respiration. It is breathtaking in more ways than one."

"Oh, Margaret. You are kind. But you only say that because Julian keeps you ensconced in the country and you never get to see my stunning works of scandal."

"He doesn't keep me there, you know," Margaret said quietly. "I don't like it in London."

"Oh?" Constance asked distractedly, examining the gold wires that had been hung for the performance. "Why is that?" She should not speak poorly of Apthorp to his sister. Her judgment was compromised by her low mood at realizing her final act in London society was going to be a mass crime of asthma.

Margaret shook her head, as though embarrassed to have spoken. "Town life doesn't suit me."

Constance did not entirely agree, given that Margaret's pale beauty and polite manners had won her obvious admiration in the short time she'd been in town. Particularly from Cornish Lane Day.

But before she could engage the girl in argument, Alfred, Westmead House's butler, came into the room with a calling card.

"My lady," he said, handing it to Constance.

"Miss Gillian Bastian?" she said, reading it aloud. "She's here? How very odd."

"Miss Bastian," Margaret repeated in a tone of alarm. "Is that the young woman who is engaged to Lord Harlan Stoke?"

"Yes, God help her," Constance said. "Alfred, please seat her in the parlor. The *small* parlor. I shall receive her. Eventually."

"Is she your friend?" Margaret asked.

Constance exchanged a look with Poppy, who had never cared for Gillian, and who had witnessed their last exchange at the opera.

"I truly haven't the slightest idea," Constance said.

Margaret seemed uneasy, so Constance patted her shoulder. "Darling, creatures like Miss Bastian are what make London interesting. Don't worry. Valeria is awaiting you in the drawing room for your fitting. Go along and I shall join you when I'm done."

"Very well," Margaret said, still looking ill at ease.

Constance took a look at herself to make sure she seemed beautiful, confident, and utterly bored, and then swept into the smallest, most inelegant parlor in the house. Gillian, having been here many times, would know that reception in this room was a sign she was not wanted.

She was waiting on a straight-back chair, dressed exquisitely in a violet gown that brought out her dark eyes and dainty figure.

It was Constance who had encouraged Gillian to favor gowns that flattered these features. It was also Constance who had given her the dangling sapphire earbobs that drew attention to her cheekbones. It was *also* Constance who had encouraged her to wear her hair swept up over one eye, to emphasize her intriguing minxlike chin.

Constance had done a remarkable job transforming Miss Bastian from the too-talkative daughter of a rich colonial from Philadelphia to the distinctive, fashionable young heiress who now sat before her. Glancing upon the striking success of her efforts, she rather regretted she was so very talented at performing miracles.

"I'm *most* surprised to see you here," Constance said, ignoring pleasantries and sitting down on an upholstered sofa.

"*I'm* most surprised I was not invited to your ball tomorrow," Gillian said, matching her tone.

"Are you? Given our last meeting, I gathered you no longer wished to be acquainted."

Gillian rolled her pretty eyes. "Well, what do you expect? Saddling yourself with such a pathetic man?"

Pathetic. That word made her seethe. Not least because she had known that's exactly what Gillian would think of anyone who possessed unorthodox tastes. In trying to protect her friend from an unwelcome marital surprise, she'd no doubt added fuel to unfair prejudices—encouraging the equation of a private pleasure with weakness, when the two things were not related. For the hundredth time, she wished she could unwrite it.

"If you believe Lord Apthorp to be pathetic, then I am *most* confused as to why you would wish to attend our engagement ball."

Gillian quirked up the corner of her mouth. "Oh, you aren't confused. We both know exactly why I'm here. I'll admit it, Constance: I miscalculated. I should have known you would manage to turn his scandal into some romantic public spectacle. It's never wise to doubt your skill at *that*, is it?"

Gillian's unpredictable flashes of candor—and canniness—had always been the reason Constance liked her. At times her interests seemed so vacuous that one wondered how she did not float away. And yet, just when one was tempted to dismiss her, she would make an observation that was so trenchant that one realized, with equal fear and admiration, that she took in a great deal more than she let on.

This quality was amusing in one's friend. It was much less appealing when it was deployed against *oneself*.

"If we are being candid, tell me this," Constance said. "Why did you pretend you wished to marry Lord Apthorp, and let me encourage his suit, if you were attached to Lord Harlan Stoke?"

Gillian laughed in her tinkling, staccato way—a sound like cracking ice. Constance had once found her laugh infectious. Today it was only unsettling.

"I never *said* I wished to marry Lord Apthorp. I merely refrained from objecting when you insisted we were fond of one another."

"But *why*? Surely you must know I had no desire to force a match where there was no attachment. Had you simply said he did not interest you, I would have let the matter drop. Why not disabuse me of my false notions, if I was so decidedly in error?"

Gillian looked at her as if she were very, very silly. "There was obviously never any chance of him marrying *me*, even if I had wanted him. Not when he looks at you like he wants to ..." She paused, and raised a brow in a rather suggestive manner. "Have his way with you. Or, if his reputation is correct, let *you* have your way with him."

Gillian snickered to herself.

"But you *pretended*—"

"Yes, because being honest with you has never paid. You are bold, but you are not plain dealing, Constance. I knew you'd frown on my attachment to Lord Harlan, and so rather than wait for you to meddle in my affairs and try to block the match with your silly circular—"

"My *what*?"

"Oh, don't deny it. I've never been the fool I let you think I was. You so love to be right that it does not take much work at all to convince you that you are when it suits one's purpose. Everyone agrees you are too vain to know when you're ridiculous."

The flinty look in Gillian's eyes made Constance feel naked. Was this how she was perceived? As some self-admiring fool so convinced of her own powers to contrive the world to her liking that she could no longer see the truth?

In the years when she'd set out to reshape herself in the image of her choosing, she'd often imagined herself to be an ice sculpture. Carved ice looked so cold and brilliant to the naked eye— stunning and beautiful even if, upon closer inspection, its glow came from the fact that it was slowly melting. It dazzled not in spite of its perspiration but *because* of it. And so, Constance had imagined, did she.

It was why she preferred the kind of friends one saw only at parties. If one did not spend enough time in the company of others, they could not see the deficits in character that lurked beneath one's superficial charm. And that was comforting. Because it took great effort to win the room, to be the grandest presence, to make a spectacle. But if one perspired enough, all anyone ever saw was the flash of light against one's carefully chiseled edges. Not the puddle beneath one's gown.

Gillian looked at her like her dress was not just damp but soaking wet. She hated being seen that way. *Hated it.*

And Gillian could tell. She sat there drinking tea as though it were nectar from a flower she'd been crowned with following a long-awaited victory.

"In any case," Gillian said, barely managing to sip her tea around her smug expression, "now you have your love match, and your spectacle, and I have mine. So invite me to your ball and I shall receive you after my wedding, and we can forget this unpleasantness and go on being useful to each other."

"*Love match?* Does that mean you still intend to marry Lord Harlan, after what I told you in my letter?"

Gillian narrowed her eyes. "Oh, don't bother to malign him to me again, Constance. I know you despise him. You never like anyone you can't feel you're above. He told me how you pursued him like a harlot and he had to fend you off. You're lucky he was discreet about it."

She wanted to invite Gillian to enjoy the fate that awaited her if that was what she believed about the story she'd told her in her letter. But on certain topics, the need for honesty outweighed the force of anger.

"He is lying to you. It brings me no pleasure at all to say that everything I wrote to you is true. I once had to defend myself against his attentions by force. I have learned that he still keeps a mistress, despite his engagement to you. And I have reason to believe, though I have no direct proof, that he has at least one child out of wedlock, whom he has abandoned—"

"Stop," Gillian said acidly. "If you do not wish to make an enemy of me—of *us*—you will drop this and invite us to your ball and make it known that we are fashionable. And you will never spread these lies again."

Constance stood. "No, I won't. I wish you the best of luck. But Lord Harlan Stoke is not welcome in this house. And if you want to save yourself a world of trouble, Gillian ... before you marry him, ask him to tell you the truth."

Gillian rose and smiled calmly. "You will regret this."

Constance swept to the door, opened it, and waited for Gillian to exit, not lifting her eyes from the girl's form until Alfred had shown her onto the street. And then she sank back against the doorframe and clutched herself.

She noticed Margaret still stood across the corridor, watching her.

"What is it, dear? Could you not find Valeria?"

The girl looked as pale as Constance felt.

"I knew him once," Margaret said. "Lord Harlan, I mean. Is he ... will he be in attendance tomorrow? Because I should not like to see him and if he is expected—"

"No," Constance said. "Not unless he desires a hatpin between the eyes."

Margaret looked as disturbed as she did relieved.

"Sorry, darling," she said, taking the girl's hand. "I forget not everyone speaks so casually of murder. Let's go be made beautiful and never speak his name again."

When Julian arrived with the Duke of Westmead to

celebrate the good news, Alfred informed him that Lady Constance was in the parlor with his sister and her mantua-maker.

"I'll wait for her," he said, sending the duke onward to share the news with the Rosecrofts, who were waiting on the terrace. "I'd like to tell Constance myself."

Now that he knew he could not change the ending of their tale, he wanted one final good-bye.

The parlor door was half-ajar, and he could hear the soft sound of feminine chatter. He sat on a bench, waiting for the ladies to conclude their business.

"I noticed Mr. Lane Day took an interest in you," Constance said. He could hear a conspiratorial smile in her voice. "I will be sure to see that he asks you to dance at the ball."

"Oh, I hope not." Margaret sounded panicked at the thought.

"But darling, *why*? It's such a pleasure to dance with a gentleman who admires you, and with you in this he will be help-less not to fall in love. Doesn't she look stunning, Valeria?"

"She does," a lightly accented voice concurred.

"It's been quite a long time since I danced with a gentleman," his sister said. "I'm not sure I remember how."

Apthorp winced. That was his fault. He could have insisted she have another season after her illness, but he had not liked the idea of her plunged into the heat and dangers of a London ballroom after everything she'd endured. To this day he could not look upon her face without remembering how vulnerable she was. But perhaps Constance was right. Perhaps encouraging her to remain in the country had not been in her best interest.

"Don't be silly!" Constance cried. "You have perfect manners, a poetic form, and a touching nature. And you've certainly caught Mr. Lane Day's eye."

Margaret lowered her voice. "Do you really think so? Since my illness I have felt rather … drab."

He winced again. His sister was not drab. She was very pretty, but beyond that, she had an inner kindness that gave her light even when she'd been at her lowest.

"But you are a perfect dove! In spirit as well as looks," Constance said, echoing his feelings exactly. "Besides, the flash of beauty is highly overprized. Give me a piece of coal, sixpence, and an hour, and I can make a beauty out of anyone."

Margaret laughed. "Whatever do you mean?"

"Beauty is a question of directing the eye to the features one wants noticed, and ensuring those features look their best. Anyone who has had the misfortune to see me in the morning can attest to this."

That was *certainly* not true. He had spent the past week trying not to spend every spare moment remembering how she'd looked on a very recent morning. He may have *remembered* at length, on several occasions.

"Please," his sister said. "You are one of the most celebrated beauties in all of London."

Constance snorted. "Only because I've trained London to celebrate illusions. If you squint, you can see that my chin is misshapen, my eyebrows are invisible, and my figure is far too puny to be fashionable. Tell her, Valeria."

He heard the woman click her tongue. "Far too little bosom."

Also not true. He had seen enough bosoms—large and small, in various stages of bloom—to know that Constance's was perfect. He could spend a great deal of time becoming acquainted with such a bosom.

"It's true," Constance sighed, in a tone that had a hardness to it he didn't like to hear. "It's all true. And knowing it is valuable, because if one knows one's flaws, one can correct them, or exaggerate them, to make oneself in one's best image. Add a carefully cut gown, a dash of charm, and before you know it, everyone sees exactly what you want them to. They'd be shocked at the meager substance underneath."

His sister, who rarely contradicted anyone, gasped in displeasure. "There is nothing meager about you."

There was a pause, and he heard footsteps. "Margaret," Constance said in a low, firm voice, "let me give you some advice. Few people even *like* me. I make them *think* they do by discerning what they want and figuring out a way to help them get it. Or failing that, I distract them with jokes and favors and parties until they've quite forgotten what they really think. And so can *you*, if you so wish. Don't let anyone tell you that you can't be whatever kind of person that you wish to be. Now, then, the family is waiting—"

The door opened and the three ladies paused, taken aback to see him standing there.

"You don't believe that," he said to Constance, not even bothering to pretend that he hadn't been eavesdropping.

"Believe what?" Constance asked.

"That you must *trick* people into admiring you."

The other ladies looked away from him, as though embarrassed by the amount of heat in his tone.

Constance blushed. "Well. If one wants the trick to *work*, one should refrain from mentioning one's tactics in front of one's admirers." She winked at Margaret.

"Constance, you are *lovely*," he said. "Truly lovely. We all see it. No trickery required."

"Did I not tell you he is quite attached?" she asked her dressmaker in an arch tone, as though he could not hear her.

The woman smirked. "Indeed. The gowns must be working."

Constance gave a throaty laugh. "Or the bosom."

He hated the brittleness in her manner. It reflected a belief she was correct in how she saw herself.

She wasn't.

And after tonight he might not ever have another chance to make her see how wrong she was.

"Constance, may I have a word with you? Alone?"

She looked at her dressmaker. "Valeria, did you not say you had something you wanted to discuss? I don't wish to keep you waiting."

The dressmaker trained her eyes on Apthorp, as though the sight of him puzzled her. "Nothing worth keeping you," she said. "I will leave a note with your maid. Good day."

As soon as the others left, Julian came and put his hand on top of hers, running a finger over a blotch of ink near her thumb.

His eyes were intense. She could not read his face.

"You *are* wrong, you know. About how people see you. I've spent nearly every day in your presence for a month, so I consider myself an expert on this subject."

"Oh, more of this," she sighed. If she'd known he'd wished only to continue this discussion, she would have found reason to withdraw with Valeria and Margaret. "And how do they see me?" she asked, thinking of Gillian. Not really wanting to know.

"I'm sorry to report that they adore you. They delight in being near you." He nodded grimly. "And having observed you very closely I can confirm that their judgment is correct. People like you very much. *I* like you very much."

He squeezed her hand, then pressed it to his lips. "I think you are the very best kind of woman, Constance. The very best kind of person."

Her nerves flared. She half wanted him to mean more than he was saying, and was half-terrified of how she might feel if he did.

"You've been spoiled," she said lightly, not sure what to do other than to ignore the intensity of his tone. "I've been on my best behavior for a month. It isn't real."

"No. I've seen what's underneath."

Suddenly all she could think about was the fact that he had literally seen what was underneath. He had seen her without a stitch of clothing, so lost to her attraction to him she had made love to an apple while he watched. After which he had declared her unbearable and left, giving her a piece of phallic rock to remember him by.

This behavior should not make her emotional. She was being deranged.

"You *have* seen what's underneath indeed," she said, striving to keep her tone light. "And I daresay you didn't like it."

He shook his head. "I think you know I'm not talking about what's underneath your gown," he said in a low voice. "I'm talking about your heart. I never noticed until this month how generous you are. How you go out of your way to bring others joy, or spare them suffering, even if it hurts you. It's a noble quality. A rare one."

She did not know what to say, so she turned away and began collecting the pins Valeria had left on the escritoire.

"But," he added in a low voice, coming up behind her, "in point of fact, I *did* like what I saw underneath your dress. Just to correct the record."

She glanced at him over her shoulder. "You did not," she whispered.

His lip curled up ever so slightly. "Oh, I *did*. I liked it immensely. I may have remembered how much I liked it and had to relieve myself of *distress* just this morning."

Did he mean ... ? Oh, the thought of *that* made her quite distressed indeed.

He ran a hand down a strand of hair that had come unpinned during her fitting, inspecting it in the light of the golden summer sunset streaming through the window.

She watched him in the looking glass above the escritoire, feeling, as usual, breathless at his nearness.

"I wish you could see yourself as I see you," he said, meeting her eye in her reflection.

She inhaled, trying to not reveal how unstrung this exchange was making her. "And how is it that?"

His hands slid down her shoulders, the sides of her arms, the swell of her breasts.

He rested his chin on her shoulder, staring at the two of them. She did not dare breathe.

"You're a goddess. Any man who does not treasure you appropriately is not worthy of you. If you take one lesson from our time together, take that."

The finality in his words deflated the tension she'd been carrying.

He was not asking her for more than this. He was simply saying his farewells.

Always perfectly mannered, her Lord Bore.

"So it's really over," she said, exhaling. "The bill passed."

"Went through without a change. Six votes to spare." He laughed quietly, such a sound of private relief that she smiled for him, through her sadness.

"I'm saved," he said, pressing another kiss to her knuckle over the ink spots. "*You* saved me. You're a genius, you know."

She closed her eyes and leaned back against him.

"Yes, of course I know," she murmured. "I go around telling everyone who will listen, so you'd think it would not be such a surprise when I am proven correct."

He wrapped his arms around her. "Hush."

His lips came down on her neck.

For just one second, as he traced a molten path down to her shoulder, she imagined a different sort of future.

In this version, she found the courage to tell him she'd been wrong.

To say that perhaps, if he asked her *one* more time to stay, she would give him a final chance to take what she found so difficult to offer anyone: her heart.

But as he dragged his lips along her skin, she couldn't find the courage.

Maybe because she didn't really wish to give her heart away.

Or maybe because her memory was long, and she simply didn't trust him not to shatter it.

She leaned against him, inviting more of his kisses.

For this much, she knew, was true: she trusted him innately with her body.

"My God, what is that scent you wear?" he murmured, inhaling her shamelessly, in case he never got another chance to breathe it in. "I've always wondered."

"I don't wear a scent."

He groaned. "You lie, you wicked girl."

She shook her head and he realized it must be true, because every time he breathed her in, he was met with some fresh, new intoxication.

"Then I am incomparably addicted to the smell of your skin," he murmured.

Saying as much exposed him, but at the moment he could not bring himself to care. Soon he was going to lose her, and soon the world would know he was not the kind of man who had ever much adhered to decency, and the combination made him physically unable to let go of her quite yet.

He pulled her against him and sighed at the feeling of her nestled up against his body. He was hard, and didn't want to overwhelm her, but he also didn't ever want to move away.

"Do you mind that? The feel of me?" he asked, pressing his erection to the cleft of her buttocks.

She closed her eyes in the mirror. "I love the way it feels."

"So do I," he murmured. He turned her around to face him.

"Oh yes," she whispered. She widened her thighs and pressed his buttocks closer so that she could feel his erection through her skirts. He clenched her against his length and groaned.

"Oh my," she gasped.

"Constance," he murmured, unable to resist his attraction to her. Wanting, somehow, to leave her with some proof of it. "I know I said I wouldn't. But before we say farewell I want to touch you. I can't stop thinking about it."

"Neither can I," she said, kissing him along his jaw. "Please don't stop just yet. It feels so lovely."

He scooped her more firmly against him and kissed her where her breasts rose from her bodice. "I would never compromise your virtue. But if you'd like I can make you feel lovelier still."

She looked up into his eyes and shivered. "Yes," she said breathily. "Lock the door. There's a key in the credenza."

He did, and when he turned back, she rushed toward him.

"Kiss me," she said.

For once, he didn't argue. He drew her back with him and pulled her down onto a sofa across from the mirror. He could not stop himself from noticing that she was shaking.

Trembling for him, and he'd barely even touched her yet. Christ, but she was precious.

He kissed her eyes, her nose, her neck. He knelt down on the floor in front of her feet and kissed the pulse points at her wrists.

"May I lift this up?" he asked, playing with the hem of her gown.

"Yes."

He brought it up over her knees and kissed the laces of her stockings. Carefully, he swept up her petticoats and parted her legs, kissing the insides of her thighs.

"I want you to watch me in the mirror."

He nibbled at her thighs, edging closer and closer to her quim until he could feel her heat, smell her desire. He teased her with his lips and breath until it seemed she was one, long, arching sigh.

She was so wet and swollen and lush and she hissed so ardently at his touch that he wanted to weep.

He ran a thumb over the cleft between her legs. "May I kiss you here?"

"Yes," she whispered.

His fingers made connection with her most tender flesh.

"My God," he murmured, at the slickness there.

"It happens whenever I think of you," she said.

"Then I hope you will think of me often."

"I can't stop," she gasped, as his tongue made connection with her body.

He didn't answer, because he had lost all sense of language.

ALL SHE COULD DO WAS FEEL.

Julian held her by the waist as his mouth rewrote what it meant to feel alive. She glanced in the mirror at the image: her skirts flung up around her, his face pressed between her thighs, her head bent back in ecstasy. The erotic sight of it overmastered her. She leaned forward, gripped his hair, and died into his neck.

He held her while she came apart and tried to avoid summoning her family with her gasps.

When she finally stopped shaking, her pleasure was replaced by a sense of shyness at what he had just done. But he only looked up at her with the kindest eyes imaginable, smiled, and then placed a long, lingering kiss on her knee.

"Thank you for the lesson, Julian," she said, because she could not think of what else to say. Other than *Please ask me one more time.*

He stood up and stroked her hair.

"I need to tell you something," he whispered in her ear.

Say I love you. Tell me to stay.

"That's what you deserve from a lover," he said tenderly.

"Wherever you go, whatever life you find, don't ever accept any man who fails to see that you are every inch a goddess."

She sighed. Any *other* man, he meant.

"I know you will find a man who treasures you *and* deserves you," he went on. "And I, Lady Constance, will be *extremely jealous of him*."

She had her answer.

She'd been so hoping for a clue that the risk of revealing how she felt might be worthwhile.

Instead, he'd kindly given her a clue it wouldn't.

She wrapped her arms around him so he would not be able to see her face. "Enough of that, you alley tomcat. You're as bad as they say in the papers. Come, fix my dress. The family is waiting."

After he helped her repair her attire and they walked outside onto the terrace, their families cheered. Julian looked proud and slightly overwrought and bashful to be seen so full of feeling.

At least there was this: her sacrifice was worth it, to give him such relief.

She wanted to remember him like this forever.

He raised his glass in the air. "Forgive me for being sentimental, but may I burden you with a toast?"

"Toast!" her family cried. "Toast!"

"One month ago my life was a shambles. I was certain that I would never have the respect of any of you again. But one woman believed in me. When I had given up on myself, she came, scraped me up, and explained, step by step, how we were going to fix the mess. At the time, I doubted her plan would work. But she was very persistent, and I was very desperate, and lo and behold, Lady Constance Stonewell was, as usual, exactly right."

She felt tears welling up. Why was he saying this? There was no reason to toast her now. They had already won. There was no point in pretending.

Nevertheless, her family cheered.

"To Lady Constance, to whom I owe my life," he said. "Not just a woman. A *goddess.*"

He met her eye as he said it, making her blush straight down to her breasts, which still ached from her unmet desire for him to take them in his mouth. To her thighs, which were still slick from her want for him. To her heart, which was breaking.

"To Lady Constance!" her family shouted.

She raised her glass and cleared her throat. "You know I can never stand to let Lord Bore have the last word," she said, to mordant chuckles. "So I shall have to have it for him. Julian, you never deserved the things the papers said about you. You never deserved to be saddled with a troublemaking specimen like myself. But I must say, the situation flattered you. Because before this month, I don't think any of us quite knew how remarkable you are. I don't think we—I—saw you for the strong, passionate, forceful, good, and clever man you are. You, Lord Bore, are unforgettable."

Emotion shone in his eyes. She raised her glass to him.

"To the least boring man I've ever met. I am so excited to see what the next several decades of your life have in store."

"Bravo!" everyone shouted.

But she could barely hear them. Because she only had eyes for him, and the way he was looking at her.

As though none of it was pretend.

As though this night was the start of the rest of their lives.

CHAPTER 16

One could always trust an event devised by Constance Stonewell to be spectacular, but the sight inside the doors of Westmead House the following evening was so stunning that, for once, Apthorp could not even muster the cynicism to roll his eyes at the expense.

Huge, luxuriant blooms lined the walls from floor to ceiling in shades of white and cream. The scent of lilies wafted through the air like candlelight you could inhale. Sheer linen drapes dyed in pale shades of violet gave the room a dreamy atmosphere, and gold ropes dangled from the ceiling, inciting speculation as to what mysteries might be in store.

Constance was giving London something to remember her by.

It broke him.

Westmead waved and walked over.

"Go upstairs and wait for Constance in the drawing room. I will introduce the entertainment, and you will wait behind the curtains while the acrobats perform. After the finale I'll raise the curtains, present you both to the room, and you will march down that staircase for the opening dance. Constance has arranged for an orchestra. And the release of ten thousand white rose petals. Naturally."

He whistled. "How dramatic, Your Grace."

Westmead rolled his eyes. "I know. But it's what she wants. I may be becoming sentimental at the idea of you whisking her away."

Apthorp could not answer him, because anything he might say would be the worst kind of lie. He clapped the duke on the back and marched up the stairs to console himself with Westmead's excellent brandy while he waited.

It was an hour before Constance arrived, and by then he was ever so slightly tipsy. But not too tipsy to notice she was gorgeous.

Her hair was pinned up with pale pink lilies the exact shade of her lips. All that pink set off her bright blue eyes, which shone next to the long strands of sapphires dangling from her ears and coiled around her neck.

"It should be illegal to look like that," he said.

She grinned at him. "You look rather illegal yourself, my lord."

He took her hand. "So tonight's our final act."

She smiled. "Let's make it a memorable one. The acrobats are nearly ready. Shall we take our place behind the curtains? We'll have to stand there for a while, but I don't want to distract them while they're walking on wires."

She led him to an alcove that had been fashioned from yards of draped linen behind the balustrade at the top of the grand staircase. Soft violet curtains drifted from the ceiling, strung with lilies and strands of gold wire. It looked like a cage for an angel's songbird.

God, his wits were soppy. He'd overdone it on the brandy.

Outside Westmead rang a bell to catch the audience's attention, welcoming the guests. The orchestra struck up, and the gasps of the crowd signaled that the acrobats had taken their positions.

"How long is their act?" he asked Constance.

"A quarter hour," she said, taking a sip of champagne.

"What shall we do to pass the time?"

She smiled, a bit sadly. "A pity you never liked playing dice."

"Oh, Constance," he murmured. He pulled her to his chest and simply held her.

"It's been fun, hasn't it?" She smiled sadly. "We made a good pair after all."

He hated the finality in her words.

He wanted to tell her that they need not part ways. To get down on his knees and beg her for one last chance.

But then he thought of Evesham, and he knew he could not ask her that.

Which made this no less painful. He held her tighter, letting her scent envelop him.

"Perhaps we could pass the time with one last lesson," she murmured.

"What kind of lesson?"

"Perhaps you could teach me to kiss someone so that he will remember you forever."

"Do you think I could ever, *ever* forget you?" he asked as he threaded his hands around her lower back and brought her toward him. He did not wait for a reply before he placed his mouth on hers.

The need to kiss her with delicacy—after all, in a few short minutes they must march down the stairs as though none of this had happened—made him feel every breath, every shudder, every gasp with perfect clarity.

"You make me overeager as a boy," he said roughly into her hair. "My God. I'm shaking. You know that, don't you? How badly I want you?"

She said nothing, only tightened her fingers around his shoulders and buried her face in his neck. No doubt it was the brandy, but suddenly he wanted to tell her everything. For when would he have another chance?

"I always have, you know," he said raggedly. "Ever since the first time I saw you, I thought you were the most captivating creature on earth."

He dragged his hands up over her bodice, fierce. "I wanted to touch you. I wanted to know every single thing about you."

I still do.

She made a small, tortured sound and he put his mouth to the hot, fragrant skin above her breasts.

"Prove it," she whispered, taking his hands in hers.

"Sweet girl," he murmured. "It's too late."

She gave him a look he had not seen in a week. A defiant, taunting look.

"No, it isn't, Julian. We have at *least* fifteen minutes."

"Darling girl." He laughed into her neck to keep from crying.

She drew him back. "Let me touch you," she said. "Just once. So I can dream of it."

Before he could think, her hands fumbled at his breeches, and then they were on his flesh. Outside the curtains, he heard the orchestra play the end of the first movement. The performance must be well under way.

Constance took his erection in her hand and ran her fingers over the tip. His entire body shuddered.

"You're softer than I imagined," she said. "And larger. One wonders how you manage to walk." She ran her hand up the shaft and gently squeezed.

"You mustn't," he groaned. "I won't be able to recover."

"What if I don't want you to recover?" He could hear the arousal in her voice. "What if I want you to fall apart?"

God, it was tempting.

"Let me please you. Show me how. One more lesson."

Her fingers gripped around him, untrained but instinctive.

"A little death before our closing act," she whispered. "One final secret."

He wanted it so badly, but it was every kind of wrong. "There isn't enough time."

She gripped him harder. "Are you certain? I find that with a bit of practice it doesn't take me long at all. Especially since you gave me that very clever gift."

He groaned in pure, desperate lust and closed his eyes and felt her fingers tracing over the crown of his cock, where she found a bit of wetness and smeared it with her thumb. He shuddered so violently she glanced up and grinned.

"Are you experiencing a death?" she asked, playing with the oozing head of him.

"You mustn't," he gasped. "I'll spend and make a mess of you. I've wanted you too long."

"I want to make you come, Julian. So I can think about it later. When I'm distressed."

What he wanted to suggest was the essence of pure dastardliness. He whispered it anyway. "Perhaps if you knelt down and used your mouth."

He deserved a slap for that, but instead she gave him a very wicked smile.

The one she saved for when she was at her most provocative. God, he'd missed that smile.

She sank to her knees and looked up at him beneath her lashes, smiling. Her lips traced tentatively against the head of his cock, her tongue alighting at the very tip.

"You taste like salt," she whispered.

Christ.

"Tell me what to do," she murmured. "Hurry." She took him in her lips.

Outside, the crowd gasped in time with the swishing of the ropes. The dancers were building up to the climax of their performance.

"Yes, like that, take me in. Suck ... Gently, just your tongue, no teeth."

The world grew dark and contained to their joined flesh. He let his fingertips fall into her hair.

"That's it. A bit deeper. Christ, Constance."

He thrust as gently as he could stand to as she laved the underside of his erection with her tongue, his need swelling in his bollocks, the shouting of the crowd just beyond them making the whole thing so wrong and so essential.

"Do you like it, doing this where we could be seen?" he asked raggedly. He could barely get the words out, but he had to ask, had to know.

In answer, she only whimpered and gasped out "Yes." If he let her keep going, he would spend in her mouth. He bit his knuckle to keep from shouting.

"Christ," he said. "That's enough. Sweet girl, stop, I'm close to death."

But she didn't stop. She glanced up at him, not breaking their connection. And then she gripped him more firmly and sucked long and hard, pressing his hip against her temple.

He pulled out and narrowly managed to spill into his shirttails, burying his face in his arm to keep from bellowing with the pleasure of it.

He sank down to his knees in shaky gratitude and drew her against him and wiped her lips with the cuff of his shirt. She was warm and pliant, panting just a bit.

"You're a very naughty man, Lord Bore," she whispered, smiling up at him. "It's really rather shocking."

Outside the crowd gasped. The performance must be nearing its end. They needed to right themselves while they still had time. But instead he heard himself saying, "You have no idea. Open your legs."

He expected her to protest, but instead she laughed a laugh

that contained a hundred filthy secrets. "They're nearly done. Quickly."

He reached under her skirts until he found what he wanted. She was wet—dripping wet. He kissed her voraciously as his fingers found the pert flesh at the juncture of her thighs and worked at it indecently. He knew she was close. He knew that the danger, the crowd, the champagne, were having the same effect on her they'd had on him. Her pussy throbbed beneath his fingers. "Fuck, what I would give to sink my cock inside you."

At his words, she began to come undone. He felt her go still and tense with it. He did not relent, and as her orgasm hit her, she cried out into his mouth, collapsing against him on her knees. As she did it, he lost his balance, his knee slamming against the hard marble floor. He wobbled, sending her arm flailing out to catch the curtain.

He realized it was happening precisely too late to stop it. As she clutched the curtain, the whole thing began to topple down around them.

Her low orgasmic cry rapidly became a shrill, full-bodied one as yards and yards of linen came collapsing down around them, sending them reeling back onto the ground in a pile.

The noise of the crowd went hushed.

He scrambled to free them from the curtains until he could see.

The startled acrobats, just ending their routine, were careening toward them on ropes, their expressions puzzled.

A tiny, dark-skinned woman in pantaloons landed just next to the balustrade.

She raised her arm, and presented the tumbled sight of them to the crowd.

"Ladies and gentlemen," Westmead's voice boomed dryly. "May I present the Earl of Apthorp and his future countess."

He stared out at a sea of aghast faces, and he was glad.

Because some things were so shocking you could never, ever recover from them.

Some things were simply irreparable.

It was selfish and inexcusable and wrong, but he didn't want to let her go.

And now ... he wouldn't have to.

UNDERNEATH THE PILE OF DRAPES AND THE MESS OF HER SKIRTS, Constance felt Julian's hands quickly working to discreetly return their garments to rights before the marveling crowd could see that they were not only jumbled in each other's limbs, but also in a state of complete indecency.

The furious chatter from downstairs made it clear the guests were already eagerly speculating about what the two of them had been doing alone behind the curtain to cause it to collapse with them entangled in each other's arms.

She did the only thing she could think to do to stop the speculation. She gave them something to watch.

She leaned forward and put her lips to Julian's cheek.

The crowd roared its approval.

She plastered the biggest smile she could muster on her face, untangled her gown from the drapery, rose, and curtsied to the crowd.

"Bow," she whispered to Julian through her smile.

He did.

The crowd roared louder.

"Say something," she hissed.

"Ladies and gentlemen, my future bride," he said. "Isn't she stunning?"

Cheers.

She stood in a daze, her body still murmuring with the aftershocks of what they'd done, and accepted this surge of approval as the orchestra cued the first strains of the minuet. Apthorp took her hand and, with another flourishing wink at the crowd, led her down the stairs and through the parted throng to the dance floor, smiling as though nothing in the world was wrong.

As the orchestra surged around them, and the room filled with the ethereal rain of flower petals falling down from the ceiling like shooting stars, he bowed and whispered in her ear: *"Marry me."*

He said it in a low, rough voice. But when she looked at his face, he was beaming at her.

Her heart leapt.

Still, it wouldn't do to force him into something he'd regret simply because a curtain had fallen down. "We don't have to," she said quickly when their hands next met. "Nothing has changed."

"Everything has changed."

"I don't want to force you to do something you don't want to."

"Good. Because I've been in love with you for eight years, and there's nothing I want more."

She stopped dancing.

"Julian, is that *really* true?"

He smoothed a lock of hair that had fallen into her eyes.

"Yes," he said tenderly. "I told you."

"I thought you were pretending because you felt guilty."

"I know, sweet girl. I didn't want to pressure you to do something you didn't want to. But it's true. I've always wanted you. The night I asked you about proposal gifts ... I asked because I wanted to buy one for you when the bill passed."

"But all that time ..."

"I was scared of failing to live up to who I wanted to be, Constance. I was scared of not deserving you unless I did. I was scared you wouldn't want me." He sighed, shakily. "I still am."

Suddenly, she understood.

All his lectures. All her hurt. All his anger. *All those years.*

Her heart broke for him and for herself even as it swelled.

"Don't be scared of that," she said. "It was never true. I'll prove it."

She leaned in and kissed the Earl of Apthorp in the middle of the party of the century.

And when she was done, the crowd cheered so loud she knew she would remember it all her life.

CHAPTER 17

*H*e put the conversation off.

He knew that he must tell her the full truth about his past, and the risk it brought to them, before they married.

But he wanted to find the perfect words. He wanted to find a way to tell her that it had never changed the way he felt about her. That she need not regard him differently, or less.

But he was not quite used to being honest with her. And when he was around her, the brightness in her eyes was so sharp and buoyant that he didn't want to dampen it.

Which must be how he had gone from having a week to having a few days, to having two nights, before they were due to stand in the chapel.

And why he was once again climbing up the trellis to Constance's balcony window at an hour peopled primarily by thieves and nightsoilmen.

He tapped softly at her shutters.

"Are you certain you were never a highwayman?" she said, appearing in the window with a yawn. "You missed your calling as a criminal."

"I'm sorry, did I wake you?"

"No. I was writing. But should Shrimpy not be more alert to intruders?" She pointed to the dog, curled up peacefully in his basket before the fire, asleep. "I think you gave me a defective hound."

Apthorp smiled at her. "Perhaps he objects to doing his duties out of protest at that ridiculous name."

"Shrimpy *adores* his name. Don't you, my wee prawn?"

The dog snored.

"May I come in?"

She smiled, stepped back, and pulled him in. "I would like nothing better."

Her bedchamber was unsettlingly bare. "Where are all of your things?" he asked.

"Most of them are already en route to your house, I would imagine. I have little left here except my wedding gown. Which you really aren't supposed to see until I walk down the aisle."

She gestured at a pale gown that stood on a wooden Paris doll. It was wide as a horse cart and ghostly in the moonlight. Despite its pomp, it looked a little mournful without her in it. He looked away, thinking of how forlorn this place would be when she left it.

He shook off the thought. She would be at *his* house. As his *wife*. Provided he managed to get through this conversation.

He reached out and took her hand again.

"Constance, I need to tell you something before we marry. I've been trying to find the right words and I'm afraid they have eluded me."

Her face went soft and gentle, like she could tell how deeply he did not want to have this conversation. She squeezed his hand in her two smaller ones.

"I am familiar with your checkered past," she said. "Whatever it is cannot be so terribly shocking."

"Well, actually, there's a rather important detail I haven't shared with you."

"Julian," she said softly, tracing the webbing between his fingers. "I think I know what you're about to say."

"You do?"

She nodded. "And if I am correct, you have done the best you can."

"Really?"

"Well, ideally you would have married. But we all make mistakes, and it seems you have handled it honorably."

She seemed very serene and certain and he was not at all sure she had understood what she had just forgiven him for.

He swallowed. "Marriage is typically not the desired outcome of the arrangement. That's the reason one chooses to pay for it. To keep marriage entirely out of the equation."

"You were paid for siring a bastard?"

He paused. "Constance, *what* are you talking about?"

"Anne," she said quietly.

"*Anne?*"

"I don't mean it like that!" she said quickly. "She's an innocent child, and I adore her. We will openly acknowledge her and settle funds on her and raise her as we would any other daughter. You needn't worry."

"You think Anne is *my child*?"

She gave him a slightly sympathetic smile. "It wasn't terribly hard to figure out, Julian. She looks *exactly* like you. Isn't that why you were so reluctant to make love to me? You didn't want to risk another …"

He felt himself stiffening, wanting to turn away and shut this conversation down.

"Anne isn't my daughter," he made himself say. "She's my ward."

"Julian." Constance looked at him skeptically. "If we are to marry, you *must* be honest with me."

He sighed. This wasn't his secret to tell, and he had promised never to tell it. But she was right; he had to learn to trust her. And she would no doubt find out the truth as a matter of course given she was about to join his family.

"Anne isn't my child. She's my niece."

She looked at him in genuine shock. "Your *niece?* But that would mean ..."

"Yes. She's Margaret's."

Constance gaped. "But Margaret's so innocent."

He sighed. "Yes. That is *precisely* the problem."

Constance looked distressed. "I'm sorry. I would never say anything ... but, well ... how? *Who?*"

He hesitated. He'd promised his mother and sister never to speak a word of the sordid tale to anyone. Maintaining the appearance of respectability was his mother's greatest wish. Secrecy had been the only consolation he'd ever been able to offer for having failed them.

"You can tell me," she coaxed. "Julian, you can tell me anything. I promise you discretion. Especially about something like this."

"Anne's father is Lord Harlan Stoke."

At his name, her shocked expression turned into something more appalled.

"Oh no. *No.* Poor Margaret."

"He took to calling on her three summers ago, while I was working in town. He summers near my estate. He courted her, told her he would marry her ... not to worry that they had not said vows in a church yet. And when he learned she was with child, he dropped her. Flagrantly denied his involvement."

Margaret had been so despondent he'd worried she might harm herself. And then her pregnancy had been difficult, endured in secret at a small, cheap house he'd let in Scotland with only their mother for company. She loved Anne, and had recovered her health, and was infinitely relieved the scandal had stayed hidden. But the ordeal had made her fragile in a way she had not been before. A way that seemed soul deep.

"That's despicable," Constance seethed. "I'd heard he had by-blows, but I had no idea about Anne. Why didn't you call him out? He should be kept away from women."

It was a fair question—an obvious one—but it still demoralized him to have to explain it. His futility had never been more apparent than the day he had not been able to save his little sister.

"I tried. I went to him and demanded he make it right. She'd been sixteen. He laughed at me. Refused to acknowledge the child or Margaret and said that if I made claims against him publicly, he would expose her pregnancy. He needs a rich wife, and I couldn't afford to dower her. And he was right; he had me. I couldn't force his hand. My mother was horrified of bringing shame on Anne and didn't want to ask for help from anyone else in the family. So we arranged for her to go away to have the baby."

"That mealy-livered bastard. And your poor, *dear* Margaret. What an ordeal it must have been."

He nodded, relieved she understood. "It was frightening to watch. But she recovered. And we hope that she might meet a gentleman and find a marriage that brings her happiness. If the story is exposed, that will never happen."

"I will find her a husband," Constance said instantly. Seeing his alarmed expression, she laughed and held up her hands.

"Don't worry. No gossip. I have thoroughly learned my lesson."

He exhaled. "Thank you."

Constance tapped her chin. "You know, Julian. This means that Lord Harlan knew you had information that might ruin his chances of marriage at the time he was courting Gillian."

"Yes. I'm sure that's why they cut us at the opera. He wouldn't wish for her to learn of it."

"Do you remember when I mentioned the actress from the Theatre Royal? And you asked me to let the matter go?"

"I do." His own efforts to pursue the lead had come to nothing.

She bit her lip. "Well … I didn't let it go. Don't be angry, but my dressmaker has been quietly unraveling the connection, and last week she left me a note with what she's uncovered. It seems the woman who was spreading rumors about you at Lady Palmerston's is a theater actress who sees a number of gentlemen in an apartment she keeps on Charlotte Street. Where it is possible she saw you coming and going and drew conclusions, or spoke to neighbors, or overheard. Valeria mentioned that one of the gentlemen she entertains is Harlan Stoke. I know you think there is not a conspiracy, but there must be some connection! For if he knew about your club, the best way of protecting himself would be to destroy your credibility."

"But how would he know to tell you?"

She sighed. "Well, *he* wouldn't on his own. But it seems Gillian has gathered I am behind the circular. It's possible she mentioned it to Lord Harlan, who conspired to plant the rumor so he he could then send my circular on to Evesham without betraying his own involvement." She slumped down on the settee, looking dejected. "So it's my fault. As usual."

"Don't say that. Even if it's true, it changes nothing. He's already gotten away with it."

"Well, perhaps not. We could use the information to put pressure on him to do the right thing by Margaret. Or to warn others."

"No," he said sharply. She looked startled at his tone.

"I'm sorry," he said, softening his voice. "But I promised Margaret and my mother we would never speak a word of this to anyone. They would be devastated if anyone outside our family knew."

It had been bad enough that he had not protected his sister the first time. He would not cause her to suffer more than she already had.

Constance looked unconvinced. It made him nervous.

"Constance, *promise* me you will say nothing."

"Of course," she said quickly. "Yes, of course. I promise."

"In any case, it is not my sister's secrets I came here to tell you. It's my own."

She smiled. "I already know about your Wednesdays, Lord Bore."

He took a deep breath. "No, you don't. Not entirely. And it is possible—likely even—that the truth will come out. Maybe sometime soon. Henry Evesham is circling around the club, prodding for more information. If he exposes me, it will cause another scandal. A bigger one."

In true Constance fashion, she looked more intrigued by this than alarmed. "Why?" she uttered. "What is the truth?"

He drew in a deep breath. "The club you wrote about? I was not a member of it. I was a host."

She shook her head blankly. "You mean, like an investor?"

He sighed. "No. I mean like … a tart."

"What?" she asked, with a strangled, disbelieving laugh.

"I worked there."

"As … a courtesan?"

"Of sorts. My role was to play a domineering sort of man in bed for members who paid for the privilege of indulging such a fantasy."

Constance was staring at him with her jaw suspended, like he was an exhibit in a museum. "It was all very discreet, I thought," he said quickly. "I wore a mask, and was known there only as Master Damian. I didn't sleep with anyone I might know outside the club. And it was safe, as those things go—I took measures to protect against disease."

"I see," she said softly, taking this in. She ran her eyes over him, as if seeing him in a new light. "What do you mean by fantasies?"

"Members would come to me with things they desired to experience that were outside the ordinary. Being ravished by a pirate or a bandit … being bound, or flogged … or being commanded to another's will while making love …" He trailed off, for her eyes were now so wide he was worried she might faint. "I listened to what they wanted and made whatever it was come true."

She nodded, faintly. "May I ask why?"

He shrugged. "For money. It began as something I did privately. As a young man I had a lover who had certain proclivities that I found I enjoyed. After the mines failed, I was desperate for coin, and she introduced me to her friend, a woman called Mistress Brearley, who happens to be the proprietress of the club. She hired me. And her members pay very handsomely. I made enough to be sure that my mother and Margaret were provided for in their daily needs while I tried to restore our fortunes."

"I see," she drawled. He could not entirely read her expression.

"Constance, I want you to know I would not have risked it had I seriously thought the truth might ever be exposed. I was honest about how I felt about you, how I hoped to marry you. That I did this doesn't change the way I feel about you."

"Julian," she said softly. "I know you think I'm innocent, but I'm not upset that you've had lovers. Have you forgotten that I surround myself with every roué and fallen woman who will have me?"

He sighed. "You're being kind, sweet girl. But you well know this is not simply a case of having lovers. I took their *coin*. I would never wish for you to be humiliated on my account."

"You found the act humiliating?"

He bit his lip, unsure of how to answer. He didn't want to lie to her, nor to cause alarm, but the truth was complicated. "Actually … far from it, Constance," he said carefully. "It arouses me to give pleasure to those who crave it, and making love in that way— being a bit commanding and rough—is something I enjoy, when my lover has an interest. I'm not ashamed of what I did. But regardless of how *I* feel, if Henry Evesham publishes that I've been whoring to pay my tailor's bill, my reputation won't recover. My wife will suffer the consequences of such a scandal all her life. And I don't want you to regret marrying me."

She took his hand and squeezed it. "Julian," she said firmly, "have I not adequately proven I have never met a scandal I wasn't able to use to my advantage? Have you somehow failed to notice that it's my greatest talent?" She leaned over and kissed his cheek. "If you plan to become infamous, my darling, then you've found the *perfect* woman."

He was so relieved he laughed. She reached out and rubbed his hair. "Julian, if Henry Evesham learns your secret, I shall simply tell him mine: that I am very blessed to spend my nights beside the finest male courtesan in London."

He crushed her to his chest. "You, Lady Constance Stonewell, are indeed the perfect woman. Why did I ever doubt it?"

She stepped back, a certain light of mischief in her eyes. "I won't lie, though, Lord Bore. I am *slightly* disappointed."

His anxiety came rushing back. "Why?"

"Well, I have just discovered I've been entertaining clandestine visits from one of London's most talented boudoir entertainers, and yet, for some reason, he has not yet deigned to ravish me."

He smiled. "Two more nights, and he will devote himself to that pursuit exclusively if you desire."

"But by then I shall merely be your wife, and I shall never know what it's like to be your mistress. If you've had a chance to be a tart, you wicked man, shouldn't I get to try it too?"

CONSTANCE KNEW IT HAD NOT BEEN JULIAN'S INTENTION TO arouse her with his confession, but in all this talk of his secret erotic life, her wedding night seemed very far away.

She ran her fingers over his arm. "Let's live up to your wicked past before we are dull and virtuous and married. Please. For Mrs. Mountebank. She'd *so* love to be proven right about us."

He chuckled ruefully. "Darling girl, it's very tempting. But we'll be married in two days."

She knew he would demur. Somehow, despite years of evidence to the contrary, he seemed to harbor a belief that she was delicate or timid simply because she was inexperienced. It was time to relieve him of that notion once and for all.

"I realize that," she countered. "But I want you *now*."

His shoulders fell and he began to laugh. He smiled up at her. "You have no idea how nice that is to hear."

He abruptly reached out and lifted her up.

"What are you doing?"

He grinned. "Carrying my newest client to bed."

"Wait just one minute. I have a surprise for just this occasion."

He set her down and she dashed into her dressing room, where the dainty gold boxes from Valeria's boutique were stored. She knew just how to assuage his fears about her. She would put on one of her brazen demimonde gowns and show him she'd been planning to seduce him all along. She was so grateful to Valeria she could kiss her.

That is, until she wrestled the thing on, and caught a glimpse of herself in the looking glass.

After several minutes, Julian tapped at the door. "Are you all right?"

"Yes," she said, although she really wasn't sure. This had seemed like such a beguiling idea, but now that she could see her reflection … she didn't like it. It didn't feel like *her*.

"What's wrong?" Julian asked.

She gritted her teeth. She would not be timid about this.

"Nothing. Close your eyes."

"Very well."

She stepped out from behind the door, clenching her jaw. "Voilà."

He opened his eyes, and they went wide with shock. "Oh *my*."

This was no doubt the moment when a proper courtesan would saunter forward and say something appealingly lewd, but her nerves completely failed her. She wanted to duck out the open window.

She tugged anxiously at the gown—what little there was of it—

trying to make it cover more of her, fighting the urge to dart directly back behind the door.

Julian smiled. Only not, she suspected, in the way Valeria had intended. He did not regard her like he was staring at a vixen. More like he was staring at an injured lamb.

"What is this?" he asked gently.

The ensemble in which I will die of humiliation!

"A … gown?"

He smiled, a touch of humor in his eyes. "Certainly parts of one."

She bit her finger in dismay. "Valeria said especially vivid people like this kind of thing? I thought it would be perfect. But actually …" She tugged the lace down, trying to find an angle that did not make her feel like a naughty woodcut.

She missed her convent night rail, with its long sleeves and high neck and comforting yards and yards of fabric. She missed her court dresses the size of castle keeps.

He came and ran his fingers over the lace along her exposed ribs. "I absolutely love it," he murmured.

"You do?"

"I do," he said slowly. "But I don't love that you seem to hate it."

"You can tell?"

"You are doubled over and scratching at it like you have contracted fleas. Which, if you have, I will have stern words for Shrimpy."

She giggled, feeling marginally better, if still rather wilted and exposed.

He ran his fingers over the contours of the gown. "Do you know what I like the most about this, Constance?"

"What?"

His fingers followed the trail of lace and landed at the cutouts, grazing against her bare skin. "The bits underneath."

She reached down to what passed for the hemline of Valeria's cyprian costume and drew it up over her head. When she dropped the lace and silk to the floor, he smiled and reached out and pulled her with him to the bed.

"You're perfect just as you are," he whispered.

"No, I'm quite—"

He clamped a hand over her lips. "Don't you dare ruin this for me."

They laughed together in the dark.

"You don't have to wear a costume to make love, Constance," he murmured. "Actually, the nice thing about making love is that, if you do it properly, you get to be exactly, exquisitely who you are."

Exactly exquisitely who you are.

That, she was capable of.

"Well then," she whispered, running her fingers over his waistcoat. "Perhaps you might dispense with this."

She trailed her hand down to his breeches, lingering at his groin. "And this."

He groaned, shrugging off his coat and pulling at the buttons of his waistcoat while she watched, growing impatient.

"Hurry," she whispered. "I've been waiting my whole life."

He squinted up at her, a lock of hair falling in his eyes, and grinned. "If you are impatient, perhaps you might help undress me."

She reached up and untied his cravat, revealing his long neck.

"Kiss my throat," he whispered. She did, rising on her tiptoes to nuzzle him under his ear.

"My shirt," he whispered, lifting up his arms. She untucked the linen from his breeches and rose up on her tiptoes, drawing it up to reveal a torso just as lean and golden and finely muscled as the statues she'd always imagined he'd resemble.

He pulled the shirt over his head and drew her toward him, so her bare breasts touched his chest. The light dusting of golden hair tickled her nipples in a way that made her want to rub herself against him.

"Your dressmaker is wrong about your bosom, you know," he said, taking her breasts in his hands. "I am wildly fond of your bosom."

He put his mouth to her nipples, as she'd wanted him to do for what felt like days, weeks, years. "Oh, Julian," she gasped. "Don't ever stop."

He didn't for some time, suckling her as he drew her toward him, parting her legs with his thigh and pressing her up against his straining cock. At the feeling of it finally against her she felt a tremor rising up in her.

"Oh yes," he whispered, sensing her arousal. He put a finger to her *fleure* and bit lightly at her nipples and it was *too much* and she widened her legs, inviting him deeper inside her.

"Oh no," she gasped, for the death was rising up in her already. "I'm sorry—I'm going to come."

"Come then, sweet girl," he urged, giving her another finger. "I love to watch you."

She did, still standing on her tiptoes. She had to wrap her arms around his neck to keep from buckling to the ground.

"I suspect I wasn't meant to do that yet," she whispered as she leaned against him, shuddering. He gripped her by the arse.

"Oh, you are meant to do that as many times as you can bear it," he growled.

"We have to finish undressing you," she said. "So that you might have a turn. Take off your boots."

He turned and removed them, allowing her to admire the fine make of his shoulders from behind. She came closer and traced her fingertips along his narrow waist to the path of golden hair trailing below his navel.

He took her hands in his and dragged them down to the placket of his breeches. "Unbutton me."

She did, taking her time, for she liked how he gasped when her fingers slid over his erection. When his cock was free he slid the garment to the floor with his stockings and turned around, fully nude.

He put his arms around her and hugged her tight to him. "Are you sure about this, sweet girl?"

She reached out and took his head in her hands and brought his face closer to hers, then placed a single girlish kiss upon his lips. He smiled, pulled her to her bed, and drew her down beside him, turning so they faced each other. He kissed her until they were both breathless.

"I'm dying to be inside you," he said.

"I'm dying for that too."

"I'm going to go slowly. Stop me if I hurt you."

She felt a shallow, insistent pressure and then, finally …

Him.

"How is that?" he whispered.

"Better than an apple."

He snorted and gave her more of his cock. It did hurt then, and she sucked back a gasp. He paused, holding himself up above her in a way that, despite the twinge of pain between her legs, she could not help but admire. She kissed him against his lovely, artful bicep.

He trembled a bit at the touch of her lips, and she felt such a wave of tenderness she forgot the pain and adjusted her hips to draw him deeper. "I'm ready," she whispered. "Please."

He paused, raised up on one knee, and flipped them over, so she was on top. He spread his hands over her buttocks and widened her thighs, so her warmth was spread out over his cock. "This is what I was thinking about in the powdering room."

It felt so good to hear him say that. She wanted to hear all of his confessions. All the times he'd wanted her and hidden it away.

She wanted him to make her a list.

He paused. "Are you all right, sweet girl?"

"I'm nervous," she admitted. For if she was meant to be exactly exquisitely who she was, she supposed there was no point in pretending that she wasn't. "I don't know how to do this. Will you show me how?"

He took her hips in his hands and lifted her up, then thrust deeper from below her. They both gasped at the intensity of the pleasure.

"Do it again," she murmured. "Please, please do that again."

He buried his face in her chest. "Oh, Constance. I will take such good care of you. It's all I've ever wanted."

And he did.

By the time he had finished taking care of her, she had lost track of how many deaths she'd died, and the sun was coming up. He curled himself around her and cuddled her against his chest, nuzzling her skin and her hair, whispering that he loved her. Exactly as she was.

This must be marriage, she thought as she fell asleep. Never mind the church or the law.

When she woke up, it was high noon, and he was gone.

But there was a note beside her on her pillow:

I can't wait to be your husband, Constance.

But I'll be your courtesan whenever you would like.

CHAPTER 18

$\mathcal{C}$onstance sipped a cup of tea in the Rosecrofts' sunny garden with Hilary, who was, one day too late, educating her about the events that transpired in a marital bedchamber.

"You might have heard that it's distasteful," her cousin said in a low voice. "But it should not be. Don't be alarmed if you bleed the first time, but after that, it should not be painful."

"No?" Constance asked innocently, shifting in her seat, for she was ever so slightly sore from having lost her virginity at least three times the night before. She dropped her voice. "How *should* it be?"

Hilary smiled and rubbed her belly. "It should be gentle and affectionate and pleasant."

Pleasant was not the word Constance would have chosen, remembering the night before.

Julian, I want you inside of me again.

I know, darling. But first, would you mind terribly if I tormented you just a little more?

After last night she felt like she could fly. Her skin was glowing and her eyes were bright and at least six times today she'd caught herself laughing, all alone, out of pure joy.

"I shall endeavor to remember that," she said.

"Apthorp may not be terribly experienced in these things," Hilary confided. "He clearly finds you ravishing, as recent events would attest. But he is such a proper type. He gets it from his mother. It's why I never put any stock in those dreadful tales about him."

Get on your knees and hold the headboard. I want you from behind.

Constance nodded solemnly.

Hilary lowered her voice. "It's no great cause for concern if he's a bit nervous at the start. He's quite young, after all. But if you have any trouble, send him to Rosecroft."

Constance smiled demurely. "I should hope that won't be necessary."

Are you sore?

No. Don't you dare stop.

Then might I tempt you to sit on my cock?

Suddenly the terrace door flung open and Apthorp came bounding out of it. His usual golden skin tone was flushed and red, and his hair looked as if he had flown from the Strand on a broomstick.

"Lady Rosecroft, I need a word with Constance," he said breathily.

"Julian dear, are you well?" Hilary gasped.

"Please," he said, not looking well at all.

Oh dear. She hoped he was not suffering some attack of post-connubial guilt. *She* certainly wasn't.

Is this dull for you, since you've had so many others?

No. It's incomparable. I've fucked, Constance, but I've never been with anyone I love.

"Very well," Hilary said. "I'll be just inside." She rose and left them with a worried look over her shoulder at Constance.

"Why, Lord Bore," Constance said, smiling. "I missed you."

He did not come forward to greet her. Just stood there, staring at her like he had never seen her in his life. He was pale, his forehead slightly damp, as though he was suffering with ague.

Perhaps he really was ill. "What's wrong?" she asked, drawing near him.

He flinched and moved away. Her stomach dropped.

"What did you tell Gillian Bastian?" he asked. His voice was hoarse.

She didn't follow. "Gillian? What do you mean?"

He closed his eyes. "Don't trifle with me. Not about this. What in *God's* name did you say to her?"

Her pulse quickened. She reached for his hand. "Julian, what's the matter?"

He snatched his hand away. "It's my *sister*. Gillian Bastian was just at my home accusing her of blackmail and threatening to send Anne to the colonies."

She clutched his hands, trying to make him calm. "Take Anne? That's impossible. What do you mean?"

"She accused my sister of slandering Lord Harlan and proposed sending the baby to Philadelphia for everyone's convenience."

"Why, that's dreadful. But don't worry, we'll—"

"She said *you* were spreading the rumors."

She stared at him. He could not be serious. "Me? Julian, *of course not.*"

"She told Margaret that she warned you, and you ignored her. Margaret said she called on you before the ball."

All at once, she remembered Gillian's threat. *You will regret this.*

She inhaled, trying not to panic. "She did call on me. And I did tell her that I suspected Lord Harlan had a child. But only because there have been rumors for years. I urged her to ask him before she weds, for her own peace of mind. That's it."

He tore his hands out of her grip and went pacing back and forth, like an angry animal trapped in a cage.

"I'd love to believe you, Constance, but you are the *only* person outside my immediate family who is aware of this connection. I told you last night and suddenly Gillian appears with some wild plan, saying you came to her with stories? Quite the coincidence."

Her sympathy began to curdle into anger. Was he addled?

"Julian, I did not mention Margaret. I didn't *know* about Margaret. I had heard whispers about Lady Jessica Ashe. I told Gillian to ask Lord Harlan. Did you not consider that *he* could have told her about Anne?"

He tossed his head, like the notion was somehow more ridiculous than the idea of her running across town the day before her wedding to gossip about her future husband's most painful family secret.

"Why would he do that, Constance? When he has done everything possible to disavow his paternity and keep their connection hidden? And why would you say anything to Gillian? Why must you constantly interfere in matters that don't concern you?"

"Because she needed to know."

"My sister is unstrung, worried her child will be snatched and her name will be destroyed. My mother is beside herself. And Stoke has yet another reason to ruin us." He paced back and forth.

"Julian, if you'd like me to intercede with Gillian on Anne's behalf, I will gladly speak to her but—"

He glared at her. "Don't even think about it. Dear God, why can't you *ever* let things be? Why did I think that you could?"

She stared at him, aghast at the unfairness of his accusation.

Aghast, but alas—not shocked.

Certainty rose up in her. A knowledge that had been there all along.

Love is a system of behaviors.

She'd thought he had forgiven her.

He hadn't.

She drew in a breath. "You know exactly why. I wrote to Gillian, weeks ago, to warn her about Lord Harlan's character when I learned they were engaged. I am not the least ashamed of what I did nor sorry for it. And you have no right to be angry at me. I know you think I can be careless. But it is not fair or reasonable of you to hold me responsible for this. *I did nothing wrong.*"

He sighed and leaned against the glass doors, his chest rising, not looking at her.

"You should apologize to me," she said flatly. "I insist."

He put his face in his hands. When he finally removed his fingers, his eyes were red.

"I'm sorry," he said stiffly. He was hoarse. "You're right. If you say you haven't done it, I believe you."

But his body told a different story. His body, which she had come to finally know so well the night before, did not look like he believed her. He was tense and agitated and his eyes did not meet hers.

He looked plainly like a man who did not trust her.

Even after last night ... he didn't trust her.

I'm scared that you'll regret this. That I'll do something to hurt you or make some mistake and you'll feel trapped with me.

Constance, I won't.

She sat down and folded her hands in her lap, where they would not be tempted to launch the teapot at the brick wall for the pleasure of watching it shatter.

"I see," she said quietly.

"Fuck," he muttered. She looked up. He was staring at her, as if in disbelief.

"Fuck. Constance ... I'm sorry." He knocked his head back against the brick wall. "You're right. I'm upset—I wasn't fully thinking. Of course, you're right. Forgive me."

He looked rattled. Shocked at himself. Guilty.

Which was, she supposed, a minor consolation.

She breathed in deeply and squeezed her own fingers to remain composed.

He came toward her. "I'm so sorry," he breathed. "Truly."

She nodded. "I understand."

He smacked the garden wall with his fist and groaned. She had never seen him look so devastated.

"Constance, I have to go find Stoke and take care of this before it gets worse."

She nodded. "Of course."

"I'll return tonight and make this up to you. Somehow."

She straightened her spine. "There's no need. I promised to spend the night with Poppy and Archer in Hammersmith. They wish to give me a sentimental farewell."

He came and knelt in front of her and put his forehead to her knees. "We should talk about this," he said miserably. "Before tomorrow."

She sighed. "We will have two full days in a carriage to Cheshire with nothing to do but converse. You may render yourself prostrate then."

She stroked his hair. "Don't fret. I understand. Go do what you must. I'm sure your sister is in hysterics, and one can scarcely blame her."

He looked up at her and his eyes were wet. "I don't want to go. But I must."

"Yes. You must," she agreed.

"I love you," he said.

And she believed his declaration.

But she also saw that he had not forgiven her. That he did not *trust* her.

And that it was possible—very likely—that he never truly would.

Love and hate, after all, were so closely intertwined that the sharp edge of one could sometimes be mistaken for the other. She had grown up negotiating the delicate balance of being adored and unwanted. She could not endure a lifetime of it.

"Go, my darling," she said into his hair. "I'll see you in the morning."

He rose and took her hand. "Constance, I'm so sorry."

She nodded. "I know."

And she did know.

And she was sorry too.

Because neither knowing of his sorrow nor sharing it could change what she must do.

MARGARET WAS WAITING ON THE STAIRS WHEN APTHORP RETURNED.

"Julian, you're back. I was so worried."

She was calmer now, though she still looked as pale and shaky as she had when he'd discovered her in the staircase at midday, wailing.

"I went to visit Lord Harlan Stoke."

At Lord Harlan's name her face went rigid.

"The matter is settled," he said quickly. "He won't bother us again."

"How do you know?"

"Because he no longer has a reason to. Come, let's talk in the study."

"Of course."

She sat down on a sofa, posture ramrod straight as usual, hands folded in her lap. Such a lady, his sister. So flawlessly correct. So rigid. As though she could not afford a single mistake after the one that had cost her so dearly. It broke his heart.

"Constance had heard that Stoke has by-blows, and urged Miss Bastian to inquire. Stoke denied it, and evidently Miss Bastian became suspicious and found a letter from you in his things. That's how she learned about Anne. She came here without telling him. He has spoken to her now, and we have agreed that it is best for all parties that no one know of the connection. Stoke was ... not exactly a model of gentlemanly conduct, but he was at least apologetic for causing you alarm. He assured me you can expect no further trouble."

Margaret sank back with relief. He was glad, but he felt more miserable than he could recall feeling in all his life. He'd gone from Stoke's back to the Rosecrofts' to apologize once more to Constance, but she'd already left for Hammersmith and it was growing late. He could not let his sister wait in agony, imagining the worst. But he felt the guilt of his accusation coating him like scum on a putrid lake.

"Oh, thank God. I was so worried," Margaret said.

"He also said he intends to settle funds on Anne after his wedding, if you will accept it."

"I don't want his money. I have never wanted his money."

"I know," he said quietly.

She took in a shaky breath. "But I will accept it for my daughter."

"You needn't. I will ensure she has a dowry."

She was grim. "I don't want to be a burden to you, Julian. Not a greater one than I've been already."

He reached out and took her hand. "You aren't a burden."

She shook her head. "You are kind. But not honest."

Honest. No. Perhaps he hadn't been. "You're right. I don't think I ever said what I needed to say to you, all those years ago."

She looked up. "And what is that?"

"That I'm sorry I wasn't there when you needed me. That I couldn't just bloody sort it out. That if our father had lived … That I'm sorry. I am so, *so* sorry. It was my duty to protect you and I didn't."

She frowned at him. "Julian, if you blame yourself for what happened, you shouldn't."

But she didn't know the truth. That he'd been *relieved* to be in London. He'd been happy learning politics, drawing up his waterway scheme, entertaining lovers on Charlotte Street—enjoying his freedom from the endless, tedious anxieties at home. He'd told himself he needed to be here to work, to meet his responsibilities. But more than money, Margaret had needed him at home.

"I could have spent more time in Cheshire, looking after you. I failed you when you needed me the most. I'd give anything to change it."

"That simply isn't true. You were off in London attempting to repair the damage Papa left. That was and is your duty; you are *an earl.* I had Mama to look after me and I had my own conscience. Falling in love may have been foolish of me, but it was *my* mistake, not yours."

He stared at her. "I *hate* that you went through that."

She smiled. "You needn't, Julian. *I* don't regret the past. I will never forgive Harlan for abandoning my daughter, but I would not trade Anne for all the world."

"Nor would I," his mother's voice said from across the room.

He turned around, and saw she was sitting in a chair in the corner, sewing.

She rose and came to sit beside him and his sister. "We have all of us suffered since your father's death—none more than dear Margaret—but we are comfortable. We have a happy home. You've borne too much, son, and it's wearing on you. And that is my fault, for leaning on you too heavily when your father died."

"Neither of you leaned on me. It was my responsibility—"

"No," his mother said. "You were a *child.* You are still scarcely more than a child."

"I am *five and twenty,*" he corrected her, fully indignant now.

"Exactly," she said crisply. "And you've acted like a man double that in years for the past decade. It's time you stop trying to find happiness for us and find it for yourself."

"On that subject," Margaret said. "I adore Lady Constance. And I have decided to take her advice. I hope you will not mind, but I had Mama write to Mr. Lane Day and extend an invitation for him to visit us this summer. I find him extremely pleasant." She paused and grinned at him. "And I believe he feels the same way about me."

He smiled. Lane Day was a gentle, serious soul—exactly right for Margaret. And if they were to marry, they might look after the estate, freeing him to spend more time in London with Constance.

"Cornish is a good man. I will leave him to your capable hands."

"I hope you will be too busy sweeping Lady Constance off her feet to worry about who is sweeping Margaret off hers," his mother said.

He winced. "I'm going to have to do better at that. My temper …" He shook his head. "I need to be better."

"Oh, darling," his mother sighed. "It's not that *you* need to be better. It's that you need to let everyone else be."

She stood and patted him on the head, in a way she hadn't done since he was a boy. "She has a big heart, your Constance. Trust in her to do right by it."

"Oh, Mama," he sighed. "I've hurt her. Over and over and over."

His mother smiled. "Love often hurts. But how fortunate you are that you have a whole lifetime ahead of you to make it up to her. *Over and over and over.* And I'm sure she will put you to the task."

CHAPTER 19

*A*pthorp stood at the head of the church and wished this part of his wedding day were over. He hadn't slept all night. At dawn he'd been tempted to borrow a horse and ride to Hammersmith, but his mother had been awake and made him tea, observing he looked wan.

"Nerves on the day of your wedding are nothing out of the ordinary." She'd smiled at him. "No need to do something rash. Let Constance enjoy her wedding morning with her family. Let's have breakfast."

He had not been able to get a single morsel down his throat. He felt impatient and irritable and overhot, like he had a fever.

All he wanted in this world was to see her walk through those doors and smile at him. Maybe then, the prickling of his skin would stop, and he would be able to breathe.

Rationally he knew she would appear at any moment now. And yet he could not stop picturing her eyes as they'd been the day before.

Empty. Like she'd departed from her own body.

The parade of guests finding their seats had begun to ease

now, close as it was to the appointed hour of the wedding. He
squinted to the back to see if there was any sign yet of his bride.

"Trust Constance to make an entrance," Rosecroft said in his
ear. "Will she sail in on a cloud of trained peacocks? Or perhaps
she intends to have the place light up in flares when she arrives."

He laughed weakly. "Neither would surprise me."

They waited. The pleasant light filtering in through the
windows grew dim. It was humid, turning wet, like it did before a
sudden rain.

In the front row the Duchess of Westmead consulted Lord
Avondale for a look at his watch, then whispered anxiously in
Lady Rosecroft's ear. Her lips formed the words *Where could
they be?*

The dim light gave way to the soft patter of rain, and Apthorp
felt a trickle of sweat fall beneath his neckcloth.

Still, they waited.

The chatter in the room grew louder as the guests began to
make conversation in their seats, and the rain gave way to
thunder.

And still, interminably, they waited.

The bishop pretended to be absorbed in his Bible. Apthorp
shifted from foot to foot. Beside him Rosecroft commenced a
grating, nearly inaudible humming.

He felt another bead of sweat prick on his forehead. The day
was not particularly warm. The only reason to perspire was in
fear that his bride would not materialize.

Don't be absurd. Of course she will. She's always late.

And yet his hands, too, began to sweat as the minutes ticked
past and "late" became more like "missing."

Don't even think it.

But, Christ, he was standing up here before their every last
relation and all the towering figures in society he and Constance
had spent the past month convincing of their epic, star-crossed

love … all of whom were casting their glances away from him and beginning to look queasy as the reality became too difficult to overlook.

The reality being, *she had not come.*

It was half past ten, one hour beyond the appointed start of the wedding, and she had not come.

Finally, there was movement in the back. Every head turned in relief, prepared to beam at the bride. But there was no cloud of silk at the doors. Only the Duke of Westmead, looking paler than Apthorp had ever seen him. A tendon in his jaw twitched as he met Apthorp's eye.

He shook his head from left to right: the universal symbol for *no.*

No, she was not coming.

The world went black before his eyes. He felt every stare in the room as though it were a burning match. His skin was on fire. He was going to burn alive.

Rosecroft's hand clapped onto his shoulder and he made himself step forward, march back down the aisle.

The church was absolutely silent.

All he could hear was the sound of his own shameful, ragged breath.

He felt arms around him and heard the sound of doors closing. Lady Rosecroft was embracing him, leading him out of the church.

Westmead grabbed his shoulder and pulled him inside a waiting carriage.

"Has something happened to Constance?" he asked weakly. "Is she ill, or—"

He couldn't bear to say it. He knew. In his heart, he knew.

"She left," Westmead said in a strangled voice. The duke cleared his throat. "She sent me and the servants running all about the house to search for our mother's missing locket. She must have had a hackney waiting, because her carriage is still in the stables. I didn't believe it at first until I realized the damn dog was missing. And then this was delivered."

He grimly held out a piece of newsprint.

THE EARL I RUINED: A NOT-QUITE COUNTESS CONFESSES

By Henry Evesham.

TODAY IT CAN BE EXCLUSIVELY REPORTED IN **SAINTS & SATYRS** that Lady Constance Stonewell, engaged to be married to Earl of Apthorp, has been masquerading as Princess Cosima Ballade, writer of a notorious gossip circular, which last month published explosive accusations about her intended husband.

Lady Constance, who was due to marry the earl this morning, has chosen to publish her dramatic confession in these pages. These are her words:

Once upon a time, when I was a girl of fourteen, I fell for a handsome man. You will know him as Lord Golden. Or perhaps, by his real name: the Earl of Apthorp.

He was not particularly fond of me then. (I daresay he is even less so now.)

I spent the next eight years trying to capture his attention.

I tried everything. Perhaps you heard of some of my antics? Flamingos on the lawn of my first house party. Gowns adorned in a thousand tiny silver bells. Acrobats and lilies. Whispers of public ruin.

But the Earl of Apthorp is a good man, and a serious one. He values comportment, discipline, manners, and integrity. Which is to say, my antics did not charm him.

Quite the opposite, I'm afraid.

And so, dear readers, I did something rash. Something I will regret until my dying day.

I set out to ruin him.

I paid an actress and a rogue to go around town telling tales about his supposed weakness for a whipping house. I wrote a cruel poem about his alleged perversities and placed it in my circular, where I knew it would get out. And you, of course, know the rest, because you're still singing about him in the alleys outside public houses late at night. (You should really stop calling him Lord Arsethorp. It makes him cross.)

The rumors were not true, but they were wickedly effective. They raised questions about his character and ethics. They toppled his political support, ruined his pending legislation, scuffled his prospects for a decent marriage, and destroyed him financially.

Exactly as I planned.

For you see, I knew that when my scheme worked, he would be desperate.

And I would be his last resort.

I would offer him my influence, my dowry, the power of my family name. He would have no choice but to marry me to save his tenants and family from ruin.

I thought I was so clever.

That is, until it worked.

The more I have come to know the Earl of Apthorp, the more I have come to realize that my tricks could not have victimized a more honorable man. He is not simply handsome and charming—the object of my girlhood fancy. He is strong-willed, empathetic, and passionate. Deeply committed to his family, his country, and his dependents. The kind of man who deserves true love. Not marriage to a woman he can never trust.

I hereby confess that it was all my fault, as most things usually are.

I confess to being reckless with his future and his family and his heart.

And most of all I confess to discovering I care about him far too much to consign him to a life with a woman he cannot forgive.

Signed,

Lady Constance Stonewell

P.S.: One last word of warning to the marriageable ladies from Princess Cosima: Lord Harlan Stoke is a ruiner of innocents, a liar, and a violent man. Some rich woman should do us all a favor and send him to the colonies.

CHAPTER 20

*A*s rain fell, Apthorp's family hunkered in Westmead's carriage, reading and rereading the confession, puzzling over where Constance might have gone and what to do about it.

He barely paid attention.

He felt like he was turning into dust. Like if he stood in the rain, parts of him would slough off in the muck.

And not because he'd been abandoned in London's most prestigious church, surrounded by members of Parliament he'd spent the better part of a decade trying to win over.

Not because he was once again the subject of gossip.

Not because he'd proved himself incapable of even getting married properly.

But because he finally, truly understood.

Love is a system of behavior.

He understood exactly why she'd done this and why she'd felt she had to.

Because she *believed* he could not forgive her. Because he'd proved it.

And even then, she'd still sacrificed her own happiness in order to protect him.

Because she loved him.

She'd never declared it. She'd simply proved it.

And so he stumbled out of the carriage and into the blinding rain and staggered over the sludge in the gutter and parted the throng teeming from the church and the newsmen hawking word of his latest ruin until he found the nearest livery stable with a horse to rent to a man who needed to get somewhere fast and rode breakneck through the rain to Grub Street.

Henry Evesham was sitting in a solemn, windowless garret, his desk a mess of papers.

"Lord Apthorp," he said, jumping in surprise at the sudden disturbance to his peace.

"Agree to drop this matter with Charlotte Street and I'll give you the story of your bloody life."

Evesham steepled his hands around his mouth. "It would have to be *quite* a story, my Lord."

"Give me a sheet of paper and a quill," he said, tearing off his coat.

He scribbled down what he needed to say, threw it on Evesham's desk, and watched the man grow pale. When he finished reading, Evesham stretched out his hand to seal the bargain.

"You have my word. And may God forgive you."

Apthorp strode back outside and into the rain and to his rented horse and rode hard and alone due southeast, never mind the wretched weather and the fact that he felt faint.

He rode for hours and hours, past the outskirts of town and down the carriage road, past the stately piles of Surrey and the ancient ruins of Canterbury. He rode until the horse was in a lather and stopped at a coaching inn for a piss and a fresh horse and a pint of good, dark ale to fend off the cold that was looming in his bones from the rain and wind, and still he rode until finally he saw it, the brown chop of the ocean, the stark, white ascendant line of Dover's jagged cliffs.

He rode to the port, where a packet sloop was docked, and prayed that her conveyance had taken longer than his horse, for she would have trunks and servants with her, and would have been delayed by the flooded road at Maidstone, and therefore would not, could not, have sailed.

Stay. He pleaded in his mind, chanting a percussive wail in his head. *Stay. Stay.*

"Can I help you, sir?" a man shouted as Apthorp jumped off his horse and went running toward the sloop.

The tide was high. Likely he had minutes before the ship sailed.

"That packet," he shouted, though it came out as a rasp, for his throat was hot and painful. "Is a woman on it? Blond?"

The man looked up and yelled to a crewman on the deck. "Brooks, someone here for a lady. Wait."

Apthorp leapt over the railing onto the ship.

If she wasn't here, by God he'd cross to Calais and keep going toward Genoa until he found her.

He staggered down the stairs, wet breeches clinging to soaked legs, panting, clutching at the rails, for his shins had turned to jelly from the cold wet ride and the unsteady rhythm of the choppy sea below him. And the fever that seemed to want to slake him from within.

He looked wildly, from a pair of young gentlemen setting off on a continental tour to a group of merchants speaking French and finally to the back where, all alone, a woman sat in an emerald-colored cloak that revealed nothing of her face or figure save for one single strand of hair that had come loose, no doubt, in the whipping wind at port.

A singular shade of blond.

So colorless and luminous it might be platinum or silver.

Hair like from a fairy tale.

And beside her, a caramel-colored spaniel, snoring.

Constance, he gasped out.

She turned.

And when she saw him, her face went white and her eyes went wide and whether they were filled with shock or love, he could not say, because, finally, his legs failed him.

HE'D COME AFTER HER.

He'd come after her.

But why?

"Constance," he gasped again. And then he sank into a puddle on the floor.

"Julian!" she cried, rushing across the cabin. He collapsed before she could reach him. Crumpled on his knees, he caught himself by his hands and looked up at her.

His eyes were wild and unfocused.

Oh God, she'd killed him.

She bent to cradle his head. His hair was soaked to his scalp, and his skin was burning to the touch beneath the raindrops dripping from his hair.

"He's ill," she called frantically. "Please don't leave the harbor. We must get this man to shore and find him a physician."

"We have a fair wind, miss," the captain said apologetically. "If we don't leave now, we could be delayed for days."

She'd been warned this might be the last passenger ship to cross the Channel for months, given the increasing tumult between England and France. If she didn't leave today, she could be stuck here. Stuck to face the family she'd betrayed. This man she'd hurt.

She had to sail. She had no choice. But she could not leave him like *this*.

"Please, please help him up," she cried, not knowing what to do.

Two shipmen helped Apthorp to his feet and wedged him

between their shoulders, hauling him unsteadily to the stairs leading out of the hold. Constance crawled up after him while a burly shipman lifted him over the railing to the dock. A sailor leaned him against a pillar. His eyes fluttered.

"You can't just leave him in the rain!" she cried. "He's ill."

"We must sail, miss!" the captain shouted.

She dashed across the gangway to the dock and knelt before him, putting a hand against his skin. It was fiery with fever. She pulled her cloak from around her shoulders and draped it over him to block the cold rain driving nearly sideways in the strong wind off the Channel.

"Someone get a doctor," she cried, to anyone, no one, for the dock was a flurry of creaking ropes and shipmen preparing to push the sloop into the sea.

Over the wind and the knocking of the waves against the ship, she heard him rasp something. She leaned her ear closer to his mouth. "What is it, Julian?"

"Stay. I love you. *Stay.*"

His gaze locked on her face. His amber eyes were sharp with fever. He put a hand over his heart. *"Stay."*

He sank back against the pillars and closed his eyes. Raindrops fell from the planes of his cheekbones and dripped onto his lips.

She used her fingers to wipe the moisture from his face.

Such a *remarkable* face.

"Miss, we have the current," the captain called to her. "We must embark."

Julian's skin was hot beneath the drops of rain. He was *so* ill.

He won't remember this. You've betrayed him. Deliberately and publicly. He'll be furious when he recovers his right mind, and you'll be trapped.

"Raise the anchor," the captain called. "Miss, you must climb aboard."

Love is a system of behaviors. He came after you. You did all that, and he came after you.

She looked from the man who had been her past to the ship that represented her future and closed her eyes and chose to risk her poor, bedraggled heart one final time.

"I'm not leaving. Unload my trunks."

"There isn't time," the captain shouted.

"Then give me my dog," she said. "And my valise."

A crewman handed Shrimpy over the rail, along with the travelling case with her money and her jewels. The pup whined, annoyed to have been wrested from his cozy basket and moved into the rain.

Julian's eyes fluttered open. *"Stay,"* he said again.

She kissed his forehead and prayed he would remember that he'd wanted this.

"Julian, don't worry. *I will fix this.*"

She found a sailor who knew a man with a cart who could carry Julian's drenched body to an inn, despite the pouring rain. She found a boy and paid him a shilling to go looking for a doctor in the weather. She coaxed the innkeeper, whose lodge was full, to make a room available—bribing its previous occupant to share a room at the pub down the road.

Through it all she held Julian's hand as he went in and out of consciousness, wiping sweat and rain from his eyes and repeating the same words to him over and over. *I will fix this. Please live and I will fix it.*

When she finally secured the room she'd paid for, she spread her sopping cloak over the filthy ticking mattress and had the innkeeper lift Julian onto the bed. She sent the man's daughter to fetch hot water and clean linens and lemon and ginger in hot broth.

She'd never nursed anyone in her life, but by God, she would learn to save a life by simply doing it.

She tugged and pulled Julian's sodden, frigid clothing off his body.

For once, she did not stop to admire the beauty of his form but only to run her hands over his cold, puckered skin, trying to abrade warmth into it, trying to infuse him with the force of her own life, her own heat.

She murmured to him as she worked, telling him how foolish he was, for it was *she* who was supposed to defy all sense with grand, possibly deadly gestures. What would become of them if they *both* started acting foolish and impulsively?

She wasn't sure if he was listening, for his eyes only fluttered when she spoke, so she told him of all the tears she'd cried as she'd fled in her rented coach along the muddy roads, contemplating never seeing him again after she'd humiliated him like this—and how all those tears were *wasted*, because now she would have to cry again at his funeral since he'd gone and frozen himself to death.

When, finally, the doctor arrived, the day had turned to night and the rain had turned to howling wind and she was half-mad with worry.

"Please," she said to the physician, "save him."

She stepped out of the room to give the doctor space and saw the assembled residents of the inn—the proprietor, his daughter, the cook, assorted guests and sailors—all staring at her disheveled form.

Their faces were locked in grim anticipation. They were waiting for her to announce his death.

Well, they could wait.

Didn't they know she'd never met a problem she could not fix?

APTHORP'S BODY WAS COMPOSED ENTIRELY OF PAIN.

Fatigue and rain and ague and heartbreak.

He was neither living nor dead, awake nor asleep. His only thought was misery.

Except when, through the fog and the pain and the thirst, there was Constance.

Constance whispering to him. Constance's hands on his brow, his chest, his back.

Constance putting damp cloths to his forehead, putting liquids in his mouth.

Her voice played in his mind, inseparable from fever dreams, spinning fairy tales that meandered with his half-formed memories.

She whispered of an estate in good repair, attended by a well-trained staff. The dairy made sweet milk and the garden bloomed with tender lettuce in the summer. The mines were in working order, for a foreman had been hired to improve the yield of salt, and the waterway had broken ground and might be finished earlier than expected, given all his careful planning.

There was money in the bank—enough to pay off all the creditors and warm the hearths with coal and thatch the roofs to keep the heat inside.

Margaret and Anne wore fine dresses and spent their days reading stories and frolicking in the fields and waiting for the gentle politician who adored them to return home from London. His mother rested comfortably in the dower house, content.

And he and Constance made their home on the Strand, which was filled with art and people and the laughter of two little blond-haired children. A daughter who could not be coaxed to stand still or pay attention and a son who was well-mannered and looked after her. Sometimes they made mischief, but no matter what they did, they never thought to question where their place was, because they knew from the time they were small that they were cherished.

And beside him in bed there was a wife who loved him so much it sometimes scared her. A wife who still presided over London society, but whose favorite nights were the ones she spent with him comparing notes on how they would conquer the world together, bit by bit. And then he took her hand and led her up to bed and brought her to such heights she sometimes wondered how she'd ever come back down to earth. But she did come down, because beside him was her home now. The only home she'd every truly had. The one she'd never known how much she wanted.

He shook and sweated and ached and raved and still this vision unfurled in the space inside his consciousness.

This will be our life, the whisper said. *This will be our future.*

Together, we can fix it.

Just come back to me.

Just open your eyes.

Stay.

He opened them.

JULIAN STARED AT HER. WAN, SCARCELY AWAKE. ALIVE.

"Constance," he said.

His voice was ragged from fever. His skin looked like watery cream gone slightly off. His lips were chapped, the skin peeling off in whorls. His beard had grown out and his hair was matted to his head.

He had never looked so good to her in his entire resplendently beautiful life.

"Oh, Julian." She rushed to him, burying her head on his chest. "I was so worried I had lost you—"

He forced himself up on his pillows and dragged a hand through her hair.

"You thought attempting to cross the English Channel in a squall would be enough to throw me off?"

A great pressure lifted from her chest. She could barely speak.

"You remember?"

"Oh, Constance. A man does not forget it when his heart breaks."

A tearless sob of pure relief escaped from her throat. "Oh Julian, I'm so sorry.

He wrapped his arms around her. "Hush. I'm the one who's sorry. So damnably sorry. Let me hold you."

She settled into the crook of his arms. But she did not hush. She had many things she needed to say.

"I thought if I went through with the marriage, I'd make you miserable. I *still* think I will very likely make you miserable, at least from time to time. But now that I have saved your life, perhaps you owe me a bit of forbearance."

"You were right to leave," he said, stroking her hair. "I'm *glad* you left."

"But why? I thought you'd hate me for it."

"No, sweet girl. I could never hate you. Constance, I am such a bloody fool that only losing you made me certain. Standing there alone, I realized *nothing* in the world mattered except the fact that you were not there with me. Nothing."

She fought back tears. "Then, Lord Apthorp, I must do the only proper thing one can when one has ruined a man, saved his reputation, destroyed his reputation once again, attempted to flee the country in a blinding rainstorm, causing him to pursue her at the risk of death by fever, and then nursed him back to health."

"And what is that?" He smiled.

"I must offer you my hand in marriage."

"I accept," he said softly, pulling her closer to him. "Because I love you more than life itself. As I have very nearly proved."

Through her tears, she laughed. "Yes, you foolish man, you nearly have indeed."

She pressed her head against his chest. "Julian?" she whispered.

"Yes?"

"I love you."

He closed his eyes and smiled. "Oh, Constance. Sweet girl. I already know."

AFTER SHE HAD WATCHED HIM SLEEP UNTIL SHE WAS ONCE AGAIN sure he wouldn't die, she stepped into the hall.

"Constance Louise Eleanor de Galascon *Befucking* Stonewell."

She looked up to a sight she had dreaded as long as her memory had functioned: her older brother glaring at her.

"Archer. What are you doing here?"

"I had a sudden yen for seaside air," he said, his jaw clicking in that way it did when he was emotional and did not wish for anyone to notice.

She had hoped she would be spared his anger for a few more days. But then, her brother had always been a driven man. If anyone was going to chase her across the downs of England solely for the purpose of excoriating her, it would be him.

"I suppose you saw my confession," she said.

He raised a brow. "Hard to miss it, Constance."

"I'm sorry for lying to you. For breaking my word. I know you won't forgive me for what I did. I don't expect you to—that's why I left."

"I'm not here to offer forgiveness," he said impatiently, in a tone that implied he was here to throttle her.

She sighed. "Well, you didn't need to chase me here merely to dress me down. I'm sorry."

He crossed his arms. "Is that why you think I've chased you? Why I paid investigators to figure out who you bribed and then tore across the country in a storm until my backside chafed? Because I want to *dress you down*?" He shook his head. "For an exceptionally intelligent woman, Constance, you can be painfully dense."

She rolled her eyes and fought the urge to smile. Accusations of lackwittedness were as close as her brother came to words of endearment.

"If you are not angry, why are you here?"

He let out an exasperated snort and ran a hand through his hair. "To stop you from running away. To *Europe*. Over *Apthorp*."

Something strange was happening in the vicinity of her heart. Was that ... affection in her brother's voice?

"Well, I didn't so much *want* to run away as I knew I would have no choice once you found out what I had done."

"And what is it that you did that was so terrible you had to run away?" he asked softly.

"The story in Evesham's paper was not exactly the truth. I exposed your club. Using gossip. I ruined Julian with it. Even though I swore to you I wouldn't write another word."

"So I gathered," he said. He took a crumpled piece of newsprint and held it out to her. "You haven't seen this?"

CONFESSIONS OF A HARLOT EARL

By Henry Evesham

She took the paper, scarcely believing it.

Following the sensational exclusive report printed in these pages from Lady Constance Stonewell, confessing to having framed her betrothed, the Earl of Apthorp, by inventing a story about his membership in an illicit whipping club in order to entrap him into marriage, SAINTS & SATYRS can report that the earl himself denies this story. Here is his confession, in his own words:

My name is Julian Haywood, the Earl of Apthorp. But you may know me better as Lord Arsethorp if you're a fan of vulgar ditties.

This is my confession. Once upon a time, when I was a man of eighteen, I met a brilliant, beautiful, singular girl. You will know her as Lady Constance Stonewell.

She tried to get my attention, and foolishly, I hurt her. I spent the next eight years compounding that mistake, rather than telling her the truth: She had my attention from the moment I set eyes on her. She also had my heart.

Lady Constance made up her story to save me from the truth. She is a liar of the most selfless kind. The kind of liar I don't deserve to call my own.

So for once, allow me to live up to her example and cause a scandal:

As a young man I made mistakes, and became in desperate need of coin. To improve my lot, I sold my body. And I'll confess to something else: I enjoyed it.

I make no apology for my past. I am a sinner, but so is every Christian in the eyes of the Lord. If I have sinned, I have also strived to be a decent man. We all must follow our hearts' morality; my conscience is between myself and God.

My only apology is to Lady Constance Stonewell: I'm sorry I ever made you think that you were anything but perfect. I'm sorry that I didn't show you how much I love you. I'm sorry that I didn't trust you with my secrets. And I'm sorry that I made you feel you had to leave.

I hereby confess that it was all my fault.

I confess to being reckless with my body and my family and my reputation.

And most of all: I confess to being hopelessly in love with Lady Constance Stonewell.

So in love that I want a chance to be forgiven, even if I don't deserve it.

Signed,

The Earl of Apthorp

P.S.: You can call me Arsethorp all you like. I vastly prefer it to Lord Bore.

By the time she finished reading, the pages were sopping wet with her tears.

Her brother reached out and dabbed her face with his handkerchief.

"Dastardly stuff, small Constance," he said softly.

He had not called her "small Constance" in a very, very long time.

Her weeping became sobbing. He pulled her into a tight hug.

"Shhhh. I suspect it's all going to be all right. I suspect you two are just interesting enough to deserve one another."

"You aren't upset with me?" she sniffled.

He cracked what, for him, passed for a rather warm smile. "Actually, this is all quite heroic. I'd say you've done me proud."

Proud.

Her brother had accused her of making him many things over the years—gray-haired, exhausted, poor—but never had he said she made him proud. Why this meant so much to her she could not say. Except perhaps it's what she'd always wanted.

"You are?" she whispered.

"Yes," he said. "And, Constance ... even if I were not ... even if I were so furious my eyes were crossed and I blacked out from rage, when I came to, I still would not wish to see you flee the country. You are my *sister*, for Christ's sake. My *family*. There is nothing you could ever do that I would not eventually forgive you for after quite a bit of grumbling. I love you far too much to have to cross the bloody Channel every time I need to yell at you."

"Oh, Archer," she sniffled. "I love you too."

He smiled and patted her head. "Now, then. How is your poor Apthorp?"

"Almost dead," she sobbed. "The physician said it's influenza but I suspect I nearly killed him."

"Well, dear girl," he said. "Let's see what we can do to bring him back to life."

$\mathcal{T}$he wedding was not publicized.

There were no sparkling jewels or elaborate gowns or political advantages to be won.

The only witness was the bride's brother, who gave his blessing, signed the settlements, and promptly left the newlyweds to enjoy their honeymoon in the cottage he had rented for them on the coast.

There was not a whiff of scandal; by tacit mutual agreement, the bride and groom were saving the scandal for their wedding night.

But by three o'clock, Apthorp had grown tired of waiting.

"What do you say we retire to the bedchamber?" he asked his wife.

Constance smiled at him with the tender solicitude she had displayed throughout his illness, during which she'd proved herself a surprisingly attentive nursemaid. "Why, it's rather early, my love. But then, today has been quite taxing, and you're still recovering. Of course you must rest."

She turned around and began tidying their tea things on the table.

He came behind her and stopped her busy hands.

"I wasn't suggesting I was tired, my bride. I was suggesting I was amorous."

In his arms, she stilled.

And then she shivered.

Oh, it melted him, that shiver.

"About that," she said softly. "I have a … question."

She dragged the words out shyly, as though she was about to ask something perilous.

He placed his hands over her shoulders and pressed her close to him, to reassure her with his body that she could ask whatever she liked. "Mmmm? Then I am at your service."

"Given we have already made love … ," she drew out, toying with his fingers nervously.

"Made wild, passionate love all night long," he corrected her with a smile, taking her small hands into his larger ones.

She chuckled. "Very well. Given we have already *made wild, passionate love*, I wondered if you would prefer to indulge in your … perversities."

Oh dear.

They had done quite a bit of talking during the many quiet hours of his convalescence. They'd gone over those years he'd dreamt of marrying her while acting like she wasn't fit for company, and she'd pretended she disliked him while craving his attention. They had apologized and pronounced themselves absurd. They'd mused on his political ambitions and her secret vision of buying a theater and writing for the stage. They'd talked about their childhoods, their families, their fears, their hopes, their favorite strategies at whist, and the foods they couldn't stand. They'd debated what they'd call their future children, and she'd told him that she'd never felt truly right or good or wanted, and he'd told her how he'd never felt worthy of his title or capable of much, and they'd held each other, both shocked that the other could be so wrong about themselves.

But somehow, in all of these confessions, the conversation had not once turned to sex. He hoped it was because it was an area where they already knew the strength of their connection. But now he worried they had not discussed it because she dreaded learning more about his past or his taste for the unorthodox. Or perhaps *he* had avoided it out of fear he would alarm her or make her feel pressured to share his predilections.

Like now.

"Constance," he said gently, "I think I once requested that you not call what I like perverse—"

"Until I tried it," she cut in. "Yes. Well, you see. That's just what's causing me distress."

"If you're worried about my past, there's no need. I'm hopelessly attracted to you. I would never ask you for anything beyond what you might like."

She swiveled her head around and met his eye. "Thank you. But I wasn't at all worried that you would. It's not that sort of distress, Julian. It's … *distress*."

He stared at her. And then he squeezed her tighter and laughed into her hair as the alarmed pounding of his heart faded into a new, more urgent pulse originating from the region of his groin.

"Oh. I *see*."

She nestled back against him, sighing.

"How intriguing, my bride," he whispered in her ear. "Tell me, how long has this distress been troubling you?"

"It has been something of a preoccupation since that day I discovered your chest of toys. Leaving aside, of course, moments when I hated you and moments when I thought you might be on the cusp of death. And the occasion when we made *passionate love* late into the night."

"Mmm," he murmured sympathetically. "You must be quite distressed indeed. Why didn't you say something?"

"Well, I didn't want to trouble you while you were ill. But now that you seem revivified …"

"Oh, I am thoroughly revivified. And most curious about what you've been imagining."

He could sense that she was blushing, based purely on the rising temperature of her skin beneath his hands. "Tell me. Please. The suspense is causing me burgeoning distress of my own."

She turned around and kissed him, still shy, but with a twinkle in her eye. "I don't exactly know. But I suspect a person like Master Damian might have ideas."

"I suspect he would."

"How might he go about it?"

"First, he would recommend you tell him what you've been imagining, and he would ask you what you might like and what you might not. And then he would do everything in his power to make your fantasy come true."

She bit her lip, and then broke into a sheepish smile. "Well, you see, back in the days when I would provoke you and spy on you and generally make a nuisance of myself, I sometimes imagined what would happen if you caught me. In fact, I rather *hoped* that you would catch me. I found the idea of it exciting."

He smiled. "What a naughty girl."

She nodded. "Exactly. Very wicked of me."

"And what would have happened, do you think, if I had caught you?"

"Well, Julian, knowing how very proper you are, I think you would have been *very* cross with me."

"Very." He nodded. "Unless, of course, I had been hiding similarly wicked thoughts of my own."

She tapped her chin. "In which case you might have forgiven me if I asked sweetly and tried very, very hard to make it up to you."

"Perhaps. If you were extremely well behaved and did everything I asked." He endeavored to say this in a tone that thoroughly conveyed his wish that she not ask for anything that could be construed as "good behavior."

She caught his playful smile and returned it. "Oh, I know you wouldn't make it easy." She stared up into his eyes, quite direct. "In fact, you would probably torment me a little, wouldn't you? You do enjoy that kind of thing, I'm told."

"Oh, do I?" he drawled. "And what do you imagine such torment entails?"

She smiled up at him and whispered all sorts of delightful theories in his ear.

HER HUSBAND KEPT HER WAITING.

Which was fair, since she'd requested torment, but he tarried so long she began to wonder if he'd changed his mind about their little game. Just when she was about to stop pretending to read the diary he'd left on the desk in the parlor of their rooms, he threw open the door, startling her.

He looked furious.

She grinned. Master Damian, it seemed, was committed to his craft.

He was dressed in breeches and a loose white shirt, as though he'd been out riding and caught her unawares. She remembered her part, and dropped the pages in exaggerated alarm, sending them drifting to the floor.

"What are you doing in my rooms, Lady Constance?"

He'd shaved and run water through his hair, and his face and voice were different. He was just as beautiful, but his posture was more arrogant, his tone more withering.

If he spoke to her that way in real life, she would slap him. Instead she made a show of smirking, rather pleased to be caught. "Nothing at all, my lord. I was ... searching for a quill. Forgive me, I'm just leaving."

He strode across the room and caught her hand. Which was, as usual, covered in stray spots of ink.

"I don't believe you, Lady Constance. For if there is one thing you possess in abundance, it is quills." He picked up a page from the floor, and slowly raised his eyes to meet hers. "Were you reading my *private journal?*"

The challenge in his tone sent a thrill of danger down her spine. The thrill of doing what one shouldn't, and not caring. When he looked at her like that as she stood guiltily beneath his gaze, it made her hot.

"I'm sorry," she said, meeting his stare slyly. "I was just trying to learn where you might be this afternoon. Where I might find you *alone.*"

"And why would you wish to do that, when you know it is far from appropriate for young ladies to be alone with older men?" he drawled, running his eyes up and down her body in a crude manner he would no doubt slap any other man for trying.

"I wished to be alone with you," she said, reaching out and boldly running her thumb over his perfect, sneering lip. "Because, you see, I seem to recall you owing me a kiss."

Even though the beats of the scene were rehearsed, making the confession still sent a hot pang of desire through her. She peeked up at him, feeling her face turn the color of an August sunset for her boldness.

He cocked up a brow. "Ah. She wants a kiss. I see." He pretended to consider this. "Did it occur to you that spying is not the way one goes about obtaining favors, Lady Constance?"

She looked down at his lips. "Yes. And since I've been so naughty, I suppose you'll want me to earn your forgiveness first."

He took her fingers and brought them to his breeches, pressing her hand to his erection, which strained in welcome evidence that this game was having the same effect on him as it was on her.

"I warn you," he said, rubbing her hand up and down his shaft, "what I ask for will be absolutely wicked."

JULIAN HAD DONE THIS MANY TIMES FOR LOVERS HE HAD SCARCELY known, and a few times with people he'd been vaguely fond of. But he had never done it for anyone for whom he felt such capacious tenderness. In fact, he'd never felt so leveled by emotion at all.

He hoped he was not making a mistake.

Their love affair—not the dramatic passion that had erupted during their faux courtship, but the quieter affection that had blossomed these past weeks in between naps in his stuffy room at the inn and during long walks along the coast with Shrimpy—was still so new. It felt tender and sweet and fragile. He worried that to mix it with his wilder proclivities might extinguish it, or make it tawdry.

But now that they'd started, he realized he'd worried about the wrong thing.

Emotion did not diminish the power of his favorite games. It only raised the stakes.

He spoke to Constance in the voice he had perfected over years of such scenes. A bit amused, a bit arctic, a bit dangerous. "I suspect you're just corrupt enough to have dreamt of this. You think of me, don't you? That's why you wanted to kiss me."

"Yes," she whispered. "I think of you coming to my room late at night when I'm alone. I imagine that the hands touching me are yours. That you are desperate to make love to me."

"Oh, I *do* wish to make love to you, Lady Constance," he drawled, walking closer. Her eyes followed him in a hungry way. "But since you have been such a very naughty girl, first you must receive your punishment. Stand up."

She came and stood before him, looking shy and aroused and uncertain and very like the younger version of herself who had once imagined such a scene.

"Give me your hands."

She closed her eyes as he bound them together with the scarf. He cinched it tighter and she gasped.

He took in her hard nipples, her parted mouth, the pulse point pounding at her throat. "Bend over."

He sat on the bed and laid her out over his knees, lifting up her skirts. He jutted forth his hips so she would feel the pressure of his erection nudging just below her thighs.

"Look at you, you wicked girl," he said, running his hand over her lovely rounded arse. He traced the contours of her bum, the cleft of it, letting his hands graze just close enough to her quim to make her squirm.

"Say you're sorry, Constance," he instructed. "Or I shall have to spank you."

"But I'm not sorry," she whispered. "Not at all."

He slapped her arse, quick and light, enough for it to smart.

"Perhaps you're sorry now."

"No," she said in a clearer voice. "Not even slightly."

He spanked her again. Harder. She gasped.

He waited for her to give him the sign she wished to end the game, but she only wriggled on his lap.

"I don't think you're very angry, my lord. I think you rather wanted me to read your journals. I think you wanted a chance to kiss me."

He smiled, grateful she could not see his grin, and spanked her three times, hard and quick. A lovely pink flush blossomed on her pale white arse.

She let out a little moan.

"I think you like this, you wicked girl," he growled, putting a finger in her quim.

"Yes, I've been very bad and I'm not sorry in the slightest," she said breathily. "I'm not penitent at all."

She was wet. Very wet. Despicably, immoderately wet.

"Spread your thighs for me," he growled.

She did, welcoming his fingers deep inside her. First one, then two.

He smacked her arse as he gave her what she wanted.

"You can apologize at *any time*," he taunted.

She spread her legs wider, inviting him to plunge deeper as she rocked against him. She was so wet it soaked his breeches. Which was fair as he could feel his cock pulsing in sympathy at the feeling of her wriggling up and down.

He heard her gasp. She was close.

He stilled his fingers and slapped her flat with the palm of his hand, so forcefully it left a bright red mark. She groaned and bore down on him, desperate now to come, but unable to, he knew, unless he gave her more.

Instead, he slapped her arse again.

She writhed against him as he struck her, absolutely flagrant and not caring. Her skin smarted deliciously and her quim rubbed against the coarse fabric of his breeches and she felt absolutely wanton and she loved it.

"Oh yes. You want this very badly, don't you, you wicked creature?" he murmured as she bore down on his fingers and edged her thigh against his cock, because she liked the feel of it when it was so hard and straining for her.

Wicked creature. The words inflamed her. All her life she'd been thought a wicked creature, and had been judged for it. But the way he said it, in that sultry tone rich with appreciation, made her feel vain. He saw her for the slightly wicked girl she was, and it *aroused* him.

She wrapped her legs around his thighs. "Please, I want you so much," she murmured. "I've always wanted you. Always."

"Don't worry, Lady Constance," he said, placing himself at her entrance. "I know just what you need."

HE WAS AS GOOD AS HIS WORD.

When he finally slid into her, the room faded out.

She was only aware of her body. And his.

He arched his strokes to hit a place deep inside her that made lightning crack behind her eyes. He gripped her by her buttocks and spread her, slowly edging a finger into her arse, making her feel full and tight, like her entire body was a rod of pleasure as he fucked her.

When they were both shuddering and panting and neither of them could fully speak a sentence, he paused, still inside of her.

"Have you had enough torment, my darling?"

If he did not bring her satisfaction soon, she might simply die from wanting him. "Please, Lord Apthorp. Fuck me," she panted.

"Christ, I love it when you speak filth to me."

He spread her taut and drove inside of her.

And then it hit, and she really did cry out his name. Not Lord Apthorp. Not Master Damian. But Julian.

Because this was not a fantasy.

It was the realest thing she'd ever felt.

He drove into her, raw and moaning. She broke open, soaking his cock and their legs and the sheet, keening with her pleasure, her desperation, her love for him.

"I'm coming too," he gasped, and the violence of his shudders triggered another wave of pleasure.

When, finally, the last of the tremors rippled through her, she buried her face against him, tears falling from her eyes.

"Oh no, my darling girl," he murmured, moving quickly to take her in his arms. He scooped her up and held her against his chest, wrapping his whole body around hers so that she was engulfed in him. She curled up against his warmth and sobbed.

She hated crying and had done so much of it this past month that she was sick of it. But it felt good and right to do it now. Because her fantasy had been that he would punish her for being naughty, and instead he had made her feel treasured and adored and able to be exactly who and what she was.

"Come back, sweet Constance. I'm sorry. It was too intense."

"No," she gasped. "No, that's not why I'm crying. I'm crying because I loved it. It felt like being free."

As the carriage drew closer to Apthorp's family holding a week later, Constance was not impressed by the beauty of the countryside. Cheshire did not boast the verdant glories of her family's land in Wiltshire, nor the Provençal bounty of the French farmland where she had spent her youth, nor the striking white-cliffed vistas of the Dover seaside, from which they'd traveled.

But if the land was undistinguished, it was in better repair than her husband's house, with its tar-covered timber beams and daub-thatched siding.

Apthorp Manor was not a grand establishment. In fact, it appeared to be listing to one side.

"Welcome to your kingdom, Lady Apthorp," Julian said ruefully as he carried her over the doorstep.

She smiled. For this place did not suit her husband at all.

Her husband was as spectacular a specimen of masculinity as had ever been carved from stone by the most optimistic minds in all antiquity. One expected him to hail from a land equally formidable. A golden sandy beach with aquamarine waters, or fields of flaxen wheat undulating beneath a pale blue sky.

"I love it," she whispered at this pitiful domain. "It's perfect."

And it was. For it looked very fragile, like it would collapse in a strong wind. Like it would be waterlogged in the slightest drizzle. Like it would instantly burn to the ground if one dared to light a fire in its hearth.

And by God, *together, they would fix it.*

EPILOGUE

One year later
The Stonewell Theatre, London

"*A*re you nervous, my love?" the Earl of Apthorp whispered into the ear of his countess as they stood in their box on the opening night of her theater, surveying the crowd awaiting the premiere of *Lord Harlot* by Princess Cosima Ballade.

"No, my darling. I know I shall only receive raves. After all, I have bribed half of Grub Street, the other half owes me a favor, and I took the liberty of penning three favorable reviews myself just in case."

He scanned out over the crowd, nodding at their friends. The Rosecrofts and the Westmeads, who had helped finance Constance's theater, sat near the Marquess of Avondale, who was flanked by not one but *two* mistresses. Cornish Lane Day, still aglow with his recent marriage, sat beside Lady Margaret, who had discovered a new taste for town now that Lord Harlan Stoke had retreated to his wife's family home in Pennsylvania. Valeria Parc, who had designed all the costumes for Constance's production, glowered forbiddingly beside Elena Brearley, who had taken

"*Someone* has to look out for the ladies," Constance replied. "Just wait until my play on the Hardwicke Act debuts in 1756. Besides, I think you'll like the rest."

> *But Lady C. had discovered his secret*
> *A talent the gent had kept hidden*
> *That he was a first-order harlot*
> *Who left no lass gently ridden*

Onstage, the actress pulled off the hero's dashing parliamentary robes to reveal him dressed up as a highwayman, complete with a whip.

Around them, their dearest friends—who peopled their house on the Strand and generally served as their family in town when the Rosecrofts retreated to the country and the Westmeads busied themselves with botany and commerce—doubled over with laughter.

> *Now the vicarish types were unhappy*
> *For this behavior was most ungodly*
> *But Lady C. enjoyed scandal immensely*
> *And was soon observed to walk oddly*

Julian groaned. The crowd began to stomp their feet.

"My dear, are you going to be tried for obscenity?" he whispered into his wife's ear.

"I can only hope so. It will do marvelous things for ticket sales."

She glanced up at him impishly and laughed when she saw his face. "Why Lord Bore, you've gone positively vermilion. Have I thoroughly humiliated you?"

He leaned over and kissed her cheek, inhaling the jasmine and smoke of her skin in that way he could never stop doing, no matter whether they were in public or private.

"No, my sweet, wicked girl. I am thoroughly proud of you."

Lady Constance Stonewell had always intended to fall wildly, extravagantly in love.

Eventually.

And now that she had, she realized that it did not feel at all like she'd once imagined.

It did not feel like being swept off one's feet by a man who had appeared suddenly in one's life as though he'd fallen from the sky, designed by God himself to adore your every breath and thought.

It felt more like being, finally, at home.

Except home was not a place, but a person.

A person who grumbled at you when you were irritating, and who laughed when you were outrageous, and who admired you when you lived up to your best qualities, and who swooned on those very rare occasions when you were sweet.

A person for whom one did not need to pretend to be more or less than what one was—good and bad, wicked and charming—because he proved how much he loved you every day.

Constance held that person's elegant, long fingers in her smaller ink-stained ones as he laughed at her bawdy jokes, some of them at his expense and some of them at hers. Just as she had held them the night before, at a dinner in St. James Square where she had watched him politely, blandly negotiate support for the funding of a charity that would provide care and midwives for brothel workers. Just as she had, the month before, as they had toasted the groundbreaking for his first canal, surrounded by his family and a host of tenants in Cheshire. Just as she had, this very morning, when they had taken Shrimpy for a walk along the Strand. Just as she was still holding them an hour later as the crowd cheered as the narrator called out the final lines of her first play.

So damn what they say in the papers,
—the rumors put forth and retracted
And raise a glass that the mismatched lord and lady
    found love,
And their vows were swiftly transacted!

THE END

ACKNOWLEDGMENTS

Thank you as always to my brilliant agent Sarah Younger, without whom Constance and Julian's love would never have been consummated. (I mean this *very* literally.) Thank you to the Rebelles for helping me stay sane while writing this book, bat by bat. Thank you to all the friends who beta read for me, and especially Emily Tomson, who helped me find the plot, and Colette Dixon, who heroically read the whole book in one day at last minute. Thank you to my editors Peter Sentfleben and Michele Alpern. Thank you to Kerry Hynds for the GORGEOUS COVER OF MY DREAMS. And thank you to my editorial assistant, Nonie, who is still a cat.

ALSO BY SCARLETT PECKHAM

The Secrets of Charlotte Street

The Duke I Tempted

The Earl I Ruined

ABOUT SCARLETT

Scarlett Peckham is a Golden Heart® winner in Historical Romance who writes steamy stories about alpha heroines. Her *Secrets of Charlotte Street* series follows the members of Georgian London's most discreet—and illicit—private club. She lives in Los Angeles. When not reading, writing, or thinking about romance novels she enjoys drinking wine, watching The Real Housewives, and admiring her cat.

She loves chatting about books on **Twitter**, turning them into pretty pictures on **Instagram**, and doddering around haphazardly on **Facebook**.

You can find here here:

Website: https://www.scarlettpeckham.com/
Newsletter Signup: http://geni.us/TheScarlettLetter
Twitter: https://twitter.com/scarlettpeckham
Instagram: https://www.instagram.com/scarlettpeckham/
Facebook: https://www.facebook.com/ScarlettPeckham/
Bookbub: https://www.bookbub.com/authors/scarlett-peckham
Goodreads:
https://www.goodreads.com/author/show/17997581.Scarlett_Peckham

Lightning Source UK Ltd.
Milton Keynes UK
UKHW022054191218
334294UK00008B/222/P